Suicide Squad

SUICIDE SQUAD

by
James Riveaux

Pittsburgh, PA

ISBN 1-56315-274-6

Paperback Fiction
© Copyright 2001 Igor Pavlov
All rights reserved
First Printing—2001
Library of Congress #00-106121

Request for information should be addressed to:

SterlingHouse Publisher, Inc.
The Sterling Building
440 Friday Road
Pittsburgh, PA 15209
www.sterlinghousepublisher.com

Cover Design: Jeffrey S. Butler—SterlingHouse Publisher, Inc.
Book Designer: Teresa M. Parkman

All rights reserved. No part of this publication may be reproduced, stored in a retrieval system, or transmitted in any form or by any means—electronic, mechanical, photocopy, recording or any other, except for brief quotations in printed reviews—without prior permission of the publisher.

This is a work of fiction. Names, characters, places and incidents either are the product of the author's imagination or are used fictitiously. Any resemblance to actual events or persons, living or dead is entirely coincidental.

Printed in United States of America

Part I
Operation Córdoba

ONCE UPON A TIME

"When woods are cut, chips fly..."

Russian proverb

The bar interior seemed very dark, even after a period of vision readjustment from the sunny outside to the subdued lighting conditions inside. The only exception to the no-direct-light-cast rule of the place was a grating suspended from a low overhang, which held several rows of crystal goblets hung upside down by the foot. Tunnel lights placed deep inside the overhang illuminated the goblet cluster, the crystal reflected a rainbow of colors.

In the evening, the usual blend of local country folks would gather, crank up the jukebox, laugh, drink beer, and, maybe, depending on the mood, light up the dance floor and boogie. But now, in the mid-afternoon, the Russian and I were the only customers.

Valerie *everyone called her Val*, a pretty, full-bodied blonde, polished goblets using a towel, then turned them upside down and added them to one of the rows on the grating. Each time she touched the grating, the goblets swayed like a flock of transparent crystal bats.

*Ting-ting...cling-clang...*The crystal bats shared concern over crowded conditions on the rack.

"My force incorporates eighty five men and women," the Russian stated. He was talking about his organization TRAG *Top Risk Action Group*.

A fly, probably attracted by the sweet scent of his liqueur, appeared out of nowhere and buzzed over his head in circles like a miniature helicopter. The Russian tried to ignore it.

"We can take out any man on this planet irregardless of how powerful and well protected he might be." The Russian paused and stared in my face, apparently measuring the impact of what he said on me.

The fly continued buzzing, then, finally zeroing in on the source of sweet scent, dived into the irresistible goblet. The Russian, unmindfully employing his little pinky, fished out the fly, dropped it on the floor, then *y-yuck!* licked the liqueur off his pinky.

I was only mildly curious, and not of what he said, but of how far he was going to stretch the fib. He sipped his Cherry Herring holding the goblet with four fingers in a very unmanly, almost effeminate, manner. To me, the way he held the goblet seemed funny. The man talked about all those macho things—international contracts, deadly operations, and daring supermen—while his little pinky *still wet* was sticking out like that of a 'miss prissy'. I studied his face. His features—green beady eyes, small nose, and a droopy mouth—resembled those of a raccoon. Hell, not that handsome, more like those of a dirty thirsty rat.

"We can..."

"Hey, Val, give me another double, and one for my friend here, too." I slapped the Russian on the back.

"You don't believe me, do you?"

"Nope." I smiled sheepishly. Of course I didn't believe a single word of what he said. His mercenary organization was probably just a figment of his imagination.

Valerie served us each a double.

The Russian did not pick up his goblet. He slowly stroked his chin—a nervous habit of his, which surfaced sometimes when he wasn't sure about his next move.

Finally, the Russian broke the awkward silence.

"It just so happens that I was about to send a reconnaissance group down to Nicaragua, to find out a few things. Instead, I'll go myself. Hell! I'm getting stale here sitting on my butt and doing nothing." He paused, glanced at me, and dumped the ball in my lap, "I'm taking you with me."

What! That was an unexpected twist; he turned the tables on me. Taking me with him? Just like that?

"Are you serious?" I asked, still uncertain whether he was joking or not. I searched for a shadow of a smile on his face. No, I guess he meant it. This guy didn't know how to joke.

Suddenly his face lit up as if he had just discovered the lost continent. "Of course, that's what we are gonna do. We..."

"Wait! Wait, wait, wait!" For me, things were developing too fast. I needed a pause; I needed time to re-orient myself, to get my bearings straight. "You want to take me to Nicaragua? I mean, you want me to go with you?"

"Yes." His eyebrows arched as if conveying a message 'Ah? Ain't this a great idea?'

I finally composed myself. "But aren't you forgetting something? There is a war in Nicaragua."

"Yes, so there is," he noted casually and dismissed the subject as totally trivial. "It will be the three of us. We'll pick up another man in Miami, an old friend of mine."

"…and people get killed in wars," I persisted. "Don't they?"

"Sure they do." He raised his goblet. "To us!"

We toasted.

"There is no action in our sector; it's all down south, by Costa Rica," he spoke confidently. "Adolfo Calera, the head Contra, sends his men across the river now and then, but the action is minimal–just laying mines and harassing Sandinista outposts."

I emptied my goblet and put it down, "Well, I don't know, I've got a lot of things to do here in Raleigh."

I was unemployed for over a month. It was hard to find a job in my profession, ornithology, studying birds. The Russian was aware of my financial status.

"The organization will pick up the tab, both the travel expenses and your monthly bills," he declared.

"Give us another double, Val…" I requested.

The blurred face of the Russian neared mine.

"And the birds! Jim, you won't believe how beautiful those damn birds are in the Nicaraguan jungle."

Although I felt no pain, I sensed the low blow; he knew what kind of bait might work on me–my inspiration, passion, and my weakness–birds! That's what he hung on the hook and dangled before me, suspended in the humming mist.

"You know, I can't think clearly…Give me more time, Alex…" Alex was his damn name, and I was no longer in condition to continue the conversation. "I think I've had enough to drink…for tonight…"

The mirror, bottles, and goblets in front of me drifted out of sight. My face touched the cold surface of the counter, the drink spilled over…

The next day in the afternoon, I met Alex at Cameron Village mall. Baskin Robbins 31 Flavors Ice Cream offered us all it advertised. My mind was made up.

"My treat," declared Alex.

"This kind of a bribe will get you anywhere."

While enjoying ice cream and watching two attractive girls sitting at another table, I expressed my provisional consent to join Alex's task force.

"Splendid!" Alex smiled like a Cheshire cat. "Splendid! I knew you'd see it my way. Ready for the chocolate flavor?"

"I am not clear on one thing though." I licked my spoon. "What exactly is our mission?"

Our mission was very simple. We had to ascertain the route and the flight schedule of the Sandinista supply helicopter shuffling between Managua and Puerto Cabezas on the north coast. The helicopter carried items too valuable to be subjected to the risks of land travel–portage along a very long and hazardous road–items like general staff dispatches, intelligence reports, mail, valuables, and currency. The supply chopper served as a vital link between the army in Puerto Cabezas and the central command in Managua.

"The Contras are going to help us," Alex stated confidently.

The more I learned about our mission, the less sense it made. We were going deep inside a hostile country just to find out whether the helicopter crew was going to be late for dinner or not? Hell, the Contras could get this information easily from their local agents; why would they bother with Alex? I did not know what kind of game Alex played. Maybe his scheme was just that, a game, and the whole thing–Contras, Sandinistas, TRAG, and the helicopter–was bullshit.

Our general plan was to move mainly by night, avoiding any contact with the enemy and the indigenous population, which was fine with me. During the daytime we would camp and rest. That is when I would have an opportunity to explore the jungle and observe all kinds of tropical birds.

Before going though, I had to clear one obstacle: talking to my girlfriend Martha. I could tell her...What could I tell her? That I was going to a war zone with a mad Russian to watch birds!? My God, it would sound unbelievably absurd. I knew exactly what she would say: "Are you off your rocker, Jim?!"

I met Martha the next day.

"I'm going to Chihuahua Province in Mexico for about two weeks to study the migration patterns of Golden-Winged Warblers," I said.

Martha seemed skeptical, at least that is how I interpreted her nose-wrinkled look.

"...Vermivora Chrysoptera," I attached for an added measure of credibility. Latin names carried more weight.

The Warbler is a Canadian bird, and I wasn't even sure if he ever migrated to Mexico, but what the heck. Martha wouldn't know the difference even between a woodpecker and a sparrow.

THREE BLIND MICE

Alex came from Russia at the height of the Cold War. I met him in New York, where I went to college. Only five-foot-eight, one hundred and sixty pounds, with a baby face that was less than handsome, Alex was not composed of material for anything tougher than a loud fart. If at that time someone gave me a hint that this apparently harmless and rather wimpy-looking individual was going to be in charge of a sinister war organization, I would not be able to hold back my chuckles. He claimed to be in command of that organization. But it didn't matter to me whether he was in command or was not. What mattered was that he was taking me where I wanted to go– to observe tropical birds. I couldn't miss such opportunity.

We left Raleigh late in the morning and landed in Florida at noon. At Miami International, we linked up with Alex's old friend Johnny. A Vietnam war veteran claiming to be a professional mercenary, he, like Alex, did not fit the part. I could imagine him holding a bucket of pig chow, but not a gun. A plain farm hand, square as they come: a square jaw, square shoulders, a square crossbar-tainted pattern country shirt, and a pair of square boots, to complete the portrait– Johnny's image did not fit any action with more punch than hosing down pig shit.

As we sat at the airport waiting for our plane, Alex sprung on me his first jack-in-the-box surprise, "We are not gonna land in Honduras."

"Ooh! But I thought we were flying to Tegucigalpa."

"Well, not directly. We'll land in Belize City first, then we charter a Cessna to Punta Gorda, a small town in the southern part of Belize, and take a sea ferry to Guatemala."

"And then what?"

"We cross to Honduras and take a bus to Tegus."

"A back door entry, so to speak?"

"Right." Alex laughed. "The back door entry. That's good!"

That wasn't funny. I felt somewhat uncomfortable, and silly. We played a game of hide-and-seek with no one seeking us. These guys liked playing games. They pretended to be conspirators...with nothing to conspire, played a cat-and-mouse game with no cat and waged a war with no battlefield.

Finally, we boarded the plane. The seat next to me remained unoccupied, and during the flight Alex joined me. Making sure that no one was watching us, Alex reached inside his jacket and presented me with the second surprise,

"By the way, Jim, please don't call me by my real name until we are back in the States." He flashed an American passport. A ratty face wearing a thin moustache stared at me from a bad quality photo. I read: *Joe A. Green, born December 29, 1946, in Santa Monica, California, U.S.A.* "Cost me two thousand bucks."

"What's A. stand for?"

"Admiral."

"You're kidding." I tried to maintain a straight face, but inside, I was laughing: Admiral? A wimp an admiral?! Doenitz, Holsey, ...Green? A make-believe admiral! In command of which fleet? Perhaps my face reflected the super-human effort I had to exert not to burst out laughing, because Alex inquired whether I was all right. I whispered to him that I had to hold my fart, and we laughed: him at my predicament and me at him. That was dirty, but I couldn't help it, I had to give him a plausible excuse *on his level* as to why I laughed.

The landing at Belize International proceeded uneventfully. In town, we stayed at a cheap, run-down, provincial, one-story hotel facing the sea but lacking beach, to which we arrived in a cheap beat-up taxi cab. Finally alone, I laughed at the cheap dirty curtains, the stained pinewood floor *God knows what was spilled on it: beer, liqueur, oil, ink, spit, vomit...*, and at the man who called himself Admiral. And I laughed at myself, a man who allowed himself to be dragged into this ludicrous scheme–the net of imaginary friends, mythical nemeses, fabricated danger, fictional tasks, and false claims.

Later in the afternoon, after dinner, Joe, Johnny and I ventured to explore the city. Among its many charms, Belize City offered us the hospitality of the Rose Garden, its number one brothel with its wide selection of Latin flowers mostly imported from neighboring Guatemala.

In the morning we were on the way to Punta Gorda. An hour and a half in the air passed uneventfully. Johnny slept next to me, in the back seat. Joe and the pilot chatted in Spanish.

Punta Gorda consisted of one dirt street by the ocean. Our ferry to Guatemala was going to depart later in the afternoon. Meanwhile, the extreme heat and humidity kept us inside the local mini-saloon.

After getting tired of staring at the poster on the wall, a cheap print of a half-naked girl, Johnny and I decided to go for a stroll down the street.

"How long have you known Joe?" I asked.

"We fought together in Guatemala."

"I can't recall any recent war in the region except for the one in El Salvador."

"Well, it was no war, not in the conventional sense, anyway. The Guatemalan's hired us to take out a guerrilla headquarters in the mountains and bring back the leader. Joe wasn't in command then; he was just one of the group."

"Tell me more about Guatemala."

"Not much to tell. We didn't catch the bastard. But we killed everyone else in the camp."

"Guerillas?"

"And their families," he concluded with a chilling calm.

I couldn't digest Johnny's last statement. What did he mean by 'families'? Did they kill women and children too?

"Wait...were there any survivors?"

"None."

I laughed; Johnny had to be joking. Probably he just tried to impress me with shocking tales, which he overheard somewhere or simply invented–a fisherman's tales of the mercenary variety. No civilized human being could do such a thing like killing a child.

We returned to the half-naked girl's bar and stayed there until out transportation piece arrived.

The ferry boat, as any other form of transportation in Central America, was loaded with cargo and passengers far beyound its capacity. We crawled our way south, chugging along the coast, until we finally reached Puerto Barrios after dark. Here, I lost most of my luggage. The customs confiscated everything bearing a shade of green.

"It's Jim's face." Joe poked fun at me, while I hissed and spat. "With a face like that how can you miss? Look at that tough jaw–typical mercenary. And they don't like our kind over here."

I sincerely suspected that this side trip was just an excuse for Joe to visit familiar bordellos. My suspicions were strengthened when I found out where we were going to spend the night–at the local bordello owner's house on the outskirts of town.

The madam greeted Joe with a big hug and a kiss, made a lot of fuss over Johnny, and barely noticed me.

In the morning we were on our way to the Honduran border. A

small pickup truck driven by the madam's brother found every pothole in the road before reaching its first decently paved stretch. Johnny and I crouched in the back, behind the cabin.

Terraced, cultivated hills passed by to be replaced with wild mountains heavily coated by jungle growth. A torrential tropical rain caught Johnny and me completely unprotected, and, within seconds, it didn't matter whether we were seeking shelter behind the cabin, or under Niagara Falls.

One unscheduled stop helped to relieve certain natural tensions and offered a delightful drink of fresh sugar cane juice at a roadside shack inhabited by a large Indian family and an ancient rusty sugar cane press. Here, on the bottom of the pass between tall mountains, where winds could not reach, all sounds were amplified. They echoed, then bounced back rejected by the sender and reverberated. For the first time since Raleigh, I heard birds. I couldn't see any of them up in the jungle wall of the steep mountain, which seemed just about to step with its heavy foot on the old shack. But birds were there; I recognized the call-melody of the Ramphastos Toco and the gentle whistling of the resplendent quetzal. Damn, how much I wanted to catch a glimpse of the feathered singers, especially of the quetzal–the emblem of Guatemala–but I couldn't. I wished to stay longer, I wanted to introduce myself to the beautiful singers, 'I am from Raleigh, friends. I can't sing like you, but I can listen. Sing for me, sing!' But we had to leave.

We reached the border late in the afternoon, waved farewell to our driver, and crossed the strip of no man's land to a building on the Honduran side of the border. The bus to Tegucigalpa was leaving early in the morning. We had to find a place to spend the night. There was only one little hotel in Agua Caliente. Its image will live forever in my memory. Nine tiny rooms, three-three-and-three, in a horseshoe arrangement, with the outhouse at the end displaying no door or any other barriers, was something to behold.

"It stinks in here," was my only comment.

The morning bus was on schedule. Borrowed from a local museum about twenty years ago, it was large enough to accommodate us, natives, luggage, chickens, and pigs. Traveling on washed out mountain roads proved to be an unnerving experience. We bumped and jumped, twisted and turned, often too close to the edge of no return, winded and spiralled, cackled and oinked our way to Tegus where we arrived, finally, late in the afternoon.

In Tegucigalpa, the pace of events picked up speed. Joe made a telephone call, and a jeep arrived within a half hour. What followed was a classic movie cloak-and-dagger action starting with the exaggerated haste of taking on passengers, the speedy departure, and evasive maneuvers. Included were such indispensible items as a tense driver and a nervous escort with an intimidating AK-47 in his lap. One essential element of this well-staged melodrama was missing though: no party kept us under surveillance, nobody chased us, and, in fact, no one gave a damn. These clowns played the same stupid games as Joe and Johnny did.

After a fair amount of zig-zagging in narrow streets while trying to shake off the non-existing posse, we finally reached our host's headquarters situated between the downtown and the airport on a quiet unpaved street in a fenced off, one story house.

"What was all that about?" I asked Joe. "The escape I mean."

"An evasive action," he said, "which is a standard operating procedure here. It is to protect us."

A tall, lean, dark, handsome man in his early thirties, wearing an out of place blue baseball cap, greeted us in perfect, though with an accent, English.

"Stedman. I hope our accommodations are adequate."

Joe introduced Johnny and me as his associates.

"Please step in my office." Stedman led us to a room with no windows.

Scanning Stedman's office, I spotted a radio station: a shortwave transceiver. The office had to be the command post. A very attractive woman entered, and apparently in observance with the preset communication schedule, turned on the station. Overcoming the atmospheric hiss and crackle on the band, she established a dialog with her distant counterpart, probably for no more than mutual assurance that all was well.

"Pranza," Stedman explained. Pranza was 250 miles away, somewhere on the border with Nicaragua.

We stayed at the headquarters for two days waiting for the next flight to our destination. The airplane was fitted to carry cargo, not passengers. We sat on the floor. Our destination, Rus-Rus, a small village in the northeastern corner of Honduras, lay about one hour ahead. I visualized an airstrip cut out in the middle of impassable jungle, in the wilderness. Instead, as far as I could see during the approach, there were only grassy hills with scattered skinny pine trees.

There was no rain forest or even palm trees in sight, and certainly no tropical birds. Somewhat disappointed, I tried to reassure myself that I would have a second chance, maybe later.

The dirt strip that we landed on welcomed our plane with a spectacular dust trail. An old jeep awaited us at the end of the airstrip. Everything here was old–the plane, the jeep, the road, the hills, and even, probably, the hot, stale air.

We rode in silence; there was nothing around that warranted any comment. Ten miles down the road, we reached a small river, and what a pleasant surprise! I saw a thick growth of trees, a jungle growth.

The bridge across the river had been blown to bits during one of the past Honduran-Nicaraguan territorial disputes and had not been rebuilt since. Now a hand-pull ferry set up next to its remains was pulled by two Contra soldiers. The village of Rus-Rus, our destination, lay on the other side. Its name carried an association with the Russian word 'Rus' *Mother Russia*, which gave me an idea.

"What was that Volga song?" I asked Joe.

"Oh, yeah." He brightened. "Hey, u-ukhnem! Hey, u-ukhnem! Eshcho razik, eshcho raz. Hey, u-ukhnem!"

I joined in.

The song carried over the river stretch, past the remains of the blown-up bridge, and up the stream. It echoed off the tall bank on the other side of the river mixing with the 'Tira, hombres!' of the soldiers. The old Russian song, performed by two amateur singers, myself, slightly off key, was so incongruent with the Central American landscape, the Contra soldiers carrying AK-47s, and our group, mercenaries, that I sank into hysterics.

"And what is so funny?" Joe inquired, apparently insulted by my inexcusable reaction to his performance.

"No, no, it's not the song. It's us. It's me. What in hell are we doing here, in Honduras, singing a Russian song? I have to get used to it, you know."

"Oh, you will." It sounded assuredly ominous, as if Joe knew something I didn't. "Yes, you will."

I stopped laughing. Suddenly I realized that we could not go back. Where were we going? What was sucking us in? I glanced at Johnny: he was helping to pull the cable, as if he had been doing this kind of work all his life. He didn't seem to care whether we had departed on a reconnaissance mission or had purchased a one-way ticket to hell.

from the manual in his head. "It looks small, but its radius of lethality is fifteen feet. Guard the ball; it may save your life."

"What do you mean by 'the ball may save my life'? I thought, we were not going to 'engage the enemy'."

"Oh, yeah, I almost forgot to mention the change in our plans. It's no longer a reconnaissance mission, but an active one. We are going to bring the chopper down."

"Swell," I said. "You son-of-a-bitch planned to do exactly that as far back as in Raleigh, didn't you?"

"No, it was decided at another meeting with Stedman. We weighed the risks of two missions and elected to combine both in one, kind of a hit-or-miss operation."

"And you failed to tell us about it."

"Well, it seemed like such a minor detail," grinned Joe. "But you still can go back, if you wish."

"You know I won't."

Later in the afternoon, after dinner *rice-and-beans, el platano, and palm leaf tea*, we stopped by the hospital compound to pick up antimalarial and water purification pills. The hospital had American visitors. In order to blend in, we became representatives of the United Orthodox Center of Raleigh, which, of course, did not exist. Joe produced a silver cross on a thin silver chain and promptly linked it around his neck, thus becoming instant Father Joe. That ordained the rest of us as Brother John and Brother James. The visitors–the Holy Rollers and an obscure charity from Boston–were dumped here overnight. They camped inside the unfinished hospital structure standing aloof from the main compound. We joined in and introduced ourselves. Both the Holy Rollers and the charity were on a fact finding mission before contributing to the Contra cause. We tried not to get involved in a sticky conversation with the visitors because answering their questions concerning the United Orthodox Center of Raleigh, or discussing other religious matters, was like talking about the craters on the other side of the moon–we were hardly qualified.

The pharmacy hut, by the entrance to the compound, housed shelves with intimidating rows upon rows of boxes, packages, and bottles, containing medical hodgepodge, from conventional aspirin to specialized antitoxins, and from field bandages to surgery tools. Here, we found what we came for: the antimalarial and water purification pills. It was getting dark, and we returned to our hut. I discovered that Rus-Rus had no electricity *ever!*. We lay on the floor.

GREEN AS A LIMA BEAN

The Rus-Rus camp contained two units: a Contra squad and an Honduran army squad, living separately, but in perfect symbiosis. In the beginning, I was puzzled by this unusual arrangement, but I later discovered its purpose. Just across the creek from the camp lay a farm housing none other than Stedman's family: his mother, two brothers, and a little girl, probably an offspring of one of the brothers or an orphan of the war. The Contra squad carried the around-the-clock guard duty protecting Stedman's family and property *few heads of livestock*. The Honduran army outpost was just a watch dog checking on the local Contra activities. Its task was simple: observe, but do not interfere.

Our group was placed in the Contra squad living quarters, a bamboo hut on stilts–standard housing here. The adjacent smaller hut served as a kitchen. The two huts were joined by a suspension bridge also made of bamboo. Stilts were a marginal protection against miscellaneous varmints *snakes, tarantulas, scorpions, centipedes, and the like* quite abundant here, by the river we had crossed. The jungle growth on both sides of the river was no less than the garden of Eden for all slithering, running, crawling, flying, and spitting *yes, spitting spiders* critters.

But, as I soon discovered, the main problem was not snakes or scorpions–it had much smaller dimensions, physically at least. As soon as the sun went down, mosquitoes came in through the openings of the hut in swarms of thousands. Since there were no doors or glass windows, these pesky irritants presumed that they were invited for a free meal–us, and they came in numbers.

I didn't get much sleep. In the morning after breakfast consisting of rice-and-beans, plantain, and palm leaf tea, we were issued war toys by Stedman's brother, the local Commander. He delivered three molded Chinese AK-47 automatic assault rifles, several cartons of new shiny ammunition, uniforms, and web belts. Then he produced a small wooden box and carefully removed three green ping-pong balls on skinny sticks and distributed them too.

I held the green lollipop in my palm not knowing what to do with it. "Do I suck on it, or swallow it?" I asked Joe.

"This is the FMK2 Model 0 Argentine hand grenade." Joe cited

"Tomorrow," said Joe suddenly.
"What tomorrow?" I queried.
"The mission is tomorrow."

I couldn't fall asleep. Lying on the hard bamboo floor, I visualized my comfortable apartment in Raleigh, its safety and peace. Why in hell did I agree to go on this question-mark mission? Oh, yeah, to watch birds. What birds? So far I hadn't seen any. I heard some in Guatemalan mountains, but that was it. These guys, Joe and Johnny, played war games. Maybe that's how they got their kicks. They didn't mind sleeping on the floor, or eating el platano and drinking palm tea, but I craved a juicy steak and a glass of burgundy. I wanted to sleep in my queen-size bed, and, sure as hell, I preferred a cup of coffee in the morning over the monocotyledonous tea.

"I can't sleep either," declared Joe. "It happens every time before a mission. Thinking of all the details, trying not to forget anything."

"What exactly is our mission? I mean the next step."

"We are going by boat to the point fifteen miles south of Puerto Cabezas. We camouflage the boat and march about thirty miles inland. Then we take position and wait for the supply chopper from Managua. The chopper will carry, besides supplies, a sizeable amount of cash to the base next to Puerto Cabezas. It's in...what in hell do they call it? Lempiras?"

"Córdobas," Johnny ingressed, he was awake too.

"Yes, córdobas," Joe agreed, "salaries for the sixteen thousand soldiers stationed at the base, plus some rubles for the Soviet advisors, and dollars for the Sandinista intelligence. We shoot the chopper down, collect the money, and return to the boat."

"Have you ever been to Nicaragua?" I asked Joe.

"No, this is the first time, but we'll be assisted by three of Stedman's men. We'll meet them in Pranza tomorrow."

Stedman's was a sizeable force in Nicaragua. It was a bitter and defiant force. Misura Indians, northwestern Nicaragua's root settlers, refused to submit to the Communists. Consequently, many of them were 'resettled' by the Sandinistas, their villages burned, livestock expropriated, and fruit plantations cut down. Those who escaped to Honduras now were fighting back. But unlike their North America counterparts a century ago, who were armed only with knives, bows and arrows, these Indians carried automatic rifles, machine guns, grenade launchers, and rockets.

I wondered who supplied the Indians with all these formidable weapons. When I asked Joe, he alluded to Stedman's association with the CIA. Although Stedman, whose mother was an American, has never admitted to having American contacts, Joe believed that they existed.

"Look at the facts," noted Joe. "What we were issued here are Chinese AK-47 Type 56 assault rifles. Stedman's soldiers carry American M-16s and his officers are armed with UZIs. The Chinese don't sell UZIs–Americans and Israelis do. Stedman is very smart; he plays all sides not allowing any of his allies to gain meaningful control over his decisions."

"And where do you stand?" I asked Joe. It was about time to ask him that question. A long pause followed.

"I am just a soldier of fortune. Take mercenary jobs here and there...but not in the States though," he added quickly as if meaning 'Yeah, I do some nasty things here and there, but don't worry–the States are off limits'. "Let me quote a Russian saying: 'Don't spit into a well, you may drink from it one day.' The U.S. is my well."

"What about Guatemala?"

"That's where I met Johnny. They had an interesting setup there, kind of a symbiotic relationship between some big American companies and the Guatemalan government. The American interests, like oil, mines, and fruit crops, had to be protected from attacks by the local guerillas. I was hired as a replacement for a guy who was killed in action. The American companies in the area, with full approval of the local Provincial authorities, set up a covert task force to deal with the guerrilla threat. Our force was small, only thirteen men, but very effective. I ended up commanding it."

"Is the force still operating?"

"No, we did our job, and later the force was incorporated in my Top Risk Action Group."

We lay silently for awhile. Gradually, Joe's breathing became deeper and noisier, and he began snoring. Johnny sighed. He, like me, couldn't fall asleep.

"I'd like to meet more of you guys from Guatemala," I said to Johnny, and that's when I had a chill, not the weather kind, because here, in the tropics, temperatures hardly ever dipped below seventy, but the creeping kind, slowly crawling around your spine all the way down to your ass.

"Joe and I were the only survivors," Johnny stated calmly.

What happened to the rest of them? They died? Was that what

Johnny said? The alarm sounded deep inside me; for another second, the chills tingled and then vanished. Coming here, did I get into something I shouldn't have gotten into? And who was Johnny? But more importantly, what was Joe?

NEPTUNE, PLEASE SMILE AT ME

I woke up late, after sunrise. The azure, crisp, clear morning, with a subtle touch of local flavor *birds did not chirp, but whistled gently, and mimosa weeds covered with dew flinched and shrunk when I stepped on them*, was, what I would call a perfect morning to start a day. After touching base with the outhouse and bumping into cross-eyed man, another of Stedman's brothers, escorting three skinny cows on the way to their breakfast in the meadows, I bathed in the creek.

Our breakfast *no surprises there: a mixture of rice and beans, plantain, this time sliced and fried in oil until crisp, and palm tea* was served by Sam, a Miskito Indian of about sixty. Sam hardly ever spoke a word to anyone except to his pet monkey, tied to the suspension bridge between the two huts. From time to time, for no apparent reason, Sam spanked the monkey. The animal always tried escaping first, but being on a short leash, it couldn't get far. The monkey then shrunk into a ball and took the beating, complaining pitifully through the whole procedure. I tried to intervene on the monkey's behalf, but Sam did not speak a word of English. He just stared at me, as if trying to comprehend my motives for interrupting, as he perceived, his instructional and beneficial actions to the monkey. He stopped the exercise, untied the animal, led him into the kitchen, and continued the punishment in privacy. The monkey complained even louder than before.

We did not linger with breakfast because the pickup truck, which was going to take us to Pranza, was already waiting. We packed in a jiffy and climbed in the back of the truck.

Pranza served as a Contra base for the operations inside Nicaragua, which stood less than a mile away, across the Coco River. We were greeted by Commandant Raul, a dead ringer for the Reverend Jesse Jackson, although considerably more pugnacious. He spoke a few phrases of English, but not enough to communicate in an effective manner.

"Escondan los hombres...tr...br...en la tienda," Raul instructed us.

"He wants us to keep out of sight until our truck is ready," related Joe. "There are American visitors here. Seeing us in Contra uniforms and armed might cause them to ask Raul embarrassing questions."

Johnny and I were ushered into a small windowless hut in the middle of the base, and a soldier was posted outside to keep any unwelcome visitors away.

Three Contras entered the hut, and Joe introduced them. Adan, a leather faced Indian of indeterminable age, somewhere between twenty three and forty, displayed a new shiny UZI submachine gun and two FMK2 hand grenades attached to his web belt. He wore a cap with the 'Soldier of Fortune' patch, a present from previous visitors from the Soldier of Fortune magazine. He held the very impressive post of Chief of Intelligence in Stedman's little army. He spoke poor English. The other two who went under their war names, Lejano *pronounced Lehano* and Chispa, were very young. Neither Lejano nor Chispa spoke a word of English. All communications with them had to be accomplished either through Adan or Joe.

"El Hombre grande," Chispa pointed to me.

"He said that you are a big man," smirked Joe.

"El Hombre joven," I responded nodding toward Chispa, and the kid suddenly smiled, approached, and patted me on the shoulder.

We hit it off from the beginning. When Chispa smiled, he was nothing but a kid from a back ranch, not a soldier with eight combat missions under his belt. Lejano, about nineteen, rarely smiled, on the other hand. He was quiet, spoke only when spoken to, although, I noticed a few times, he made comments to himself. He, too, was a veteran of eight combat missions. Lejano and Chispa carried M-16 rifles.

"I would advise," said Joe to Adan, "to exchange the UZI and M-16s for AK-47s."

"Por que?" responded Adan.

"AK's don't jam in the jungle conditions as M-16's do."

"It happens only with the old ammunition." Adan's weapon expertise apparently surpassed that of Joe's.

"We all should use the same type of ammo. If one is killed, the others could use his clips."

"If I get killed, you can have my UZI."

"All right, have it your way." Joe yielded; I think he was somewhat irritated by the way Adan was holding his own.

The truck finally pulled up, and we started our forty-mile journey to Puerto Lempira.

"As far as I know, they always give a military operation a name,"

I said to Joe. "What do you call this one?"

"Why don't you give it a name?"

"All right...How about the Operation Córdoba?"

"Córdoba it is."

The question mark operation was no longer question mark–it became Córdoba, and I was the one who gave it its name. Joe suckered me into that one, too, I mean into giving the operation its name. Suddenly the operation became, at least in part, mine. Whatever the outcome of it was going to be, I would be partially responsible for its success, or failure. James Riveaux had joined the players of this foolish war game, becoming a factor in Joe's Nicaraguan equation. The other factors included four more players, a boat, weather at sea, the possible Sandinista naval patrol, a toy chopper from Managua, and the equivalent of half million dollars. The players were able and ready, the boat...there was no boat waiting.

The Contra outpost commander in Puerto Lempira informed Adan and Joe that the boat was out to sea and would not be back for a couple of days. Adan hollered at the commander and Joe observed silently. I think Joe was patiently waiting until Adan let out the steam. Then he suggested asking the commander whether another boat was available. And, voila! one was–a wide low-sitting fairy tale shoe with its top sliced off unevenly.

"That will do," Joe said enthusiastically.

"We'll never make it in the open sea," I prophesied.

"Look at the alternatives," reasoned Joe. "We'll go back empty-handed and stay at the camp waiting for the next month's chopper's flight. Would you like that?"

I thought of rice-and-beans and el platano and said, "The boat looks fine. It's really built; they don't make boats like that anymore."

"I hope the weather will hold." Joe scanned the sky.

"There is a distant storm in the mid-Atlantic but it is moving well north of where we are," answered Adan.

"That was another mistake," Joe suddenly cut him off. "If your transmissions are monitored by the Sandinistas, and they probably are, then the enemy knows now that someone is going out to sea."

"We request weather forecasts routinely, Señor Green," Adan snapped back.

"Please don't request anything before consulting with me," Joe finalized firmly.

"I know Nicaragua, Señor Green, and you do not."

They crossed swords for the second time. An unpleasant pattern of relationship was developing, confrontation instead of cooperation–another damn fucking power struggle: who was in charge? Adan attempted to be a host and treated Joe as a guest. Being a senior officer in Stedman's army and probably outranking Joe, Adan projected himself as a commander. The war against the Sandinistas was Adan's war, not Joe's, who was an outsider, merely a visitor, a temporary element in the big Nicaraguan equation. Nicaragua belonged to Adan, a Nicaraguan, and not to Joe, a foreigner. Besides all these points in his favor, Adan had ventured behind the enemy lines more that once, always in command, while Joe had not. Thus, Adan's forte boiled down to a corollary that Nicaragua was his turf, not Joe's.

But no matter how one turned it, it was Joe's operation, conceived and planned by him and authorized as such by Stedman. Adan, whether he liked it or not, was merely an advisor and a guide, no less and no more than that–a hard pill for him to swallow. And above all, Joe was responsible for the outcome of this operation, not Adan. So, the conflict between the two top men set in from the beginning.

We loaded our gear and two fuel canisters on the boat. We were ready to sail. The sea greeted us with smooth, low waves; they rolled under the boat with comfortable regularity–up, down…roll, unroll– gently touching the sides and murmuring the Gulf of Mexico lullaby. Our mission was to prove that Murphy's Law was sheer nonsense.

We sat the course south. The cradle motion of the boat never missing a wave, the rhythmic change of the motor pitch, and the gentle whisper of pushed aside water gradually put me to sleep. Meanwhile, while I slept, the distant mid-Atlantic storm, originally small, intensified and turned southwest, toward us. Maybe that was a survival test bestowed upon us by Neptune, or he wished to impose a toll for passing through his kingdom and warned us that he was not going to be responsible for the consequences, if we refused to pay the toll. In response, Joe spat overboard. I missed witnessing this unwarranted, unfriendly request and our insulting response.

When I opened my eyes, the boat stern heaved, the motor whined, and the boat plunged into a foamy abyss. I tried to figure out where I was. I could see it was early in the morning. Water was everywhere: left and right, and below and above…I found the dipper. The boat dived and smashed into the oncoming wave. The offended wave roared in anger, and the boat responded with a strained moan. A wall of water rose above the bow, hesitated for a moment, and suddenly broke into a million globs and droplets showering everyone and everything in the boat. We headed into the storm. The boat sloped upward, and I discerned a chain of lights in the distance. The shore seemed to be unreachably far. The wind strengthened, and soon the rain obscured the lights of Puerto Cabezas. Adan modified the heading by another twenty or so degrees; the bow now, presumably, pointed straight toward the invisible shore. The waves started rolling the boat from side to side while, at the same time, tossing it up and down. At the end of each roll, the boat picked up more water.

I worked feverishly scooping the water and throwing it back overboard. Johnny joined in employing a cooking utensil, and even Lejano participated, using his hands in the 'Allstate' manner. But for all that valiant and almost superhuman effort, we were losing the battle against the sea. The boat picked up more water than we could throw out. Water rushed back and forth on the bottom of the boat carrying backpacks and tossing them around like toys. We were going to sink.

I lifted my head and could see the shore. Suddenly, the motor quit. Adan, cursing through his teeth, pulled the handle in the futile attempt to restart the motor. The motor gargled in response but refused to cooperate. The boat drifted helplessly, completely out of control. As a big wave lifted the stern, a fuel canister sailed by in the air, missing me and Chispa just by a few inches, and crashed into the middle seat easily breaking the seat in two.

"Get the fucking thing out of the boat!" shouted Joe.

The boat turned sideways, and at that moment I spotted the approaching wall of water. It had to be the 'ninth wave', in sailor's jargon, the largest wave of the storm.

"Grab your guns and gear!" hollered Joe.

The wave lifted the boat with a jerk, rolled it on its starboard side, tossed it with tremendous acceleration, and smashed it against the shore. The boat groaned and collapsed with a loud crash. Tons of water fell upon its corpse, transforming it into a shapeless heap of wood and metal: split beams, jagged boards mixed with rocks and sand, backpacks, and human bodies *including mine*–all tumbling while pushed up the shore. Then the retreating water forcefully pulled us back into the sea, right into another wave, and this non-yielding process repeated itself over and over again. I attempted to claw my way up the shore. A thick, heavy beam, probably a chunk of the boat's keel, helped me to accomplish the task by giving me a mighty thump on my butt and adding momentum to my effort *as well as leaving a blue mark*.

It seemed incredible that we survived, paying Neptune off only with cuts and bruises. But we lost all our food and medical supplies. Joe's Nicaraguan equation was falling apart: one of its main factors, the boat, was no more. My own little personal equation crumbled too: I lost my camera.

"At least we saved the tools," proclaimed Joe.

What a misnomer for weapons! A tool is something one builds, or fixes things with. A weapon is a device one uses to kill, or destroy that which was built with tools.

"Are we going home now?" I asked Joe.

"How?" He smirked. I watched the bits and pieces of what used to be a boat, tumbling up and down the beach every time a new wave broke at its front step. That was a good question: how? Under different circumstances, the answer could be found in the Canadian version of the Last Frontier: 'Go north, young man, go north.' That's where Honduras lay: north. But instead, we moved south. Nothing was going to stop these crazy goons from completing their mission.

As we marched, the rain stopped, and flatlands with meadows and patches of woods gradually became hills covered with impenetrable jungle growth, which, in order to pass through, we had to chop with the two surviving machetes. The point we tried to reach lay somewhere south of the town of Yablis. We reached our destination before dark. We were exhausted and hungry. That's when I started liking Chispa even more than before. He was the only man among us wise enough to independently stash away a bowl of cooked beans. It wasn't much, but it was better than nothing at all.

But we did not have to worry about the loss of food because the chopper that we were going to bring down carried, besides the money, miscellaneous supplies. Joe joked that we were going to have vodka and caviar *destined for the Russian advisors stationed at Puerto Cabezas* for breakfast.

Our position in the open patch, close to the top of 'la montaña', carefully selected by Adan, faced south. The scenery from the mountain overlooking smaller hills was breathtaking. Patches of fuzzy lint peeling off the underside of the slowly moving cloud blanket did not obstruct the view: they disintegrated long before they could reach the slopes of the rolling hills below. The hills did not actually roll, but appeared to do that, in slow motion, if one stared in the distance long enough without blinking. They competed in the show of their individual and unique assets. From my vantage point, the grand prize went to the nearest hill with a mysterious recess on its side, curved and contoured in the sensual image of a yet untouched, young, beautiful woman; entry forbidden–reserved for the one she would choose someday.

I PRONOUNCE YOU...DEAD

In the morning the cloud cover thickened. The dark grey mush drifted slowly above us, like a smooth wavy quilt, comfortably close and seemingly solid. And maybe it was, at least until it touched the mountain peak. The mountain peak pierced its surface and plowed into its body like an ocean liner cleaving the open sea. One could expect to hear a ripping sound of torn fabric, or, at least, a splash of spilt water, but instead there was only silence.

Joe explained the procedure of bringing down the helicopter. Due to the low cloud ceiling, the chopper was going to fly at our level or maybe even lower. The distance to the chopper, according to Joe, should not exceed two thousand feet. Johnny was going to use his M-60 carefully, trailing the chopper first, then carefully bringing the fire on its tail. The rest of us were instructed to lead the chopper in our sights by half length and hit the cabin, not the engine or the fuel tank.

"Fire on my command. With luck, we'll bring her down in one piece," Joe stated confidently.

According to Adan, the chopper was going to arrive within two hours, but the two hours passed with no helicopter in sight.

"Maybe they changed the schedule," I suggested, disappointed and relieved at the same time.

"Or maybe someone else has already shot it down," Johnny remarked grimly.

"We'll wait," said Joe.

The helicopter showed up almost without warning. There was silence in the hills, and suddenly there she was, emerging out of nowhere. Initially masked by the near hill, which also shielded us from hearing the chopper, she peeked out first, then lifted up and straightened out, slicing her own roar with the blades. She flew slightly above our level and closer than anticipated; it seemed to me, that she flew straight at us, like in the movies.

The chopper climbed on top of us; I saw nothing but her belly and fired. All did. What followed was a total surprise: a bright flash and enormous fireball in place of what only a moment ago was a helicopter. A warm, hard, heavy, pillow pushed me in the chest, and I fell backwards. A deafening boom almost split my head. The boom echoed from the nearby hills. Then suddenly all became quiet, except for the ringing in my eardrums.

"The motherfuckers carried explosives," I heard Johnny say.

A huge grayish cloud slowly changed its shape while rising and drifting by us; its curly festoons extended all the way to the sloping ground like tentacles of a gigantic octopus, the octopus of death.

"Does it mean that we are not going to have vodka and caviar for breakfast?" I heard myself say.

"All right, let's get the hell out of here." Joe said the obvious. And that was the moment when we plunged into another internal crisis: Joe and Adan could not agree on the method of our return to Honduras. Joe aimed to proceed directly to Puerto Cabezas and, under the cover of darkness, steal a boat. Adan objected to this plan on the grounds that it was too risky. He suggested a safer plan: travel on foot by land.

We voted. Split in the middle, three against three; we faced a stalemate. And, of course, Joe found a wise solution to the problem: he produced a penny.

"Heads or tails?" He flicked the penny.

All watched the coin; it flipped in its confined and predictable binary choice of outcome. Maybe it didn't gain in value; the real worth of this flipping penny was still a penny, but it certainly reached the peak in its importance: it decided the fate of six men.

"Tails," Adan chose.

Lincoln fell flat on his face; Adan won. I picked up the coin and, for the first time in my life, examined a penny. There were no tails on it–just another faceless fucking government building *the Mint? or something else? I didn't care what it was* and the inscription 'e pluribus unum' *I really didn't give a damn what that meant either.*

We were going to walk. That's when I had an opportunity to learn another interesting military concept–a concept of a point man. A point man is a scout sent ahead of a group to see whether or not it is safe to proceed. He must stay in sight of the group at all times, and he is the one who pushes the panic button, when circumstances warrant it.

"So, he's the guy who sticks his neck out," I remarked.

"No, not at all," elucidated Joe. "During an ambush, the enemy usually lets the point man pass and hits the main body."

"That's very comforting for the point man."

Due to my lack of military experience I was made a tail man, which was fine with me. In this position, I had freedom to stop and examine idiosyncrasies of the jungle any time I felt like it, sometimes dropping back a bit. I was fortunate to observe a specimen of Eurypyga Helias, a grayish brown bird with the unmistakable two dark stripes on its long tail, and its multicolor wing insignia formed by coverts. And when two Pipra Mentalis landed only ten feet from me and commenced a trilling duet, I almost forgot that my stomach was empty. I was afraid to move, because the moment these birds spotted me, the magnificent show would end. Both singers wore bright red crests and yellow pants befitting the show.

"Los pájaros." Chispa startled me, and the birds. "Los pájaros hermosos."

"Yes, they are beautiful, aren't they?"

Another mile down, we finally reached the swollen Wawa.

"There is a ferry down the river, Adan says, but, of course, we are not going to take it," Joe informed me and Johnny.

"What then?" I asked. "Swim?"

"You've got it."

"Swell."

I would guess that there are limited number of ways one can build a float. Given time and material, we could build a float capable of holding us, though we still would lack the oars to propel it across the river. Being in a hurry to get to the other side we built two platforms to hold our gear, using the material available: logs that had washed ashore, bamboo, and vines to tie it all together. I realized how indispensable our machetes were; without them, we couldn't build even a two-log floating contraption to hold a proverbial chicken willing to cross the river.

Pushing the floats, we, three per float, started our wet journey across the river. From the surface, the distance to the other side seemed even greater. No one talked. Occasionally, a curious seagull, visiting here from the Gulf, swooped down on us to see whether the two floating masses carried any eatable refuse, and, disappointed, veered off to the side. Nearing the shore, we spotted a small clearing in the jungle and, fighting current, finally reached it. I was tired.

I could hear birds, but, too tired to move, ignored them. Undoubtedly, this was the most exciting day of my entire life. I did two things that I have never done before: shot down a helicopter and swam across a river, each deed greatly overshadowing the closest qualifying event from my past—driving my father's pickup truck into a ditch. The fireball and even the swim across the river were exciting events.

But at the same time I felt somewhat uneasy, kind of not used to it. After all, we had killed. Who knows? Maybe it was my bullet that hit the explosives, and it was I who killed those guys inside the helicopter.

"Don't look so happy," said Joe sitting down next to me.

"I was thinking of the families of those guys in the chopper, their mothers, wives, kids..."

"Those are outside factors; they don't count." Joe rationalized irrationally. "Look, when we face these guys, the stakes are equal—it's either them or us. Don't you see it? In case you forgot, we have families too. I have an ex-wife, two sons, and a daughter."

"But these guys didn't shoot at us..."

Up to now, all recent events didn't seem real. Probably because they came too fast and there were too many of them: the sea wreck, the chopper, the river—all within the span of less than two days. And until yesterday it all was just games. But today these games were for real: it was hard to deny the fact of destroying the chopper and killing its crew. And I participated. It didn't matter whose bullet hit the explosives, we all shared the blame equally. Heck! I was never going to tell anyone that I shot at the chopper's belly, through the deck, straight in the cargo bay...

WHEN THE BULLET HITS THE BONE

Right after breakfast a small incident occurred. Life is full of surprises. But some individuals—call it coincidence, or luck, or curse—have more than their share of one kind of surprise. Johnny's curse was snakes. He was bitten by a snake at the age of nine; he always found snakes in unlikely places: under the door mat, in the love seat, and even in the walls of his house. This morning he discovered a snake in his backpack.

"Christ!! What is it with me? Do I smell good to snakes or something?" He kicked the backpack, but the snake refused to come out.

"See if she has a pointed snout," I said.

"You see it," said the sissy.

I emptied the backpack on the ground, all contents including the snake.

"There...She's got a round snout, a garden variety, completely harmless. Probably doesn't even have any teeth. Look, she is more scared of you than your girlfriend." Although I spoke confidently, like an expert on snakes, I wasn't at all sure whether the snake really wasn't poisonous. But I felt that I had to show these jungle know-it-alls that I knew something they didn't.

To my great relief, Adan confirmed that the snake was harmless, and my stock went up. Adan was the authority on all local matters. He knew the route, the natives, the nature—Nicaragua was his country. On the surface, nothing seemed to bother him, but beneath the dark leather mask of indifference hid a very sensitive, intelligent, and proud man. Joe's mistake, or maybe intent, was his lack of recognition of Adan's special status in the group. As Stedman's right hand, Adan commanded a lot of respect. But Joe did not differentiate between the three, Adan, Lejano, and Chispa, at all, be it the assignment on point, collecting shrubs for fire, or the night watch duties. And, I think, Adan resented that.

This morning Adan led first. We crossed a brook and entered the jungle. Chispa and I trailed the group. *I took the rear position whenever I could.* We walked silently, listening to the chorus of hisses, trills, whistles, clicks, and staccatos—all fused into one magnificent, intricate jungle melody.

"Mira…" whispered Chispa. "Los pájaros."

"I wish I had my camera," I said.

"La cámara, si…si…" agreed Chispa.

He was the only man in the group who shared my interest in birds, well, to a point. The others didn't care one way or another, except that maybe some were curious from the offending culinary angle of how tasty those birds would be, if cooked. Johnny, though, apparently after long and exhaustive analysis, came up with the question of dubious scientific value, 'Do birds fart?'

While walking in the rear, it occurred to me that our group's intrusion on the jungle's privacy probably frightened off most of its inhabitants, and, if I took the point, then I would see more of them. So, I volunteered.

"Yeah, I guess you're ready for that." Joe did not object. "Just follow the trail and listen ahead. Keep us in sight."

Walking alone, I enjoyed the jungle. Jungle! No other environment can offer as many sights, and sounds, and smells as the jungle can. When in the jungle, one tends to put up resistance not to be overwhelmed by the flood of strong, often contradictory, sensations. One may trace a unique, rhododendron-tainted scent to a red or pink ginger flower and then suddenly step right into a stream of pungent, acrid odor of rotting vegetation. I soaked in these sensations, incomparable to anything else. Totally unexpectedly, I found myself face-to-face with a stocky, bigheaded Cochlearius Cochlearius, the boat-billed heron. His tuft went up, like in courtship, which produced mixed emotions in me.

"Scat, you, dumbfuck," I said to the heron.

He seemed to realize that my resemblance to Mrs. Cochlearius was only superficial and totally inconsequential and took off. Disappearing in the brush, he said, "Kwa-kwa-ko-ko-ko-ook."

I didn't know what he meant by that, but just to have the last word in our brief exchange, I answered, "The same to you, pal."

The jungle ended abruptly, cut by a narrow opening. I saw the sun, the sky, and a divi-divi tree. Suddenly, I was facing six Sandinistas. They all carried AKs, but only one held his on ready. They were as much surprised seeing me as I was seeing them. We just stared at each other.

Finally, the leading man inquired, "Como te llamas?"

"Enchiladas," I said, using up twenty five percent of my Spanish vocabulary.

The Sandinistas seemed puzzled by my reply, then the second man made a remark, and all laughed. I held my AK muzzle down, so the Sandinistas, considering me not being a threat, did not bother to ready their AKs. Perhaps they mistook me for a Russian advisor on a stroll through the jungle. I suspect that even if I told them who I really was, they wouldn't believe me: what in hell would an American be doing deep inside their territory, alone? But I was not.

"Hit the dirt!" I heard Joe's shriek behind me. I fell on the ground and covered my head with both hands. I couldn't hear shots. Instead, a giant stone crusher grinded rocks. They cracked, split, and crumbled into gravel and dust under enormous pressure of the grinding wheel. I heard screams of pain. One of the Sandinistas fell right next to me, and we stared at each other for awhile before I realized that he was dead–he wasn't blinking.

The deafening noise probably didn't last longer than fifteen seconds. I lifted my head and watched Lejano and Chispa approach. They stopped and crouched holding their M-16s on ready. Johnny and Adan leap-frogged ahead; Joe followed. Then Johnny stood up and advanced alone. I watched him lower the barrel of his M-60 machine gun and make a stew out of a wounded Sandinista. Another one, still capable of raising his arms, sat up in the grass.

Johnny levelled his deadly tool. What was it that Dr. Kubler-Ross said about the stages of death? 'Anger, denial, bargaining, depression, and acceptance.' All nonsense. Here, in the jungle, the stages were shock, stupor, panic, pleading, and resignation. I read this chilling sequence in the face of the doomed Sandinista. Johnny pulled the trigger, and there was no more face at all–just flying splinters of shattered bone, shreds of torn flesh, gobs of splashed brain matter, and a pink mist...I ran behind the divi-divi tree and threw up, then I cried.

"Hey, hey...stop wasting ammo, will you!" I heard Joe holler at Johnny.

I raised my eyes to heavens and was stunned by the sudden realization that our venture was no game; these guys didn't just play. It all, from the beginning, was terrifyingly real, and I simply hadn't realized that it was real. Up to now, I had willingly participated in these guys' 'fun', even enjoyed myself to a certain degree, particularly shooting down the helicopter. It was exciting, Rambo stuff–the scenery, sequence, timing, and all. I didn't see the faces of those who died; they were no more than an abstraction, almost a figment of my imagination. They were just part of the game–players, not victims.

But here, I saw the faces of those Sandinistas very close. They were surprised exactly like me, they joked and laughed like ordinary human beings, and then they were no more.

"Are you all right?" Joe found me behind the divi-divi tree.

"Yeah." I pulled myself up.

Chispa and Adan dragged the bodies off the trail. Lejano chopped tree branches with his machete, making stakes. I stopped by the body with no head, just a bloody stump with uneven edges. This was the Sandinista who 'lost his face'.

"Grab his legs," Johnny told me. "Come on, we don't have all day."

"What are those stakes for?" I asked.

Johnny did not answer, but the hacking sounds coming from behind us, exactly like those in the butcher shop, did.

"Why?!"

"Psychological warfare." Joe stood right behind me. "Go and give'm a hand."

"...malgastando la cabeza," Chispa lamented.

At least one of them has human feelings and remorse of what they've done, I thought.

"What did he say?" I asked Joe.

"He is complaining that Johnny wasted one head, now we have only five." Joe turned to the busy Indians. "Rápido, rápido!"

People die of old age, due to illness, in accidents, and in wars, and each death brings pain to the loved ones, family and friends; each death is a very significant event. I was brought up believing that to be true. And suddenly, here, in the jungle, six deaths that I had witnessed had no significance at all. The whole thing boiled down to simple arithmetic: twelve lives minus six equals six lives–a very impartial and cruel jungle equation.

But that was only the beginning; what followed defied description. I watched the scene with magnetized fascination; I found myself captivated by the cool savagery of the process, its shameless efficiency, and the cynical composure of the participants. These men broke the mold of civilization, they invalidated all commandments, they defied gods!

And what did I do? Try to stop them? Pray for these men's forgiveness? No, I joined the process. My God! I think I smiled. I smiled because I was experiencing a feeling of tremendous satisfaction, a sense of accomplishment, as if I had finally completed a hard task scheduled a long time ago. But how could it be? I didn't search for it, I didn't want it. I didn't even know there was such a task. Then what was the source of my satisfaction? It was as if I'd passed a hard test; I was able to accomplish something that I thought I would not be able to accomplish.

"That's what I'd like to do to some folks back home," Joe said.

And suddenly it was all clear to me. We were always capable of unspeakable deeds and did not commit them only because we were not in the opportune setting to commit them. Social laws and moral standards of the 'civilized' human society stopped us from committing such deeds. But here, in the jungle, social laws and moral standards did not apply. The main law here was the law of survival; all human actions were governed by it. Human emotions were subjugated by this all-pervading law, and only the most primitive, the most barbaric emotions were allowed to flourish: hate, cruelty, and, above all, fear. Fear was the moving force, a defense, and a killer. Hate and cruelty only supplemented fear in, what Joe called, the Jungle Survival Equation. Psychological warfare was part of survival, in the long run. And me? For as long as I was in the jungle, and with the group, I became a non-cancelable part of that cruel equation.

"And that's what some folks in Puerto Cabezas will probably want to do to us," I replied.

"Let's make sure that doesn't happen." Joe lifted his eyebrows and slightly tilted his head forward as if saying, 'If it's all right with you.'

It's not every day that one comes across the opportunity to behold a row of severed human heads with nothing but a bloody stake to show for the rest of the body. Chispa and Lejano hauled the last headless body to the side, and Chispa spat on it. The gruesome task was completed at last. Chispa stepped back and critically scrutinized the 'sculpture' in the same manner that an artist examines his artistic creation.

"Muy bien." He was satisfied. The rest of us stared at the 'work of art' blank-faced.

"Vamos," Joe finally said.

He tossed his Chinese carbine into the bushes and picked up a newer model of the Sandinista's Russian AK-47. I abstained from the firearms exchange and retained my oriental model on the grounds that I had gotten used to it *the real reason, frankly, was my squeamishness of using a dead man's weapon.*

Meanwhile, the jungle melody, briefly interrupted by an

insignificant human drama, resumed. We started walking. The pace was fast; we were trying to distance ourselves from the art exhibition. Initially sick to my stomach, I wasn't certain how I felt now. There was no remorse, no sorrow, not any other 'appropriate' emotion–I was numb inside. I had participated in the horrendous act of desecration of human body. Blood stains covered my hands. All walked silently. There was nothing to say. Later in the afternoon we set up a camp.

It seemed as if here, in Nicaragua, the dusk was shorter than back home. Lying on the ground and staring at the stars, quite exhausted, I couldn't think of anything but the massacre. Was there a choice? Could we have avoided the massacre? No, for us there was no other choice. It was the jungle law: kill, or be killed. We could not take prisoners. Where would we take them? And we could not let them go. Compassion, generosity, and chivalry did not apply here. It was necessary to kill, I understood that, but the head stuff was not necessary. I tried to imagine what would be the first reaction of anyone stumbling upon the grotesque row–shock? horror? Like Joe said, the best of psychological warfare. The point stated was: see what we can do, what you are up against. We are stronger than you, remember that. The purpose of the head row was to instill fear in the enemy, for whatever it was worth. I replayed the day's events in my clouded mind, returning again and again to the emetic experience.

The subdued voices of my companions, the crackling of a camp fire, the hoot of a distant owl, and the much closer low-to-high accelerating whistle of an unknown bird, merged with the hum inside my head.

"Tomatoes kaput." I could hear Adan lamenting the fate of tomatoes squashed during the skirmish.

A desperate animal cry covered by a greedy panther growl upheld the finality of death. I dozed off. In my dream, I nailed a head on the sharpened stake tip. The head winked, smiled, and stuck its tongue out at me. I cried out and ran...

"Wake up, Jim." Joe shook my shoulder.

The dinner was, finally, ready. Rice, this time generously spiked with tomato pulp, tasted better than beans. The familiar local Indian tea made of boiled palm leaves easily washed it down.

Joe sat next to me, "Don't let it get to you. The boys did what they had to. It was necessary."

"The hell it was."

I wondered what made this man tick. His attitude toward the

'head episode' seemed quite casual *yeah, we nailed a few heads on stakes, so what?* as if he had done this sort of thing before.

Johnny disappeared in the bushes to take a crap, at least that's what he said, but I had a feeling that something else was on his mind, like jerking off after a stressful day. Adan stretched on the ground on the other side of the camp fire. Chispa carried dinner for Lejano still on the watch.

A bird fell off a nearby tree and landed clumsily next to our fire. Perhaps a snake hunting for a meal had startled the bird. The bird sat motionless trying to ascertain whether it was safe to share company with us.

"Like us–with enemies all around," commented Joe. "Here, pal, have some." He threw a handful of cooked rice at the bird. The bird mistook the handout for an attack, took off, and disappeared in the dark of the night.

The fire was slowly burning out, and the jungle seemed to step closer. I stretched on the ground. My head cleared, thanks to the short pre-dinner nap, the emotions subsided. I thought of home–my cool apartment in Royal Hill, the swimming pool, the sun, the cool breeze…and Martha…All was so far away, and so long ago.

INSIDE THE LION'S MOUTH

A cool and clear morning paved the way for another nice day. I watched with a smile how Johnny carefully examined his backpack. But it was Chispa's turn to entertain night guests. One of them was late on leaving the premises, this time the interior of Chispa's boot. Probably its warmth *and the aroma* were hard to part with. The scorpion claimed Chispa's boot and resisted eviction, but presented with an ultimatum and fare amount of vigorous shaking, he changed his mind and volunteered to fall out.

We proceeded down the trail. The hills and the jungle ended; we broke out in the open. The trail straightened out; now we could walk slower while still covering more distance then we could in the jungle.

I changed Adan on the point. The scenery—wide meadows and scattered groups of pine trees—was a welcome change from the ever-sloping slippery jungle trails. I breathed fresh air, listened to birds sing, and enjoyed the space—the clean, cool space of the morning prairie. Yesterday's events lost their immediacy and part of their significance. Life always conquers death, and I was surrounded with life. Whatever happened yesterday was history to be filed away and forgotten. It had no bearing on today, or tomorrow. Therefore, I could shed the yesterday and go on with living. I walked with my head high enjoying my renewed positive emotions, restored faith in the future and even, maybe, in the basic goodness of man.

The unmistakable 'whop-whop' of a helicopter approaching from behind caught me off guard. The danger of being spotted from the air had never occurred to me. And now we were caught in the open; there was no time to search for cover. I stopped. What were we going to do? Shoot down the chopper?

The group continued walking toward me, casually carrying carbines over their shoulder, as if the helicopter presented no danger whatsoever. All waved when the chopper closed in, and I figured that Joe tried to sell to the helicopter crew the impression that we were no one else but friendly Sandinista soldiers. I waved, too. The chopper passed low and continued on its course. I waited until the group joined up with me.

"Maybe they bought it, maybe they didn't," Joe speculated. "We can't take that chance. I think we should leave the trail."

"I agree," Adan nodded.

Bless my buttons, I thought. For the first time they agreed on something. We turned right and proceeded east for two or three miles. Encountering a swamp, we resumed the northerly course. The general idea of this unsophisticated maneuver was to circumvent a possible ambush site further down the trail. We did not know that the trail, too, turned northeast and converged on the edge of the swamp–an ideal spot for an ambush.

The party was awaiting us. The hosts were dressed in exquisite green-yellow-and-brown-patch and elegant green tuxedos. Adhering to social etiquette, they brandished shiny AK-47 assault rifles indispensable for such an amiable shindig like the one we were just about to attend.

Chispa, who was on the point, raised his arm signalling a warning and started sliding sideways behind a bush. We astonished our hosts by entering through the back door instead of using the front entrance, but it didn't matter, because they were ready for us, even if we had dropped through the roof. The hosts greeted us with exclamations of surprise, and we exchanged a few friendly rounds. Leaving Chispa behind to cover us from the rear *to cover our ass, as Joe put it*, we advanced along the swamp edge toward a small hill.

Suddenly, the whole left flank came to life and about two dozen soldiers ran in our direction. They formed a line and took positions two hundred yards away. No one fired. Lejano, sent to check out what lay ahead, came back. A grassy inlet behind the hill led into the jungle and appeared to be a safe passage. Lejano did not inspect the peninsula on the other side of the inlet, because there was no reason at all to suspect that Sandinistas could be there. That was Lejano's report.

A firefight erupted behind us indicating that our hosts had bumped into Chispa. He screamed and collapsed. Our way back was cut off; Chispa was hit.

"Okay, let's get moving," urged Joe.

"What about Chispa?" I asked Johnny.

"Forget him, he's finished."

"We don't know that," I protested. "We can't just leave him behind."

"Jim is right." Joe sided with me. "The bastards can take him alive and make him talk. If they will find out who we are, then the whole Sandinista army will be on our ass."

The distance that I had to cover before reaching Chispa was about one hundred yards. I must confess that I had second thoughts.

A machine gun burst behind me, announcing that Johnny was giving me cover. Crawling in the grass is not the most efficient way to travel. It took me awhile to reach Chispa. He lay on his side clutching his belly. I figured that it would be easier and safer to pull Chispa in the grass. If I carried him on my back, he would present a highly visible target, since the grass was not tall enough to conceal us. I started dragging him, holding him by the collar of his shirt; he ground his teeth and held his breath in pain.

A second later, the hosts surprised us with impressive special effects. First, I didn't understand what was happening. A bolt of lightning struck the shallow water, splashing dirt and creating a billow of grayish blue smoke slowly rolling toward us. Then a bag of concrete mixture hit the ground to the left and exploded, showering us with sand.

"Run!" I heard Joe's scream.

Shots crackled from all sides. Chispa curled up in a ball on the ground. I lifted this moaning ball of pain, sprung up on my feet, and started running toward the hill. I ran in the open, leaping over logs and puddles, expecting to be hit by bullets any moment; I ran for my life. Chispa screamed from pain without stopping; I wanted to drop him and run alone, but couldn't open my arms and clutched his body even tighter.

Time slowed down...I was only vaguely aware, almost oblivious, of the events around me. I think another bag of cement exploded behind me. I just watched the hill ahead: could I make it? I remembered tripping over Johnny who lay on the rim of the bank. The bank sloped gradually toward the edge of the swamp, a grassy bed covered with water. I lost my balance, dropped Chispa, and tumbled down the bank.

"Are you all right?" Joe tossed me my AK *I had left it behind, when I went to get Chispa.*

"What are we waiting for?" I asked.

"We're trapped," answered Joe. "That peninsula, which Lejano was talking about, houses a machine gun nest."

Only then did I notice Lejano lying on the ground face up, yellowish pale, with possible kidney damage, his pelvis shattered by a bullet. His condition was, obviously, as lamentable as Chispa's. But we were trapped. Although we did not walk into the ambush set up by the Sandinistas along the trail, in which case we would be dead already, we still walked into what is called a killing zone, prepared just for us. A killing zone is an open field in the enemy's lane of fire. The action, which usually takes place in the killing zone, is roughly equivalent to a turkey shoot, a very unpleasant experience, particularly if you are playing the part of the turkey.

We were trapped in the killing zone, unable to retreat due to a machine gun and two or three AK's placed behind us, prevented from proceeding by another machine gun and two or three AK's ahead, and were just about to be pushed into the swamp by another two dozen AK's right into the firing lane of that second machine gun from the peninsula. I excluded the human element behind those AK's and machine guns, Joe's way, to simplify the scenario. The human element was just a biological abstraction that pulled the trigger–guns did the damage. To complicate the matters by a notch or two, a mortar nest was positioned somewhere behind the Sandinistas' AK-line, on the other side of the trail. This little bugger was the omnipotent entity, which threw those 'lightnings' and the exploding 'cement bags' at me while I was hauling Chispa across the killing field. To worsen our position even further, if only it were possible, our M-79 grenade launcher, with which we could take out the peninsula machine gun nest, had been put out of its misery at the same time when Lejano was wounded.

We were trapped in a small blind spot behind the hill, facing about three dozen, I would guess, less than friendly Sandinista soldiers. With Chispa and Lejano both out of action, the ratio of nine to one exceeded even Joe's 'survivable' ratio of seven to one *by his claim, every member of TRAG was worth seven soldiers of any army.* Since both Adan and I were not members of TRAG, our chances lessened even further. We were going to die.

The Sandinistas were regrouping for an attack. While the preparations were taking place, no shots were fired. All became quiet; even Chispa stopped moaning. Adan attended to the wounded, but there was very little he could do since our medical supplies were lost.

The Sandinistas split the line in two with a small gap separating both groups. The mortar gunners stopped sending their loud presents, too: they either ran out of ordnance, or, more likely, were saving it for the final push *they had already wasted three rounds on me, plus some.*

Joe split our defense perimeter of one hundred and eighty degrees into four sectors. He took the hill and everything beyond it, Adan and Johnny faced the main front, and I was assigned to defend our left flank. Of course, this arrangement was fluid: in case of an all-out assault, we all would be facing it, lending assistance to other sectors, when necessary.

"Save ammo," Joe cautioned. "Don't shoot until they reach one hundred yards. Concentrate on the targets in your sector. Fire at your discretion. If the chopper comes back, shoot the motherfucker down this time."

The instructions were specific and simple. I studied my sector. From my position, I could not see the trail, but I knew that a few trees and bushes about two hundred and fifty yards away were screening a machine gun and several AK's. The field in front of me was generally flat with grass in patches, not capable of concealing anyone. But the main action was expected in Adan's and Johnny's sectors.

I relaxed a bit *if one could call the state of less tension a relaxation* and watched a hawk diving toward the Sandinistas' side. I couldn't see the prey. Suddenly, the hawk veered off before completing the dive. Apparently, he had spotted humans, the soldiers. I made a mental note of their location. Then I glanced back to see the wounded and missed the moment when two Sandinista soldiers rose up in Johnny's sector and crossed into mine. The second soldier carried a heavy box of ammunition, probably for the machine gun because that is where they were heading by taking a shortcut.

I looked at Johnny, and he nodded. Taking very careful aim at the space between the soldiers, thus allowing for distance and my inexperience *the bullets would scatter and hit at least one*, I squeezed the trigger. Nothing happened. Fumbling feverishly, I pulled the lever back and released it. Then re-aiming and yanking the trigger with greater force than was necessary, I sensed with satisfaction as the carbine came to life. The second soldier dropped the box and fell on the ground. The first stopped and returned to the fallen. He was going to pick up the wounded *just like me and Chispa*, and I wasn't sure if I would be able to shoot again and kill someone who was saving his buddy's life. But the soldier only picked up the box and started running directly away from me. I aimed *it was easy, because from my angle he presented a stationary target* and fired a short burst; he fell.

"Good shooting, man, congratulations with your first...

"Johnny never finished, because the world ruptured. The volley of shots, a sudden elevating and then subsiding crescendo, a finale of 4th of July fireworks, crackled on all sides. Someone nudged my elbow, but when I glanced to see who it was, there was no one next to me. A string of little spatters was approaching me, fast; I ducked. The ground shook, and I lifted my head to see what caused the shake only to discover a big splash of dirt, grass, and smoke right in front of me. Apparently, the mortar gunners had not run out of ordnance yet. Someone pulled me back by my leg.

"Get the hell down here! What's the matter with you? You wanna get yourself killed?" It was Johnny.

Now it really started...In the killing field, the stages of death are shock, panic, a lot of cold fear, praying for a miracle, and more fear–the stuff heroes are made of.

In a sense, I had already accepted the inevitability of death, but still, a faint gleam of hope remained. Maybe there was a chance of 'cavalry' coming to our rescue, although I couldn't imagine in what form it would come. A mistake by the enemy could change the odds in our favor, though I didn't see how it could influence the outcome, considering the overwhelming number of enemy soldiers. Also, there was a potential life saver called luck, but again, I couldn't envision how it would apply to us. Then, of course, a miracle could happen, an earthquake, for instance, which would disrupt the whole thing and give us a chance to escape. And, finally, there could be an option of surrendering, but here they didn't take prisoners, especially after what we'd done the day before. If we were to die, I only hoped that my death would come swiftly and painlessly.

Joe was hit by a shrapnel in the left shoulder and bled.

"Here, check if you can see it," he told Johnny.

"Yeah, it's not deep. I can get it out, but it will hurt like hell."

"Do it."

I watched the shivers-sending process of field surgery without anesthetic. Joe tried to pretend it didn't hurt. The metal splinter was finally removed.

"Let it bleed a little." Johnny comforted the obviously suffering Joe. "It will wash the dirt out."

Then Johnny turned to me and pointed to my elbow, "You're wounded, too."

I remembered someone touching my elbow, and when I turned, there was no one next to me. The bullet had just grazed the muscle of the forearm without inflicting much damage. Blood trickled down my arm inside the sleeve. Now that my attention was attracted to the wound, I began sensing the sting.

The 4th of July finale continued. I lay on my back watching a few white, shady clouds sailing slowly across the azure ocean of the sky. Set on the course to their own destiny, these vagile wanderers were completely indifferent to what was unfolding below them–our end.

"God, please help me! If I get out of this alive, I will go to the nearest church and light up candles–the whole bunch of them," I prayed.

Another mortar bomb hit the swamp; it meant that the next bomb, zeroing in, was going to hit the blind spot, where we hid. The peninsula machine gunner, apparently on edge, misinterpreted the explosion in the swamp and opened up fire. The water erupted with a hundred little fountains.

"Look," said Johnny pointing up the slope.

A large basilisk, with his legs moving in diagonal sync, was attempting to climb over the bank's rim.

"Lousy timing for visiting his date," I commented, very proud of the fact that I could joke in the face of death. Surprisingly, at once it felt easy, as if I were less vulnerable than before. It didn't make any sense, but the carefree sensation and shedding of fear was welcome. I suddenly understood all those who were said to be laughing in the face of death. They were not heroes, or crazy, or showing off. They simply refused to accept death, they defied, they conquered her, "Look, motherfucker, I'm laughing at you, and there ain't a fucking thing you can do about it."

A bullet struck the ground next to the lizard and startled him by splashing dirt in his face. The lizard turned and paused, as if considering whether or not to proceed, then he stood up on his hind legs, and, wobbling, ran down the bank. He passed us in a hurry and disappeared by the water's edge.

"Just like us," smiled Johnny.

The noise stopped abruptly.

"Well, here they come," sighed Johnny and climbed up to his machine gun. I followed.

Once in a while, one comes across a frog nursery by a pond, or swamp. Those little rascals, when startled, do not scatter, but leap in the same direction *not necessarily away from the approaching human.* The rearmost baby frog jumps over the front ones, while those wait until they become a rear echelon, then they jump and overtake the others. Something like that was going on in front of me, in the open field. The Sandinista soldiers leapfrogged approaching our defense line.

This is it, I thought, and the fear came back. There still was a chance for an earthquake, or cavalry to arrive, but the time was running out, fast. Johnny and Adan opened up first, and the hopping in their sectors stopped for awhile. Several soldiers returned the fire. In my sector, however, leapfrogging continued. I made sure that I was ready, then aimed at the closest two 'frogs' using my tested technique: shoot in the space between the two, bullets will scatter and, probably, hit at least one. One screamed and fell. The clip was empty, and I changed it. Then I fired again and again. Someone screamed and cursed; I realized it was me.

The Sandinistas retreated, leaving their wounded and dead behind, I couldn't believe it. We beat them off, we survived! I even thought that we won.

"We did it, we beat them!" I shared my elation with Johnny.

But my elation, of course, was premature. The Sandinistas brought reinforcements.

Joe proposed a plan. His plan was simple and, of course, as all his plans, high risk. Adan, Johnny, and I were to simulate an attempt of crossing the swamp–create a diversion. While the peninsula gunners concentrated on annihilating us, Joe would cross the open space between the hill and the grassy inlet. Then he would circumvent the nest, approach it from behind, and terminate it.

"When you hear the commotion on the peninsula, go straight into the swamp, don't wait for me," he finalized. "Oh, yeah, I'll need this." He borrowed my hand grenade.

The bare stretch between the hill and the inlet could be seen by both the peninsula gunners and about three dozen AK's, plus, maybe, the omnipotent mortar. We did our best in creating the diversion and almost getting killed in the process. Maybe it helped Joe, or maybe it did not, because we heard many AK's fired, obviously not at us, and then the peninsula machine gun shifted its fire in Joe's direction.

"I'll go and see, if he's hit," said Johnny.

He came back and was silent.

"I saw something in the grass," he said finally, "but I'm not sure what it was. It didn't move…Let's wait."

The sun was falling slowly, too slowly; the dusk would settle down long after we were gone, gone to the promised land.

COUP DE GRACE

A 'cut-out line', or 'save-your-ass line', defined by a defense commander, is simply how close the enemy should get to you before you are allowed to run. This life saving concept did not apply in our case: our only exit, the swamp, was just another killing zone. But a 'cut-out time' did apply. We had to get out before the next assault, or die. Now, we waited for Joe's action. If he was shot, then it didn't matter, because the chances of making it across the killing zone were infinitesimally small.

I thought of my parents and regretted not letting them know where I went. And what about my Martha? Now, they would never find out what happened to me, my disappearance would remain a mystery forever. And my body would be thrown in the swamp right here, next to the damn hill. I turned and glanced at the swamp. I hope they have no alligators here, I thought. They could tear my body apart.

A muffled bang followed by two AK-series from the peninsula announced that Joe, after all, had succeeded in reaching the machine gun nest.

"That's it. Move out; get the wounded!" hollered Johnny. He and Adan carried Lejano, supporting his limp body from both sides; I swung my carbine over my shoulder, lifted Chispa as gently as I could, and followed the pathetic trio.

The peninsula machine gun sounded again, but this time it poured the lead not over us: Joe fed the Sandinistas teaspoons of their own medicine, their cries reached us from behind the hill. We hurried toward the taller grass deeper in the swamp.

What was going to happen to Joe? The massive roar of fifty AK's signalled his end. I could see in my mind his bullet-ridden body sprawled next to several Sandinistas he had just killed. In the supreme, noble gesture, Joe sacrificed his life in order to save ours.

We continued our slow and laborious march. My feet sunk into ever softer and deeper, easily yielding, but reluctantly releasing mud. Chispa was silent, he drifted in and out of consciousness, and I knew that he was dying.

"How much farther?" I asked Adan.

"Maybe a quarter of a mile, maybe half," he guessed.

The ten-foot-tall swamp grass offered us a reliable sanctuary at last. Whatever lay ahead—quicksand, water holes, alligators, snakes, and leeches—still beat what we left behind. The quagmire had finally ended; we reached a dinky island, or a cape with a few dead trees and scattered bushes.

"We'll rest here and wait for Joe," said Johnny.

Did he really believe that Joe could survive the mayhem of bullet rain? Adan attended to the wounded, and Johnny and I went farther up to ascertain whether we had reached the mainland. We discovered no surprises, except, maybe, for a snake pit—not a genuine surprise *how could it be, with Johnny around.*

The snakes refused to pay any attention to us. They were deeply involved in what appeared to be an amorous gathering. That was Johnny's lifetime opportunity of getting even for all the instances of fright and humiliation, snakes, his curse, caused him. Never in my entire life have I seen so much pleasure and sadistic satisfaction on anyone's face as I observed on Johnny's when he pissed all over the slithering, curling, and wriggling participants of the reptilian orgy. He certainly added spice to their romance.

Returning to the camp, I was amazed to see Joe, still dripping mud. I wanted to convey to him my gratitude for saving our lives and admiration for his courage, but he rashly brushed me off. Something wasn't right.

Joe and Adan argued in Spanish. I listened, trying to figure out what the argument was about.

"...muertos...la captura...los Americanos..." was all I could sift out.

And then something horrendous and totally unexpected took place. Joe lifted his AK and with two single shots executed Chispa and Lejano. The deed was so senseless, hideous, and despicably repulsive, that my first reaction was of disbelief. What was happening had to be some kind of charade, a horribly cruel joke, the meaning of which I did not understand. The next moment, both Chispa and Lejano were going to lift their heads, smile, and wave to me saying, "Fooled ya!"

But their heads didn't move. Lejano's body kept lying on its side, and a small hole in his forehead kept on oozing blood. Chispa's feet twitched; his face was turned away, and the back of his head displayed a large gaping hollow. Was Joe mad, or had the whole world gone mad? Or, maybe, I was going insane.

"Hold it." Joe pointed the AK muzzle at Adan who tried to reach for his UZI. I closed my eyes expecting to hear another shot, but it didn't follow. Adan, finally, controlled his emotions. He wanted to shoot the goddamn son-of-a-bitch.

"Okay, move out. We don't have much time," ordered Joe.

Chispa and Lejano were traitors, I thought, and Joe had uncovered the truth. Both Lejano and Chispa were the Sandinistas.

"Move it!" spurred Joe.

Now, we could run without the burden of carrying the wounded. Was that the answer? The cold-blooded son-of-a-bitch had constructed another jungle survival equation: one's speed is inversely proportional to the amount of weight he carries? Dump the wounded and save your skin?

"...de caldrones!" came from the left. The Sandinistas apparently were trying to intercept us.

We ran...the jungle was near, in a few moments we'd be under its canopy, in safety...it was a horrible dream, a nightmare. Just look at those black clouds overtaking us—they can't be real. In a second or two, I'll wake up in my Raleigh apartment, in my bed, and say to myself, "Boy, I'm glad that it was all just a dream."

Three events commenced precisely at the same time: the Sandinistas emerged from the bushes, we dived into the jungle, and the first droplets of rain fell on all of us. If we didn't run, the Sandinistas would lock us in the swamp and, as Joe expressed it, 'we would be cut to pieces', or in Johnny's even more colorful words, 'we would be caught in deep shit, and they would squeeze the shit out of us until there was no shit left'.

The storm hit hard. The wind roared above, in the treetops, like an enormous, wild, infuriated animal ready to pounce upon us and tear us apart.

The trek through the vine web of the primordial jungle was torturous; we got spoiled by all those conveniently criss-crossing jungle trails that we had used until this afternoon...but no longer. Now, every step had to be fought over and conquered, every yard hacked, torn, and pushed through. We were cutting a tunnel in the thick growth with the last surviving machete. Finally, we broke out of the jungle island, pushed through a hedgerow-like wall, a coppice, and fell out on the other side right into the raw fury of the storm. A pine tree snapped and crashed next to us; we started running across the patch of savanna, as if it were possible to escape the swirling inferno of the storm, its bashing wind, and lashing lightning. Something slashed my hand. The tall grass that we were running through, with edges as sharp as a razor, had joined the storm in the alliance against us.

We dived, again, into another jungle island to find at least marginal protection from the howling beast determined to catch up with us. We found the protection—the vine mesh so thick, almost solid, that the wind could not penetrate it. But neither could we; we had to backtrack almost to the entry point, and start searching for a break in the living wall probably capable of holding even King Kong.

Even through the threatening roar that followed us, I heard a murmur ahead, and even could make out familiar words '…blue…fluent…flirt…' interspersed with musical bells, or, maybe, my high-strung imagination animated the inanimate river talk.

"Ulana," said Adan.

We had to cross another river. Ulana River was as wide, or maybe even wider, than Wawa.

"We've got to do it fast," warned Joe, "before the mountain runoff can reach here."

Constructing another raft took less time than before; we had become quite proficient in the art of raft building. Then we launched the raft and ourselves. Our timing was impeccable. The mountain runoff literally lifted us and flushed us down the stream on the wall of dirty bubbly water mixed with grass, broken branches, and logs. Suddenly, we were in full control of nothing; the river was making all the decisions. Her mighty currents played with the raft *and us* like with a toy. But we stubbornly pushed toward the other bank. A mile or two down the river our persistence paid off: I could see the approaching bank clearly.

"Hang in there, baby!" Johnny yelled. We struck a submerged log, and the raft disintegrated.

"Save the guns!" Joe screamed. "Save the fucking ammo!"

I had been holding onto my gear from the start. Perhaps I had learned the most important rule of the jungle: expect the unexpected. Every event here was a surprise. Johnny lost his gear, both the backpack and the M-60. Joe and Adan held to their precious cargo.

The log that hit us *or was it the other way around?* jutted from the bank, so the distance that we had to swim was short, at least its lateral component, but the current still carried us another hundred yards down the stream. We climbed out into more jungle and more of the same hopeless mesh of branches and vines.

By now, lightning ceased to be an individual event; the whole sky flashed in one continuous discharge, with us right in the middle. What was happening? Whatever it was, it didn't make much sense. After breaking out of hell, beating the odds, and cheating death, we should ride out in silver armor, on white horses, and into the golden sunset. Instead, we plunged into another hell.

I experienced a strange sensation of deja vu, as if I had been through these events before, maybe more than once. And, as if struck by the next lightning, I suddenly realized what was happening: WE WERE DEAD! We imagined that we had escaped from the Sandinistas' trap, but we couldn't have; it was impossible. All things fell into their places at once: the out-of-nowhere low black clouds, the likeness of which I have never seen before; and how these menacing clouds chased us into the jungle; and the untimely pitch darkness, slashed by lightning; and the lightning bolts themselves, which flashed in unending succession; and the torrential rain, which cascaded in bucketfuls, not drops; and the raging river, which boiled and pushed, not ran; and the wind, which roared, as if it were alive and conscious of our presence; and the razor blade grass, which cut not just flesh, but clothes, too. But the most significant clue, which supported my theory with conclusive evidence, was my waterproof Timex wristwatch. Its hands didn't move: THE TIME HAD STOPPED!

We were in hell, and our punishment was to wander forever in the jungle maze hit by ever raging storms, and to cross a thousand madly running rivers, eternally...I wondered how the others would accept my findings. Probably, in the beginning they would only laugh at me, those poor bastards. They didn't know yet. But I should find more proof, I thought.

If we were dead, then Chispa and Lejano should be with us too, plus all those Sandinistas that we killed. And maybe they were: I could swear that more than once I felt someone's breath on my neck. I stopped, listened, then continued, just a little more apprehensively. During the next lightning dance, I glanced at my watch again. The hands had not moved: they stopped at nine-o-five, the time when we crossed the Ulana River. But wait! If we died at the killing zone, then the watch should show six-thirty. Maybe we drowned?

The storm subsided as suddenly as it started. Whatever that natural *or unnatural* phenomenon was–a squall line, a tropical depression, a hurricane, or something else–it passed. The rain stopped, the wind was still blowing, but only with a fraction of its original force. And we had also found an exit from the 'rain forest'.

I began having suspicions concerning the validity of my moribund theory. There was a chance, a slight chance, mind you, that we were alive after all. Johnny was blowing his nose–a good sign, because, to the best of my knowledge, dead people don't blow their noses. Adan started a camp fire *it felt nice and warm*, then took off his wet uniform, and the rest of it, and hung it on the makeshift clothesline, to dry in front of the fire. I followed his example.

Joe sent Johnny to 'recce' ahead, as he called snooping around, and report back, then he joined Adan and me in the striptease session.

I still wasn't completely sure whether we had cashed in our chips, but when Adan opened his backpack, produced the leftovers of our last meal, split them four ways, and I tasted food, I became absolutely convinced that we were alive and kicking. I unsnapped my wristwatch and threw it in the fire: one's got to have a scapegoat for one's mistake.

Johnny returned and reported that all was clear: no roads nearby, or villages. But Joe, being a security freak, decided to post a sentry outside the camp anyway. This time he took the first shift; I was to replace him two hours later.

"If you'll lend me your watch," I told Johnny, "I'll share my AK with you."

"Fine," he smiled.

Putting on my dry uniform, still hot from the camp fire, I caught myself glancing around the camp. What was missing? Chispa and Lejano, Chispa's mischievous smile and Lejano's cautious sideways gaze: they were no more. The horrifying sequence of their cold-blooded execution by the bastard passed before my eyes afresh. Adan stared into the fire, and I knew exactly what he was thinking about. We shared the same emotions of bitterness and sorrow, and maybe anger. If I'd been wounded like Chispa and couldn't walk, would the goddamn son-of-a-bitch execute me too?

I couldn't fall asleep. The fire was dying, and I added wood. The jungle was recovering from the storm, trills and whistles resumed. Two bats almost singed their wings flying too low over the fire. I checked the time–thirty minutes before my sentry shift. Hell, I'll go and change Joe early, I thought.

I found him by the creek; he was sitting on a log hunched with his head bent almost to the level of his knees. The son-of-a-bitch fell asleep on duty, I smiled. I got'm. He didn't detect my presence in the murmur of the creek until I was practically on top of him. His shoulders shook convulsively, and, suddenly, I heard his sobs. The fucking son-of-a-bitch was crying, really crying, like a baby; the scene was unbelievable. The cold-blooded monster was going to pieces, the tower of strength collapsed in ruins, the steel spring of nerves snapped, the fearless tiger became a little pussy cat.

I coughed, and he kind of jerked, trying to compose himself and got up on his feet. We didn't say a word for a long time. He turned away, attempting to wipe off his tears with the sleeve.

"I couldn't sleep," I said. "Go and get some rest; I'll stick around here for awhile."

His hands suddenly seized the front of my shirt and almost lifted me off the ground, all one-hundred-and-ninety-five pounds of me.

"If you breathe one word of this to anyone, I'll kill you," he hissed through his teeth.

I didn't answer, and he let go of my shirt. His squinting glaring eyes stared right into mine, and I knew that he meant what he said.

So, our rock of Gibraltar leader was human after all. The Superman was, in reality, no more than Clark Kent; his ostentatious costume with the big 'S' on the front was made of cotton and tore easily. He tricked everyone into believing that he could fly, but attempting the feat he would fall flat on his face. Joe cried because he felt sorry for himself, sorry for what he had done, even though he believed that he had to do it. To Joe, in his survival equation, the wounded were a dead weight factor; to me, the killings were another important lesson in jungle mathematics.

In the morning, while Johnny fixed breakfast, Joe and Adan discussed the next route. Of course, again, they disagreed. Johnny served breakfast. Seeing this man in action, I learned to respect him, a lot. The most impressive *and puzzling* quality that he possessed was his nerves of steel. For me, it was hard to understand someone holding a stick with an ant on it trying to get off, totally immersed in the process of observing the ant, while bullets ricocheted only inches above his head and mortar bombs exploded only feet away. He had played with an ant, while I panicked and barely held myself from standing up and running, simply running away *and, of course, getting killed right then and there*. Johnny's nonchalant attitude toward danger–I strongly suspect, he was putting on a show for me, just to calm me down by trying to convey, 'Would I play with an ant, if we were in real danger?'–had a sobering effect on me. Johnny helped me to survive.

CATCH ME, TEASE ME

We moved out about mid-morning. The IFR weather, with the low overcast, was going to hamper the Sandinistas' search for us from the air. Most aircraft would be grounded at the base in Puerto Cabezas.

I volunteered for the point duty before Joe could assign Adan or Johnny; I needed to be alone, to 'sort things out'. There were several things that bothered me: the loss of Chispa and Lejano, how I felt about the son-of-a-bitch following the loss, but most of all, the new me—I had killed.

Twenty hours ago I believed in the sanctity of life. I believed that no one, under any circumstances, had the right to take someone else's life. Then, my own life was threatened, and I killed. What was I now? A killer?

Scattered pine woods suddenly ended. I stopped, surprised, contemplating an eery sight of several rows of banana trees that had been cut down almost at the ground level. Weeds and bushes had already overtaken the newly created open space. I could not surmise the purpose of this carnage; it was as if a giant with an enormous scythe had passed through, leaving behind a path of mass destruction.

Signalling caution to the rest of the group, I proceeded slowly across what used to be a banana plantation. A hamlet behind it, or what was left of it, testified to the drama, which took place here a few months ago. I surveyed the two rows of churned stilts and the piles of ashes in place of bamboo huts, and rotten carcasses of slain cows in the middle of the street, still identifiable as such by the horns. Bundles of lush grass fertilized by the disintegrating flesh pierced through the hides.

The hamlet had been levelled by the Sandinistas; its inhabitants were either forceably relocated south, or maybe escaped to neighboring Honduras. A few dead animal carcasses by a pond indicated that its water had been poisoned. A small vegetable garden next to a burned out hut somehow having survived the human-inflicted catastrophe stood out in the landscape of total destruction.

I kicked the charred bamboo wall out of the way and froze. The wall covered two human remains, both female, judging by partial clothing still on; probably a mother and her little daughter. Their flesh was in the final stages of putrefaction. The clothes *the mother's blouse and the daughter's torn dress* were in slightly better condition. Chills ran down my spine when I realized how they had died. They were raped and then killed. As though hypnotized, I stood over them unable to take my eyes off their corpses: their hands and feet were missing, chopped off. They had bled to death.

Tears filled my eyes, and the scene of horror blurred. Joe approached from behind and surveyed the scene of butchery. I turned to him and said, "You have no idea how much I hate this fucking little country…"

We slowly walked away leaving behind the legacy of ultimate human cruelty. Nothing in the world could make me turn and look back.

Adan took the point, and we proceeded northwest. The next hamlet, a few miles farther, no longer existed either. This time, we didn't stop.

Soon after we passed the second village, Joe made his first mistake. Perhaps it happened because we were so close to the end of our 'journey of the damned', and he became impatient to get it over with, or, maybe, he, like me, hated this fucking little country and wanted to leave it behind as soon as possible.

"Take over the point, Johnny," he said. "We're going straight north, directly to Rus-Rus."

"And if we bump into a patrol?" Johnny softly voiced caution.

"Then we will terminate the motherfuckers; we'll exterminate them all." I suspected that there was a compelling reason for Joe's decision, which I dismissed initially as inconsistent with his cool makeup–revenge. The vision of a mother and a daughter slain by the Sandinistas haunted Joe as painfully as it was haunting me. I handed Johnny my AK. Adan rejoined Joe and me.

"Por que?"

"Cállate." Joe did not want to explain.

Every cluster of trees, every bush, could conceal an ambush.

"How far is Coco Rio?" I asked Adan.

"That jungle." He pointed ahead.

Another two miles, then one more swim, and we would be home free. We'd made it.

Without a watch and with the slowly breaking but still heavy overcast sky it was hard to judge time. I could guess that it was late in the afternoon. I could scarcely discern Johnny's figure still hiking ahead of us. We shortened the distance between us and Johnny. He was following a barely visible trail in the grass and between scattered bushes. The wind died down, tranquil dusk descended on the whole world, and under its supple canopy all became unbelievably serene. I looked up and, through the cloud window, could see a faint star.

A bright flash and a deafening bang split the dusk. Joe and Adan fell on the ground. I followed their example. All became quiet again, except for the ringing in my ears. The bang echoed from the jungle wall ahead, as if someone snapped a whip in response to the bang.

Joe sprung up and rushed forward to where Johnny had walked a moment ago and where the flash came from. Adan and I followed. Johnny was conscious. He lay on the grass and appeared to be unharmed, except that his legs rested bent under his body somewhat unnaturally, and his clothes smoked.

"Are you okay?" I asked.

"I can't hear," he replied calmly.

"Let me help you up." I bent over to Johnny.

"Don't touch him." Joe's voice was stern. He and Adan were examining a bare bush.

"A mine," said Adan.

"It could be a mine field, we have to go around," reflected Joe.

A mine? I thought and glanced at Johnny's legs again. It seemed odd that he could lie in this uncomfortable position, with his legs bent, and it dawned on me *perhaps, I already knew it, but refused to acknowledge*: his legs were not bent, they were missing! I started walking in a strange vacuum aimlessly shuffling on my legs *I still had them*.

"Stop, Jim!" I heard Joe calling to me. "Stop right there."

I stopped. What in hell did he want from me?

"You want to blow yourself up?"

I turned around and shuffled back.

"I was looking for my AK," I muttered.

"Forget the fucking AK. Let's get out of here."

"What about Johnny?"

"I'll carry him."

Joe and Adan tore off their sleeves and hastily tightened the knots above Johnny's knees to stop the bleeding. Shreds of torn flesh and exposed shin bone swayed lifelessly when Joe picked Johnny up. We walked to the next meadow, clear of bushes, then turned toward the river again.

"Go without me." I heard Johnny saying to Joe.

"Shut up, we'll get you out, do'ya hear?"

We made camp short of the river.

"Why are we camping?" I asked Joe. "We've got to take Johnny across the river as soon as possible."

"Johnny's staying here," Joe replied calmly. The fucking son-of-a-bitch played God again: who lives and who dies.

"Isn't it up to Johnny to decide?" My anger grew.

I glanced at Adan. In the dark, I couldn't see his eyes, but in his silence I could sense a fatalistic resignation. What in hell was going on? Johnny, besides being Joe's close associate, was also his friend. Why, then, was Joe acting as if Johnny's life wasn't worth the little effort of taking him across the river? We could build a float big enough to hold Johnny, and, on the other side, tie a stretcher together, and carry him to Rus-Rus, where the doctor would fix his legs.

I sat down next to Johnny. He lay on the pile of banana leaves, still conscious.

"Can you hear me, Johnny?"

He breathed unevenly, sometimes pausing and clearing his throat.

"Something struck me in the neck too," he answered finally. "Don't blame Joe. I'm all messed up…It's not just my legs."

"The doctor will fix you."

"There is nothing the doctor can do about it…It hurts."

And suddenly I understood: the damages extended higher than Johnny's legs…

An owl hooted in the distance; the dark, silent silhouettes of Joe and Adan who sat only a few feet away, only added to the grimness of this appalling scene.

"But, man, we'll take you back to the States, and there…"

"No, Jim, I'm finished…" Johnny paused. "Please do me a favor."

"What is it, Johnny?"

"Untie those damn knots."

Johnny wanted me to undo the tourniquets on his legs and let him bleed to death, he wanted me to help him die.

"Do it, now…"

The owl called again. Maybe, it wasn't an owl at all, but a messenger, an escort from heaven, calling Johnny, ready to take Johnny with him. What was I witnessing, the ultimate? The ultimate tragedy? Johnny was a good man, a simple man. He did not contribute to any 'worthy cause', or charity, because, being just a poor farmer from Kansas, he had nothing to give. He did not spread the word of God, because he didn't understand it. Yes, he killed, but so did everyone else, directly, or by approval *supporting causes which kill, or at least electing someone who gives orders to kill.* But whatever Johnny did in his life that could be called bad, he did not deserve this punishment, and whatever I was witnessing now, should not happen, either by chance, or by design.

But it did. Why? Was this event the Creator's punishment, or was he unable to help, or unwilling, or unaware, or simply didn't care? Was all completely out of control? And I thought, if God is not in control, then he has my sympathy, not worship. I bent over Johnny's legs and untied the knots.

"Thank you, Jim," He said quietly. "Here, something for you."

He handed me his wristwatch.

Johnny died quietly; he simply stopped breathing. Death with dignity. Is there such thing? And what about burial with dignity? We didn't have tools to dig Johnny's grave. We just found a hole in the nearby swamp and covered Johnny's body with grass, then Joe tied two slimy logs together in the shape of a cross and thrust it deep into the soft yielding ground.

Here lay a quiet, serious man who used to be called Johnny and who used to go under the funny war name 'Mad Geek'. When Joe and I died, no one would even remember that Johnny lived, no one would care, not even his square girlfriend.

"That wasn't a Sandinista mine." I heard Joe say to Adan. "It was one of yours, wasn't it?"

A long pause ensued.

"Creo que si, boys planted it," finally replied Adan. "But I didn't know."

We broke out to the river's edge…

BACK TO THE FUTURE

Absolutely nothing had changed in Rus-Rus. The Honduran guards greeted us with 'Buenos dias'. They enjoyed a laid-back tour of duty here. They were not involved in the Contra war and hardly ever ventured outside the village. After standing at the check point for a few hours, they had all the time in the world to play volleyball, write letters to their sweethearts back in Tegucigalpa, and sleep. To the Hondurans, the spectacle of three soldiers in uniforms torn to shreds, their sunken cheeks covered with a week old stub, and their tired void eyes, easily compared with the sight of a freshly rescued cat, which, while prowling in the back yard by an outhouse, had accidentally plunged into the shithole.

Sam, the cook, performed his customary ritual of beating, pardon me, spanking the monkey still tied down to the suspension bridge leading to the kitchen hut. He served us rice-and-beans and el platano, which tasted as bad as seven days ago. Sam didn't ask any questions, not even about Johnny—he just served one plate less.

Never in my entire life had I gone through the cleaning ceremony with so much pleasure as this time; the process, which required almost as much effort as it would demand from the above mentioned careless cat: a fare amount of licking. Freshly shaven, back in civvies, with my hands free *not holding an AK, for a change*, I rejoined Joe who, too, regained a presentable appearance.

"When?" I asked. I didn't have to complete the sentence with 'are we going home'; it was self-evident.

"Tomorrow morning," Joe answered smiling.

We had to perform one more task before we were free to go: report to Stedman in Tegucigalpa. I don't think Joe looked forward to this task. Meanwhile, Joe and I spent the rest of the day together, mostly resting, sleeping, eating, and talking, talking a lot.

First, Joe presented me with a surprise. "Are you coming with me on the next mission?" he asked.

The question was so totally unexpected, so out of place and time, and almost absurd, that I was speechless for awhile.

"You're joking!" I squeaked, there was definitely something wrong with my voice. "We almost got killed this time."

"Not so," Joe objected. "Our chances were better than fair."

I couldn't believe what I was hearing. "We were trapped like rats in the bag." I pushed Joe's nose right in the middle of the clear, solid facts.

"We were not."

The silly 'We were too…We were not…We were too…' followed. Obviously, we looked at the same events from completely different standpoints, and, boy, they were different.

From my viewpoint, we were incredibly lucky. Joe's analysis of the events, however, differed radically from mine, particularly of his own role. He had to cross a stretch of an open field exposed to the fire by both the main force and the peninsula nest. Joe distracted the machine gunners by our diversion, and while we played "Nya-nya-nya-nya-boo-o-o-boo, you ca-a-an't get me", Joe dashed across the field. According to Joe, it takes at least five seconds, even for the best trained soldier, to accomplish the task of reacting, aiming, and firing at the surprise target. Joe's run lasted four seconds, leaving him one second to spare. Taking the nest out was a relatively simple task. In the resulting confusion, we all escaped.

"Our chances of getting out alive were not close to zero, but were about eighty percent, which was better than fair." Joe rested his case.

It was hard to defend my side of the argument: after all, we did survive. Luck or no luck, Joe managed to open the door from hell, and we escaped. At that time, our lives depended on those five seconds, five seconds of aiming and firing at the surprise target—the time that even a highly trained TRAG member could not beat. Joe knew that. He spoke of his organization with unconcealed pride. In his mind, it was a living body, an organism with all functions tuned to a quiet rhythm, skills honed to perfection. He did not create the body–he just assembled it like a watchmaker assembles a perfect watch.

We lay quietly listening to the voices and laughter of the Contra soldiers outside the hut. Life went on…

"You know what I want right now?" Joe turned to me. "A cone of cherry vanilla ice cream."

I imagined the cone filled with a thick pinkish-white sweet frozen cream spangled with chunks of cherry.

"Yes, that's what I want," affirmed Joe.

"In Raleigh," I said, and we looked at each other. Suddenly, the helicopter, the Sandinistas, Chispa, Lejano, and even Johnny became less significant episodes from the past, history, played out characters of a cancelled drama. They no longer existed. But the cone of cherry vanilla ice cream did. It became real and important, more important than any event which had already passed. We were alive, really alive! Alive to enjoy a cone of cherry vanilla ice cream.

Why did I feel like this? Had someone else's death to be an affirmation of my life, a confirmation of how wonderful it was to be alive, a victory of life over death?

"I am going with you on your next mission..." I said.

The next day we flew back to Tegucigalpa. The same old DC-3, which brought us to Rus-Rus, carried us back to civilization. The streets of Tegucigalpa were as peaceful as before, but this time I couldn't help noticing the military, the presence of the Honduran army in the city. Soldiers guarded the airport and all other important strategic and public centers, and by George, to me, they all resembled the fucking Sandinistas. The soldier on duty by the central post office and the telephone company, all in one, holding an automatic assault rifle, smiled at me. The military was a caution sign, a warning that that terribly cruel little war in the forested slopes of the Nicaraguan mountains could spill over into Honduras. Who knows? Maybe a few months later, Joe and I would return and would be fighting the Honduran Sandinistas, and I would shoot this soldier in the smiling face. I forced myself to smile back.

While Joe reported to Stedman, I had enough time to explore Tegus. La Avenida Seis *Sixth Avenue* was the main drag of the four-block downtown. It displayed a row of modern shops. I followed the Parque Central to a tiny square in front of a dilapidated colonial church. If La Avenida Seis was too expensive for the Hondureño, it was here, to this little square, that he went. The goods were on display–the whole assortment of 'centavo capitalism', Indian handicrafts, and trinkets covered spreads laid out on the pavement.

One of the 'stands' was 'manned' by a blind old Indian woman and a three-year-old girl. All items were priced. The girl was in charge of sales. The little smudge-face was the breadwinner of the family. I bought dollar earrings for Martha, paying five dollars, and was rewarded with a microscopic 'Gracias', the most precious 'gracias' of my life. I know that I underpaid the girl for those pretty Indian earrings: given the choice between the most expensive diamond earrings from Tiffany's and the girl's, I would take hers, and I mean it.

We stayed at the Holiday Inn, only two blocks away from the post office building. This place was the meeting spot for all Americans coming to *or passing through* Honduras who congregated in its dark bar, a focal point, a gathering joint for miscellaneous tourists, businessmen, correspondents, and even clergy coming to spread the word of God in the countryside. The bartender spoke English and his Bloody Mary's were pretty good.

In the morning, Joe and I were on the SAHSA jet bound for Miami, and for the first time since we left the States two weeks ago, I was able to really relax. Joe claimed the seat next to the window, on my left, and I didn't object to the arrangement. Let him watch the fucking clouds, who cares! I had the advantage of seeing the stewardess' legs in the passage between the tiers. One finally reached me.

"What would you like to drink, Sir?"

"A shot of Napoleon brandy, please."

"Do you wanna know one of the secrets of history?" Joe squinted his eyes at me.

I nodded.

"Napoleon feared an assassination attempt. That's why he carried a pistol in his coat and held his right hand close to it, ready to whip it out and defend himself. He was paranoid about it."

"That's bullshit," I said.

"Do you have a better explanation for his hand always resting under his coat?"

This guy smiled and joked with the ease of a man returning from a pleasant vacation in Acapulco, and not from hell. Was that how he really felt, or was it all a put-on? Are we all guilty of hiding our true selves? For example, what about this attractive young woman on the other side of the tier, clean as a whistle, and, if it weren't for the presence of a fidgety little boy sitting next to her, I would say 'innocent'? I wondered if she had any skeletons in her closet. Or that mild middle-aged lady by the opposite window who, I would bet, couldn't even hurt a fly? Or that young black dude in the next front row across the pass?

The flight to Miami dragged on; I wished there was a faster mode of transportation than a jet.

The captain's voice over the intercom has finally announced, "Ah...Ladies and gentlemen, fasten your seat belts. We're on the final approach to Miami International. The weather reported is scattered clouds, the surface temperature is eighty three degrees..."

"I'll stay in Miami for a couple of days." Joe fumbled with his buckle. "By the way, Jim, you can call me Alex again."

Alex? Who was Alex?

"Are you kidding me, man?" I didn't know Alex. Maybe I heard of him, but I didn't know him. That man was a hazy image from the past. That quiet, slightly insecure Russian did not exist any more, and I wasn't sure if he ever had. But I knew Joe very well; we went to hell together and returned. And I also knew that in the future we'd go to another hell and would come back. I couldn't call Joe by the name of Alex: that was someone else's name.

THEORY OF RELATIVITY

At Raleigh-Durham International, when I re-entered the American Airlines terminal, I experienced a strange sensation of change. I tried to pin down exactly what had changed, but couldn't. All appeared familiar and, at the same time, all seemed new. I had to concentrate in order to remember where the exit was. I almost dialed a taxi because I forgot that free taxi cabs were always present outside the terminal.

"Where to?" asked the cabbie.

"Uh…" What the hell was the name of my street? It was on the tip of my tongue, but I couldn't remember it. It was as if I had been away for a very long time, two years, maybe longer. But I had been away for only two weeks. "Royal Hill apartments. Do you know where that is?"

"Sure, it's on Charles Drive, next to Crabtree."

Of course it was on Charles Drive. What the fuck was the matter with my memory? I had lived on that fucking street for three years already and still couldn't remember its name?

The ride to Raleigh passed uneventfully.

"Stop over there, by the first entrance," I told the cabbie. "Here…keep the change."

At least I remembered where my apartment was. The whole thing was becoming ridiculous. I checked my mail box: it was stuffed with junk mail and a few first class envelopes *bills, of course.*

My apartment hadn't changed. I opened curtains, windows, and doors to air it out, enjoying the incomparable feeling of being back home. Everything was returning to normal.

Or was it? When I opened the refrigerator, I was stunned to discover that the milk had not spoiled. How could it stay fresh for such a long time? But wait! There was nothing wrong; it shouldn't spoil in two weeks. Why did it seem to me longer than two weeks? In fact, I had a strong feeling of being absent for a very, very long time.

I telephoned Martha, but she was out–of all evenings, she had to be out when I needed her the most. Mulling over whether I should tell her about what happened in Nicaragua, and about how I felt now, I drank the unspoiled milk. She would probably never let me hear the end of it, first, because I lied about Mexico, and secondly, because I took chances without even consulting her. I called one hour later, and she answered, and again, of all evenings, her folks *conceivably, my future in-laws* were in town.

"Why don't you join us?" she asked.

"No, can't make it tonight." I wasn't ready for large company. "I'll see you tomorrow. Love you, angel."

"Love you, too."

Of course I was going to tell her all about Nicaragua.

I couldn't fall asleep until about three o'clock in the morning. The images of Joe, Johnny, Adan, Chispa, Lejano, Stedman, and Sandinistas, continued floating before me in the dark—I couldn't get rid of them. They talked, I could hear their voices, and they moved around. And suddenly I understood what was wrong with my memory. The last two weeks were not ordinary—they were packed with never-before-encountered, strong events; in fact the last two weeks were crammed with more 'big' events than the previous two years of my life. I simply was not accustomed to absorbing so many intense experiences in such a short time. My brain 'panicked' and allowed more space for the incoming information than necessary, thus creating an illusion that more time had passed. Previous events were pushed back, displaced by a torrent of new, powerful, shocking, impressions. All previous memories became less significant, and, therefore, more easily forgettable.

Extrapolating from my conclusions, I wondered if it was possible to flood the brain to the extent that one would forget most of the previous events, or even all, causing some form of insanity *well, maybe an acute amnesia*. My forgetfulness was a caution sign, a warning to take it easy in the future.

"Don't let anything get to you," I self-instructed. "Sometimes you just gotta say, 'What the fuck!'"

Resolved to adopt this new philosophical *or was it cynical?* attitude toward the world, I was finally able to fall asleep...

Of course, Carolina birds woke me up first thing in the morning. I fixed eggs and bacon for breakfast, and the whole apartment filled with a delicious aroma; it surely beat el platano.

After breakfast, I had to stop by the unemployment office—to confirm that I still was on their payroll and to check whether any 'bird associated' positions were open. None were. Finally, I was able to pick up my Martha at her work place and give her the biggest hug and kiss; I missed her tremendously.

We had dinner.

"You seem different." Martha noted. "Much quieter. Did you finish your contract in Mexico?"

"Yea," was my lengthy reply.

"Care to talk about it?"

"Not much to tell." I hesitated whether I should tell her about Nicaragua. "We mapped the pelican migration patterns all the way to Honduras."

"I thought it was warblers," she wrinkle-nosed.

"Yes, those too." I still hesitated. If I told her about what really happened, she would strongly object to my going on another mission with Joe.

"It had to be a boring job," she observed.

"Yes, it was." I decided against telling her. "Here, I have something for you. It's not fancy, but it's very, very special."

I handed her the Honduran girl's earrings...

Two days later, Joe called and invited me to his place. Although a bedroom was available, Joe slept in the living room. The living room extended into a dinette and L'd into a kitchenette. From the hall in the back, doors to both a study and the bedroom were closed, always, to save on heat.

"I open those rooms only when my kids are visiting, or the girl of friends of mine is staying with me."

Joe was talking about pretty ten-year-old Angela *I met her later*. Her parents separated periodically, and she usually stayed with Joe until they could reconcile their differences and reunite again.

Joe maintained an apartment, and a car. I found out later that he sent his ex-wife generous financial child support, more than she was entitled to. His mercenary business consumed the rest of it, in fact, more than it produced.

Why, then, did Joe stay in that business? Obviously not for financial gain. But then for what? Glory? But the witnesses to his deeds could not testify: they were all dead, and his former employers would not even acknowledge their acquaintance. The circumstantial evidence pointed to Joe's simply being hooked on action, the deadlier–the merrier. Every task he tackled was a maze studded with booby traps and killers on every turn, a challenge to overcome and survive. Joe was hooked on death.

My conclusion was supported by Joe's taste in art. A poster in the narrow hall to the bedroom depicted an Armageddon-like event where death *a solemn figure with no face* ruled. Another poster, right above the television set, in plain view, portrayed a young gentleman *faceless, too* entering a black-and-white passage from the fairyland-like outside *in vivid color*; the young gentleman found himself in the company of a beggar sitting on the ground, in the trash, with his hand stretched out for a handout, and a prostitute in a short nightgown standing by the entrance and observing the guest. This poster was titled 'Step into the Real World' and, obviously, reflected Joe's view of the world with him being that young gentleman in the poster.

"Let me buy you a drink," Joe offered, distracting me from the pessimistic poster. "Remember the country bar?"

Val greeted us with a nod of recognition. We did not drink nearly as much as we did on the day when Joe attempted to recruit me for his Nicaraguan mission. Thus, what happened later could not be blamed on the amount of Cherry Herring we had consumed. I dropped off Joe, returned to my apartment, and went to bed.

A telephone call woke me up. I turned the lights on and glanced at the clock which showed ten past two a.m. It was Joe. Although he sounded calm, I could sense fear in his voice. Fear! I had learned to recognize that sucker.

"Those guys are after me, Jim."

"Which guys?"

"Chispa and Lejano, man." He paused.

I was silent for awhile. What in hell was he talking about?

"They are both dead, Joe. Don't you remember?"

"Yeah, I know they're dead, but I saw them."

Something wasn't right.

"Run it by me again, Joe. You said, you saw Chispa and Lejano?"

"Yes, I woke up, and they lay next to me, on both sides."

"How could they?"

"They were here; I touched them…but when I jumped on my feet, they were gone."

"It was just a dream, Joe, a nightmare." I tried my hand at psychoanalysis.

"But I saw them the day before yesterday too. They were real, and I was completely awake, Jim."

"Look, the dead are dead, no one can bring them back."

Joe was silent for a few seconds.

"Yes, you're probably right," he agreed finally.

"Of course, I'm right. Go back to sleep, and you'll feel better in the morning."

"There are no ghosts, right?"

"Right."

I turned off the lights and stretched out. But I couldn't go back to sleep. That was an unexpected twist. Joe was going schizo, he began seeing ghosts, invulnerable Joe suddenly became very vulnerable. I tossed and turned. I couldn't help but feel sorry for Joe. I imagined his room. Joe lay on the mat, in the dark, alone, listening to the apartment noises coming from all sides: a refrigerator clicked on and hummed, then a dog barked outside, a wall panel cracked in a thermal contraction, the wind moved a tree branch and it scratched the roof, a shadow lurked in the corner…maybe it was Chispa, waiting for Joe to fall asleep. The room was full of moving silhouettes, the souls of those he killed–the private hell of Joe Green.

I called him in the morning, just to see if he was all right.

"Yeah, I'm okay. Forget my call; it was nothing, just one of those things," he clammed. I understood that he regretted letting me see his vulnerable side.

And two days later he vanished…He did leave me a note stating that he was in a bind, but he did not explain in what kind of a bind: financial, personal security, or maybe even mental, judging by his recent nightmares. Whatever were his reasons for leaving so suddenly, I had no choice but to accept them.

Part II
Operation Golden Camel

IN THE SHADOWS OF ZAGROS

"A ban has been placed on any town We have destroyed; they shall not return."

Prophets, Koran

As months passed, I began believing that I would never see Joe Green again. Sometimes at night, I thought of him and recalled the details of what happened in Nicaragua. Perhaps I wanted to find answers to questions which still bothered me: how could I have participated in actions totally alien to my convictions, repulsive to my inner nature? What happened there?! I couldn't find answers. Maybe that was why I still did not tell Martha anything about those freak events. Martha and I planned announcing our engagement, I had found a steady job, and my life began acquiring firm contours.

Then one Saturday, as I was taking my trash out, I heard right behind me, "Hi, Jim." I instantly knew to whom this voice belonged.

"Jesus! Do you have to sneak up on me like that?"

"Sorry."

Joe appeared to be in good health and even better spirits.

"I have something for you." He handed me a manila envelope.

I completed my household chore and we entered my apartment.

"What's in the package?" My curiosity was aroused. What was up Joe's sleeve?

"Information, something I wanted to show you."

I opened the envelope. It contained a stack of documents.

"If you watch my stew cooking, I'll read the papers now," I said.

Some pages were stamped 'top secret' and 'for your eyes only'. I read the documents.

"I don't understand," I turned to Joe. "What all of this s'got to do with me."

"Well, I thought that you should know the background," he smiled conspiratorily.

"The background of what?" I asked. A little nagging thought crossed my mind, 'What if this weasel is trying to involve me in something nasty, similar to what I read?'

"Relax, Jim. The thing like that is not going to happen to us."

'Thing like that' was described in the damn documents. From what I could piece together, here is what had happened.

The dark, bare hills on both sides of the road receded faster and faster as Karl's jeep picked up speed. Karl glanced at his wristwatch; the fluorescent dial displayed 2:35 AM. Thus far, the Operation Der Gabel *the Sabre* proceeded without a single glitch. Karl's mercenary team had successfully negotiated their passage from Turkey to Iran thirty minutes ago.

On the Turkish side, the chief border official *the Chief Turk*, as Karl called him had scrutinized their cargo manifest. The cargo manifest was a free pass for their cargo, supposedly part of the German humanitarian relief efforts. Although everything seemed to be in order, the official had insisted upon inspecting the contents of the crates in the van and the jeep, allegedly containing medical supplies for casualties of the Iran-Iraqi war. A financial incentive in the form of a hundred dollar bill had shifted the Chief Turk's curiosity from the cargo to personnel, which clearly exceeded the nominal number of four needed to accompany the cargo. But Karl's charm *and another hundred* had deflected the Turk's attention from the subject of his legitimate concern to completely unrelated matters. Both sides were pleased by the ease of communications in the air of amity and mutual understanding. The Chief Turk, finally, had stamped all passports and the manifest and waved both vehicles through.

One more hurdle remained—the Iranian check point fifty meters down the road. Of all the obstacles they had to overcome so far, this one was the most unpredictable and could present problems. The client who hired the team warned Karl that a straightforward bribe offered to an Iranian border official could backfire. The new Islamic regime took a dim view of corruption. Violation of the strictly enforced Islamic code of ethics could cost the guilty party his life. Thus the flexibility of an Iranian border official depended on the degree of his fear of Islamic retribution and his greed. But no obstacles materialized. The guards at the check point appeared friendly. And why shouldn't they be? Ostensibly, Karl's mission was an amicable gesture from the generally unfriendly western world, its generous gift to the war-torn country.

Still, something seemed wrong. What was it? Maybe this curiously empty road? Other traffic was totally absent as Karl's little convoy continued its journey and passed the town of Maku, twenty two kilometers inside Iran.

Hans, Karl's colleague and close friend, drove.

"Sei doch güter Dinge! Snap out of it!" Hans smiled. "Present company excepted, one has to be a damn fool to bibble around this late, leaving his Frau in bed alone."

"I still don't like it." Karl shrugged his shoulders. "Things are going too smoothly."

"Both you and I simply need a long vacation. After all this is over, why don't we go south and taste those beautiful Bavarian frauleins, ah?" Hans twisted the wheel, negotiating a turn.

"Ya, that sounds good, and..." Karl did not finish the sentence. The jeep's headlights illuminated a roadblock ahead.

Hans slammed on the brakes.

"A fucking ambush! " were Hans' last words.

Karl spotted a fast-approaching small yellowish fuzz-spot–the unmistakable signature of an incoming rocket.

"Jump! " Karl bailed out a split second before the explosion, yet did not escape its fiery jolt. He landed broadside, hitting his head against the compacted surface of the roadside. Everything blurred...

Regaining consciousness, Karl heard a crackling rat-a-tat of automatic weapons followed by a blast and screams. Then a long machine gun burst cracked the night open, and the screams stopped. It became quiet, except for the rustle of flames. Karl lifted his head. The jeep and the van burned. Crated munitions in the van exploded in the blazing display and showered the vicinity with burning debris.

Several figures emerged from darkness and approached. Eben commen sie angestiegen! thought Karl. Here they come! Three Iranian soldiers passed Karl and stopped by the burning wreckage. The fourth, an Army Captain, nudged Karl with the tip of his boot. Their eyes met. The Captain lifted his arm and aimed a pistol at Karl's face...

The German mercenary team led by Karl Wolfgang Steiner on the mission to assassinate Imam Ayatollah Ruhollah Khomeini was terminated thirty four kilometers inside Iran on September 15, 1983– there were no survivors.

"Now you know what happened," Joe commented, and as if the story merited no more than the tale of Jack and Jill, casually scanned my kitchen.

"Where in the fuck did you get this information?" I asked.

"From the British intelligence." He lifted his legs and placed them on the edge of my kitchen table–an unsanitary habit of his which I strongly disliked. "I have a high-ranking friend in MI-6."

I finished fixing dinner and was ready to serve it, but Joe's legs still occupied part of my kitchen table. I attempted to give him a few hints, like 'Well, dinner is almost ready' and 'I like your boots', but he didn't get the message. Finally, my patience was exhausted.

I pointed to his boots, "Do you mind?"

"Sorry." Joe lowered his feet and put them where they belonged–on the floor.

"Thank you, you were saying?"

"Yeah, I was asking if you have a job."

Instantly, I smelled a rat. Was he trying to recruit me for another of his insane ventures? After all, back in Honduras, I did mumble something stupid about being ready for another mission, purely on emotional level and on the spur of a moment.

"Yeah, I have a steady job." If Joe tried to recruit me, he was wasting his time. There was nothing in Iran that I was interested in, not even their birds. Besides, the Iran-Iraqi war still continued. But I was curious. "And what is your mission?"

"Well…" Joe paused and hit me with, "We're going to assassinate Ayatollah Khomeini, the Imam of the Islamic Republic of Iran."

I must grant Joe credit: he did wait, he gave me enough time to regain my composure, then he outlined the assignment. And, my God! I've heard crazy plans in my life, but this one topped them all. Imagine the following scenario. The team has been assembled in the open, where almost everyone could see that they were up to something, their destination and target were no secret to the opposition, and the reception committee waited to welcome them in appropriate manner.

"Can't fail." Joe grinned.

After a pause *the son-of-a-bitch liked to leave me speechless* I carefully cleared my throat and noted, quite delicately, "You're fucking crazy, and I don't have to tell you that, because you already know it."

"Both the German and the British teams, I didn't mention it before, but there was a British team too, were betrayed and ambushed. I'm sure there is a leak somewhere, which we can exploit, which we can use to our advantage."

"How many men are you taking with you?" I asked just for the sake of asking.

"With you and me–eight."

Joe presented the details of his plan. He dispensed a detail, I nibbled at its ambiguities, and he explained until I agreed with him. And, I don't know how he accomplished it, but when he finished, I was facing the fact that I agreed with all the details. I knew perfectly well that this insane plan simply could not work and, at the same time, when examined in detail, it seemed feasible.

In a last effort to find a fault, my final assault on the plan, which was more an act of desperation than logic, I asked, "What makes you so sure that this plan can work?"

"That the opposition is certain that it cannot, meaning that they are not going to change or reinforce the present security setup because they think it's adequate."

"And what's in it for us?" I asked, suddenly startled to realize that I used 'us' instead of 'you'.

"Fifty two million dollars in gold bullion."

"Where is the gold?"

"On Ayatollah's premises."

Yes, fifty two million bucks in gold bullion was not a dog's dick. My share of this wealth could pay for my fiancee's engagement ring and then some.

"How do you feel about becoming my business manager?" Joe's eyebrows rose as if trying to convey, 'Isn't it a great opportunity for you, eh?'

"You mean joining TRAG?" I guessed, not surprised. It was time to graduate from that habitual state of shock, my former usual aphasic reaction, to Joe's bombshell statements.

"Yeah, that's it."

What he offered was an invitation to become a member of a suicide company.

"No, thanks."

"Why not?" He appeared to be genuinely surprised.

"Not qualified, to begin with." I felt that I had to give him a reason that was valid, in his eyes.

"Qualified is a relative term." Joe wasn't willing to give up on me. "You were cool under fire."

"Yea, I nearly shit in my pants on that Sandinista hill."

"So did Tom, Dick, and Harry."

But I was not going to commit myself to membership in any association advocating activities more intense than birdwatching. The only reason why I was willing to join the Iranian operation was the fifty-two-million-dollar-prize, worthy of risk taking. But then I wanted out, for good.

"I will help you out on this operation, as an acting business manager." I said. "But that's all."

"Fair enough." Joe smirked as if he knew something I didn't. "Welcome to Operation Golden Camel."

MAFIA CONNECTION

Joe introduced me to the arms purchase procedures. My pending task encompassed a meeting with an arms dealer and requesting a few items from Joe's list.

"Go to this motel in Dunn next Monday." Joe handed me a typed page. "It's all set. Call me when you get back."

I was slightly uncomfortable with the ease with which Joe suckered me into becoming his purchasing agent, but what the heck, I had never met an arms dealer before and I was curious what those guys looked like.

"Can you handle this?" The exit door was still open, I could still change my mind and pull out.

"A piece of cake," I said, sealing my fate.

I arrived at the motel, next to Interstate 95, early in the evening and right on time. A very handsome, dark-haired gentleman of about fifty met me at the door to his room.

"Frank Grazia." He introduced himself in a soft baritone.

I presented myself, too; we shook hands. I scanned the room. It did not contain anything out of the ordinary, if one ignored a short-barrel UZI resting on the bed.

"I carry it wherever I go," Frank commented, noticing my stare at the weapon. "In my business, one can't be too careful. Ever used it?"

Frank handed me the UZI, which was ready for action, the clip in and all.

"Yeah, a few times." I lied, holding the submachine gun while having no idea how to operate it. I hoped that Frank was not going to ask me to demonstrate my knowledge, or, in substance, the lack of it. Before he could come up with this idea, I handed him both the UZI and the list of wanted items.

"…eight AK-47's, uh-huh…Karl Gustav system…a dozen hand grenades, uh-huh…" Frank read aloud.

"If it's hard to obtain Gustavs, then American LAWs will do," I said, quite satisfied with the way I stated it–very professionally.

"Here's what you're looking for." Frank opened a cabinet drawer and produced a green tubular object.

I wondered what the heck it was: a tubular container of some kind of a weapon.

"Y-y-yeah." I nodded, playing for time and trying to figure out what the green contraption really was. It was too short to be a rocket launcher, but that's what we were discussing.

Frank dissipated my doubts by pulling the housing back with one jerk and doubling the length of the contraption. Now it began resembling a rocket launcher, but which one was it: a LAW or a Gustav?

"Let me see it." I bravely took possession of the gizmo.

"Careful! It's activated," exclaimed Frank.

It was American made, it had to be a LAW *Light Anti-tank Weapon*. I instantly felt like an expert. What did Frank know? I've seen enough war movies to know how to handle that thing. I lifted the LAW and aimed it at the tree outside the window. I touched the trigger. So, Frank said it was activated. Good, all I had to do now was to press the trigger, and the rocket would be launched.

"Yea, it feels right," I commented handing the rocket launcher to Frank. He seemed relieved, as if he was afraid that I could pull the trigger and set off a chain of totally unpredictable events.

"When do you need them?"

"We are going to release the downpayment in about a month," I stated, implying that we already had the money. In fact, we did not: the deal with our clients was not yet sealed.

After Frank and me agreed to all terms, I returned home.

I called Joe, and the knock at my door signalled his arrival fifteen minutes later. He brought a mysterious manila folder. I related the details of the meeting with Frank. Joe kept nodding, but did not comment.

"So, what's the deal?" I asked. I felt that since I was already involved in the operation, on top of everything else being Joe's business manager, my status entitled me to know more about it. I simply wanted to know what was I getting my ass into.

"Okay, it's like this..." Joe began. "I have an operative in Greece. Although he is a British national he settled down in Thessaloniki. A month ago he was approached by two elderly gentlemen. The strangers introduced themselves as Mr. Halsim Fa and Mr. Farik Salem-tuk, co-owners of an Iranian shipping company. They had left their country at the onset of the Islamic revolution and now resided in Greece. Owing to the fact that they were close friends of the former Shah, their names figured prominently on Ayatollah's death list. Thus, justifiably so, they wanted Ayatollah himself dead. The gentlemen produced a dossier, and Keith was astonished to discover that the dossier was his. It contained, among other things, the details of his British military service. He wondered how in hell they managed to obtain his military record. During the trialogue, the inquisitive strangers disclosed that they were aware of Keith's membership in my Top Risk Action Group, although, they said, regretfully, their information concerning this American mercenary organization was sketchy. They queried Keith for more information about TRAG, and he outlined the scope of TRAG's operations. Both gentlemen expressed interest in the organization."

"So, what in hell did they want?" I asked impatiently.

"Well, they wanted to hire several militarily qualified individuals. The task at hand encompassed a commando raid on heavily guarded presidential quarters."

"Not much to it at all," I commented.

"Another meeting followed soon, and the gentlemen made an offer. The offer by the potential clients stood as follows. They would pay for the team's expenses, which included equipment and arms, of course, plus transportation, lodging, and meals. The individual fee was set at ten thousand dollars."

"Wow!" I said. "What would they offer for blowing up the world, eleven thousand?"

"I told Keith to let those guys know that we don't work cheap. We'd take the job for ten-thousand-and-one." Joe paused, searching for any kind of emotional reaction on my face, but I maintained my face impenetrably blank. Joe's clumsy sense of humor lacked even elementary sophistication. Finally, giving up on my response, he brought to a close, "Just kidding. We said that we'd do it for a double fee."

"Yeah, there is a helluva difference between ten-thousand and twenty-thousand," I remarked with a touch of sarcasm.

Joe opened the folder. It contained maps.

"That's what they gave Keith." Joe pulled out and unfolded a large map of the Iran-Iraqi front showing the Iranian troops' disposition, profile, and strength, arterial and secondary, patrolled and patrol-free roads, and, of course, the target zone in the southwest of Tehran.

"Here is another one," Joe pulled out a blueprint, a layout of the target area, a neatly drawn on a grid of coordinates.

The target was a heavily guarded 'little fortress' surrounded by a seven-foot-high glass-topped wall with a single entrance facing northeast, toward Tehran. The 'little fortress' was the only place in the whole country where Ayatollah felt relatively safe.

Joe and I studied the fortress layout thoroughly *wouldn't one be curious about the place where one, conceivably, was going to die?* If I could, I would prefer to visit this fascinating citadel under friendlier circumstances, using a less violent mode of entry than Joe had in mind. Two sentries manning the roadblock a few yards in front of the double-door gates would smile and let us through. We would pass the gates into the inner world of the fortress.

Inside, the fortress would not seem as impregnable as from the outside. On the left, a guard tower dominated the landscape. One bored guard slowly paced the confined floor space of the tower, occasionally pausing by the general purpose 7.62 mm machine gun mounted on a turret. On the same side, a structure with antenna housed a radio room manned by four technicians and guards.

On the right, only a few yards away, stood a smaller structure, a weapons and ammunition depot. Right behind the weapons store, facing us, like a big can full of worms, lay barracks housing thirty five soldiers. Past the barracks, hid a small garage for the presidential auto.

And finally, straight ahead, about fifty feet from the gates, stood the main building–the presidential living quarters, the main target, with the adjacent Holy Shrine on the left side. With eight soldiers inside at all times, four sentries on its flat roof *one per corner*, and two half-tracks armed with large caliber Browning machine guns in front of the building, the structure was a tough nut to crack.

So, what did we have here? Fifty four soldiers armed with AK-47's and three machine guns. Eight against fifty four–a ratio of 1 to 6.75 *better than survivable 1 to 7, from Joe's survival equations*. I guess the quarter-point margin could be considered the allowance for my inexperience, a pretty slim allowance.

"Here is more." Joe handed me two photos. "Look closely; what do you see?"

I examined both photographs. The first photo portrayed a group of Iranian soldiers and a jeep. On the other side, it read 'Photo taken at road block–1600 hrs. guard change over 10 km from target and 5 km from Teheran outskirts'. The other photo displayed a speeding jeep carrying two soldiers: one driving and the other manning a large caliber machine gun on a turret. I turned the photo over and read 'Photo taken of patrol around target area 1200 hrs. Patrol distance from target 5 km'.

"I see a bunch of grunts and a 'rat patrol' on the move," I said.

"Look at the grain of these photos. See the lines? That's a long-range tele-scan photography using equipment like that of the CIA."

"You mean the CIA is involved?"

"It seems so. We'd better check the clients out."

Who were the clients? How did they obtain Keith's military records? And where could they procure a military map with the up-to-date and detailed military information on the Iran-Iraqi front? The map had been drawn professionally, on the grid, showing reference points, and contained only the essential military information. More than that, it was tailored to serve a task like ours. In fact, it was made for us *the target was a centerpiece of the map*. The layout of the target area was a civil engineering blueprint spiced with comments of clearly military nature. Interestingly enough, the sequential numbers on both documents hinted on them being only a subset of a larger set of maps prepared for a big project encompassing much more than our task. What could it be?

"And look here." Joe's finger touched the lower right corner of the target layout. "See a faint stamp of a paper company? If we could find out where the company is located, we would know who is behind the task."

"Using the British Intelligence?" I guessed. After all, Joe did claim having friends in high places.

"Yes, the MI-6." Joe smiled.

Yeah, sure, I thought. It wasn't that I did not take Joe's claims of having a high-ranking friend in the British Intelligence seriously, but I simply couldn't shake off the James-Bondish flavor of the whole thing.

Totally lost amidst all this important information was one trifling detail, an item hardly worth mentioning: fifty two million dollars in gold bullion.

"It is likely that we won't be able to remove the whole thing," Joe noted. "Still, it would be a handsome bonus."

"More like the main fee," I said, "with the twenty thousand dollars being a bonus."

"Speaking of fees..." Joe began, and I knew that whatever he was going to say next had nothing to do with fees. 'Speaking of...' was his manner of changing the subject of conversation. "Speaking of fees, I'd like to send you to Europe for a couple of days."

"Just like that? To Europe?"

"Yeah, you'll meet Keith, and he will fill you in on all the details."

"The details of what?"

"Business negotiations. I think you should be in on this. It's one of the options of entry, an important one."

I had never been to Europe, and here was my opportunity to see it. I pretended that I was not excited, "Yea, I guess I can take a couple of days off."

"Well, enjoy the trip," Joe wished me while leaving.

Later in the day, I faced Martha.

"Birds!?" Martha wrinkle-nosed. "Chasing birds in Greece?"

"Not chasing, watching them," I corrected my fiancee.

"That could be interesting."

I sensed that the task of explaining my trip to Greece was not going to be an easy one.

"Gyps Fulvus, Griffon Vulture." I stepped into the twilight zone of Latin. It had always worked on Martha before. She considered everything associated with Latin to be boring and usually dropped out at that point. But not this time.

"I like vultures," she declared, raising the ante, and suddenly I didn't feel comfortable anymore.

"It's a two-day assignment, an exchange of a sort, involving hanging from cliffs." I tried the 'possible hardships and danger' maneuver.

But she was undauntable, "I'd like to go with you."

The 'danger' tactics didn't work; I had to think fast. I hated all this, lying to Martha I mean, but I didn't have any other choice. I could not tell her the truth. In the first place, she would, probably, think that I was joking: her fiance—a birdwatcher—was going to arrange an entry into a Mid-Eastern country for the purpose of assassinating its President and hauling out fifty-two million dollars in gold. I could hardly believe this fairy tale myself. Still, it was funny, particularly the combination of a birdwatcher, assassination, and gold. I chuckled.

There had to be a solution to the vulture problem. What if I'd take her with me? Hell, why not? Once in Greece, I could find an excuse why we could not watch the fucking birds. I could persuade her to go shopping. Could she resist the lifetime opportunity to shop in Athens? Probably not.

"Yes, let's go. I know you'll enjoy Athens." My mind was made up.

"You really mean it?"

"Of course I mean it." I was becoming quite enthusiastic about the prospect of taking Martha with me.

"Well...I'd love to, but I can't, not this time. I just wanted to know if you'd take me with you."

Martha tended to be unpredictable sometimes.

AN AUDIENCE WITH THE GODDESS OF WAR

Sitting next to the window, a notable disadvantage—stewardesses' legs were missing from my flight menu—and utterly bored, I was glad to hear the captain notifying all that we were finally approaching our destination. As our jet banked and descended below the level of scattered clouds, I watched their shadow-patches on the ground. These imperceptibly slow-drifting shadows were crossing the plains of Athena, the Greek Goddess of War, spot-blemishing the whitish mosaic of the city bearing her name, and, unable to stop, climbed the sun-burned slopes of the Ymittos mountains.

At the airport, passing customs, I scanned the crowd of faces by the exit searching for one familiar face *Joe had shown me Keith's photo.* My own distinction from the crowd, my mark, was the auburn briefcase in my right hand and a folded newspaper in my left.

The crowd slowly melted away.

"Jim?"

I turned. A man of about twenty five, five-foot-seven, compact, muscular and handsome, was Keith. I nodded.

"Did you have a pleasant flight?" This ordinary question, spoken with the British accent, somehow sounded polite-friendly, cordially-concerned, and totally European.

"Yeah, I asked them to stop over the French Riviera, but they told me that their reverse thrust didn't work."

For a moment, Keith's face expressed puzzlement. Finally, he caught on to my 'Yankee' sense of humor.

"The reverse thrust didn't work?! Jolly good."

We boarded a shuttle jet to Thessaloniki. Keith came straight to business, "We have an appointment with the Iraqi Consul in Athens in the morning. I met the chap a week ago. We talked for three hours, he is fairly informed, and his attitude toward us is positive."

"What's in Thessaloniki?"

"Me." Keith smiled. "That is where I live. I have a spacious apartment."

Spacious is a relative term. What is spacious to a native of Europe is cramped to an American. Keith's whole apartment, including the 'Mattel' bathroom, could fit into the living room of my apartment in

Raleigh. The size of Keith's couch, my overnight sleeping accommodations, was about one half of what it should be. Thus, my legs dangled from the edge of the 'love seat' all night.

But my discomfort did not matter, because all love seats in the world and all apartments–all put together–dwarfed in comparison to what we planned. Before coming to Athens, I did not give the whole affair much thought, postponing the analysis until Keith would fill me in on the details. Now he did, and the magnitude of our operation stunned me. We were going to plunge right in the middle of the Iran-Iraqi war. A full-scale diversionary field operation would be initiated by the Iraqis: aircraft, artillery, an infantry attack, and all– just to clear a 'safe' passage across the front line, for us.

Jesus Christ! What was I getting into?

The next morning we returned to Athens. A taxi cab brought us to the affluent part of the city, the Psychico area *a name easy to remember, dub it Psycho, as in our case* and to Mazaraki Street. A guard at the gate of the Iraqi Embassy greeted Keith with a nod of recognition and briefly scrutinized my face. Then he directed us through a dense garden to an elegant 'Beverly Hills' style villa.

The Consul was expecting us in his spacious *by American standards* office. He welcomed Keith and introduced himself to me, "Abdul Kadhim Mohsin at your service."

His English was good, although accented. His dark eyes studied me. I wondered what this impeccably dressed gentleman thought of us. It could be either 'What do we have here? Two screwballs?', or 'Allah does things in mysterious ways. These two foreigners could be the answer to our prayers.'

"I convey greetings from the Highest Authority." Abdul, barely perceptibly, bowed his head.

I began to realize how important this meeting was. Abdul Mohsin on one side and I on the other were a link, a tie between an evil, powerful Arab government and a sinister mercenary war organization–absolutely unrelated, even alien, entities, still harmoniously symbiotic in an attempt to accomplish a mutually beneficial task.

"I forwarded your plan to the highest office," said Abdul. "If they will approve it, I will contact you at once."

'They' were Saddam Hussein himself, the President of the Republic of Iraq. No one but he could make this important decision. He could consult his top military advisors, but most likely, he was not going to, for political reasons. The operation was ultra-sensitive, particularly from political angle. Still, Saddam could chicken out and say no to the operation, but, from what I knew about him and his ruthless ways, this guy was going to bet on us in order to unbalance the stale-mated war with Iran in his favor.

As if reading my thoughts, Abdul accentuated, "You probably understand how sensitive this is. By merely passing this information, I put myself into a very precarious position."

Yes, I understood. If our operation were going to be put in motion, Abdul was the only person in Iraq, besides Saddam, who had the knowledge of our connection. Would Saddam sever the link by liquidating Abdul?

"And another thing," Abdul continued, "and this is from my personal perspective, have you considered the consequences of this operation in the larger framework?"

I wondered what he meant by the 'larger framework'.

"You mean the historical consequences?" I guessed naively.

"No, no, not that large," he laughed. "I meant the immediate consequences: your safety. You will be hunted by Islam, you know. You realize that, don't you?"

Frankly, I hadn't given it much thought, but now it occurred to me that Abdul was probably right. My imagination readily offered me a glimpse into the possible future–after successful completion of our task in Iran, back home. Here is what I saw.

I was preparing to go out on a date with Martha and check listed all the apparel items which I was going to wear for her: custom-made cowboy boots adorned with golden, ornamental snaps, a silk shirt with golden buttons, silk underwear, a solid, western style, golden belt buckle, a gold watch and cuff links, and, of course, a golden medallion on a gold chain around my neck–all made-to-order from the Ayatollah's gold. Clearly, farting through silk had its advantages.

Descending the stairs, I noticed two burnoose-clad figures lurking in the shadow of my apartment building. Both men stepped out, and the bright moonlight reflected from the steel blades of their long, curved yataghans. They had to be those Islam guys that Abdul talked about a few months back.

What was I going to do?!

"Are you the Allah-damn son-of-a-bitch who murdered our Esteemed Ayatollah?" The first Islam guy addressed me.

I was in trouble.

"It was an accident." I couldn't think of anything better. "I was watching birds at that time."

Now I really got myself into a mess. These guys didn't have any respect for birds. They were not like us, they didn't care about the bald eagle, or Russian steppe hawk, or Guatemalan quetzal, or even the phoenix, and, from what I heard before, they shot vultures on sight.

"Ahem..." The second guy anchored his hand on the jewel-speckled handle of his yataghan.

At this point of our verbal exchange, I became convinced that the Islam guys meant business. Still, I didn't want to leave them with the wrong impression that I was afraid. So, I ran...

Emerging from the 'Arabian nights' scenario created by my troubled imagination, I said, "One step at a time, Mr. Mohsin, one step at a time."

"What do you think?" Keith asked when the meeting ended, and we left the Iraqi Embassy.

"If Saddam says yes, that's the route we're gonna take." I was quite sure of it.

Keith Fletcher was an unusual individual *is there any other kind in the mercenary business, excluding myself?*. An adventurer, like Joe and Johnny, Keith was more so. One could call him an extremely enthusiastic adventurer. While Joe and Johnny were cool, even cold, about it all, Keith thrived and blossomed in the light of adventure. Coming from the SAS *the British equivalent of the U.S. Special Forces*, where he was baptized under fire while his unit fought guerillas in Belize, Keith, according to Joe, was fully qualified to join TRAG.

Joe had related one interesting incident involving Keith, which alone put him into that category of individuals I call unusual *it should be called extraordinary, but in mercenary business the extraordinary, consumed in large enough quantities, becomes a mere unusual*. The task involved freeing an American prisoner from a Turkish jail. The components of the task included a diversion at the main gates, silencing a watch tower sentry, scaling up a wall on the back side, eliminating a few guards, breaking into a cell block and a cell, freeing the prisoner, and evading one angry posse–an enormous task for a team of four. Keith accomplished it ALONE.

We walked in silence.

"See that flower arrangement?" said Keith suddenly as we stopped in front of a flower shop. "Isn't it lovely?"

"What!?" I exclaimed.

"The flowers, the color composition, see it?" Keith's green eyes, with a tint of hazel, were wide open.

Surprise, surprise! What did we have here? A florist-killer?

"Yeah..." I faltered. "How the reds hide behind...I mean how the whites overlap the reds."

"This is what I am going to do someday." Keith turned to me. "Open a flower shop."

"Swell," I said.

We approached the Omonia Square, the heart of Athens, and I checked into King Minos Hotel for an overnight stay giving me just enough time for finding a little present for Martha and for visiting the Parthenon.

"See you in a few weeks," I told Keith. "Don't forget to fix a bouquet of flowers for Saddam."

"I'll get you for this," grinned Keith.

AMERICAN ATHENA

Upon returning to Raleigh, I called Joe.
"Come to my place," he said. "I have a cold and do not wish to spread it."
"So you want me to do the job," I hung up.
Joe lived in Cary, about fifteen minutes drive from my place.
"Please report," he greeted me in a dry manner.
"Okay, I met Keith and Abdul, and if Saddam says yes, the road is clear." I did not want to report. What was it? A military camp?
"Could you expand on that a little?"
It seemed I did not have any other choice but "to expand on that". After all, my trip to Europe had been a business trip sponsored by Joe.
"Our status with the Iraqis is as follows. We, the team of eight, are allowed to enter the country via Baghdad. Neither visas nor inoculations are required *the inoculations part tickled my fancy: I really worried about contracting typhus in Greece and transmitting it to Ayatollah.* We are not allowed to bring weapons; whatever is necessary will be supplied by the Iraqi military. A government liaison person will meet us at the airport and escort us to our destination. We are to coordinate our activities in Iraq with this person until the arrival at the destination, where the local commander will take over. Under no circumstances are we to explain our mission to anyone, including the commander." I paused. "One minor detail is lacking though–Saddam's okay."
"Excellent!" Joe exclaimed. "Excellent! You've earned your week's pay."
"Look, I didn't do a thing."
"The weapons, you saved us a sum on weapons."
"That was the Iraqis' initiative, not mine." I could not take credit for anything.
"Well, you represented TRAG. Your face fits better than mine."
I glanced at Joe's face and suddenly realized why Joe sent me to Greece: not to negotiate but to present an appropriate face. Negotiating with the mercenary organization, the Iraqis would not be particularly impressed by Joe's baby face; my face 'fitted' the occasion better. This was the most ridiculous, and insulting, revelation I had uncovered in a long, long while.

"In that case, I resign as your business manager," I declared bitterly.

Joe's puerile facial expression changed to a stern one, "Hold it right there! What is the matter with you? You like to play a goddamn prima donna? Your feelings are hurt! Listen, this is not a fucking game, this is for real, man. And your role in this operation is as important as mine. When we go out on a mission like this we must use every scrap of help and every resource available in order to pull it off. Your face, my friend, may have opened the safest route for us, your face may have saved our ass. Do you understand?"

Joe's anger grew, and he attempted to control it.

"Well, I thought..."

"There is no reflection on your abilities," Joe interrupted. "None. I saw you in combat. You handled it better than I did the first time."

"All right, all right, I think I understand," I capitulated.

"Good, I'm glad you do." Joe calmed down somewhat. An awkward silence followed. Finally, he said, "Tomorrow I'll introduce you to another face, infinitely prettier than yours."

The next day, in the afternoon, it happened.

Every woman *or man, for that matter* possesses a forte–a top asset. Unique personality could be that asset, or a beautiful face, or something else.

"Jim, this is Charity Hall." Joe introduced her.

Her large, pale-blue, deep-set eyes were her forte. I stared into their infinite depth, irresistibly attracted by their azure, luring void, unable to pull away my gaze.

"Joe told me about you." If she didn't say anything, I would probably continue being in the trance and make a fool of myself. But her melodious voice brought me back to my temporarily lost senses. I shifted my gaze to the front of her tight sweatshirt.

"UCLA" I read. "Are you a student at the UCLA?"

The C and the L were attractively sunk between the U and the A.

"Yes, I major in Physical Education, and I'm on the college gymnastics team." She moved, and the U and the A bounced.

"Are you attending the summer school here? *What else would she be doing in Raleigh, I wondered?*

"No, I'm with Joe, " and she smiled for the first time.

"Staying here long?" I still wasn't sure why she was so far from California. She couldn't be Joe's girlfriend, not with his rat face.

"No, not for long." She stopped smiling. Apparently, my probing questions began to annoy her.

"Let's eat at O'Brian's." Joe barged in. "Their pork baby back ribs and curly fries are pretty good."

Charity turned to Joe. No, hell, it was her hair! Her straw-blond, long, straight hair was her top asset.

We drove to Glenwood Avenue.

This mid afternoon, I don't know what it was: maybe the sun rays came from the right angle, or the way Charity walked ahead of me and Joe, but I was sure this time *please forgive me, Martha, I thought. I know that's your department* Charity's legs were her top asset.

The dinner proceeded in a normal fashion. I loved the baby-back-ribs and the skin-on curly-fries. In fact, I pigged out on them.

"I don't think they serve this stuff in Baghdad." Joe opened his big mouth and surprised me. I stopped chewing. What was the matter with him? He should know better than making such comments in front of someone who was not involved in our operation.

Joe noticed my open mouth and a curly potato shaving dangling precariously from its corner.

"Oh yeah, didn't I mention it?" The fucking son-of-a-bitch revealed, "Charity is coming with us."

"What?!" I couldn't withhold the exclamation, and the potato shaving, obeying the law of gravity, fell on the table. "Is she TRAG too?" I finally recovered enough to resume chewing.

"Yes, I'm from TRAG." She smiled somewhat shyly.

"Swell," I said. "Now we have the best action team for the task: a sailor, a gymnast, a birdwatcher, and a florist. If we can't shoot them, we'll shower them with flowers."

Charity laughed, then stood up, approached me, bent over and kissed me on the cheek.

"Everything that Joe said about you is true. I like you; you're okay. Welcome to our team." And I don't know what, maybe the way she turned her head, but I realized that Charity had no top asset–she was the top asset...of our team.

And the team sat right here, at O'Brian's, maybe not all of it, but at least the core. We had nothing in common with each other. Origin, education, interests, and whatever–nothing matched. Yet, we fit neatly together, like a puzzle, or a chain: Joe-Charity-me-Keith. We had a common goal; we depended on each other in order to achieve it. The potency of our team lay in the diversity of its elements, the strength in their sum. And, in addition to that, there existed a personal bond built on mutual attraction.

I shared my thoughts with Joe and Charity.

"Right on target," she commented.

Joe, judging by the thoughtful expression on his face, seemed to comprehend the essence of what I was talking about, but then, out of the blue, he muttered, "You mean you have a personal attraction to Keith as…?"

"Not that kind of attraction, damn you!" I cut him off. "Did you have to spoil it?"

"Sorry, I thought…"

Du-u-u-mb! And this guy swam in math like a fish?! Un-n-n-believable.

In Charity's opinion, the whole spoil-thing was very funny. She laughed, and laughed…

Two days later, Charity flew back to California. I had a chance to say good-bye to her at the airport *that is why I came with Joe*. She gave me another kiss on the cheek. Damn! She was something…

On the way back to Raleigh, Joe hardly spoke a word. I attempted to infuse some life into our 'stuck on the reef' conversation by paying him a compliment on his selection of exquisite female personnel for TRAG, but received only 'hm-m-m's' and 'yep's' in response. Finally, I gave up on the idea of dislodging the dialog off the reef.

"Care to stop by for a cup of coffee?" I asked, knowing that he would probably turn down the offer.

"Yep." He, unexpectedly, agreed. "I've got to show you something."

He reached inside the glove compartment and pulled out a half-rolled folder.

"I have the information on our clients," Joe began. "Are you ready for this?"

What he told me made me feel quite uneasy. The Iranian shipping company co-owners, Mr. Fa and Mr. Salem-Tuk were not the co-owners of anything. In fact, they were not Iranians, but the nationals of Egypt, A.F. and E.F., brothers. Both held high profile positions in the Egyptian government.

"Even if I live to be fifty," I commented in surprise.

"A hundred," Joe corrected me, "but that's beside the point."

Both A.F and E.F. were big shots in Egypt. In the diplomatic corps, it was not at all unusual for a person in high position to receive a covert assignment from the government, but the scope of this particular assignment–hiring an assassin team–surpassed the usual diplomatic boundaries.

"Why in hell would they want to terminate Ayatollah?" I was puzzled. "Husni Mubarak, the President of Egypt, is not a friend of Ayatollah, but neither is he his enemy."

"You're absolutely right." Joe smiled somewhat conspiratorily. "Because Mubarak's got nothing to do with any of this."

Thus, properly setting me up for the kill, Joe revealed the rest of it.

"Read this," he handed me a stack of documents and reports.

"...covert operations with the CIA from June 1966 to 1968 *month unknown.*" I read. "Covert ops with the Mossad from April 1967 to present. Active with joint U.S. and Israel operations dating 1977, 1978, and 1979. Worked with his brother under the CIA and Mossad instructions on Iranian operation, which involved securing and removal from Teheran four male individuals *information classified.* Involved in hiring of a mercenary unit composed of German nationals, Commander Karl Wolfgang Steiner, an ex-commando. The unit was terminated thirty four kilometers from the Turkish border inside Iran. A.F. is also included in the Blue File."

"Goddamn!" I exclaimed. "The story you told me was true, Steiner's story."

"Sure it was, except that I didn't know who hired them."

"By the way, what's the Blue File? I bet it has nothing to do with flying saucers." I was curious.

"Beats me." Joe did not know. "Maybe A.F. worked for the British Intelligence too."

E.F., too, was involved up to his ears.

I read, "...E.F.'s first recorded covert operation involvement took place in 1979. Under the CIA and Mossad instructions, he hired an all-British mercenary unit for the task of removing four male subjects from Teheran at the height of internal hostilities. Operation completed successfully. No known activities between 1979 and 1981. June 1981 reports indicate that E.F. was reactivated by the Mossad. Participated in hiring the German mercenary unit in 1983 for the purpose of Ayatollah's termination; that failed. Both brothers reside in Cairo."

"And here is something that ties the whole fucking thing together," announced Joe. "Submitted for analysis, the imprint on the low right corner of the Ayatollah's residence blueprint was identified as a trademark of a paper company based in Jerusalem and Tel Aviv, with no international contracts recorded."

"That's the Mossad?" I concluded.

"The Mossad." Joe agreed. "The document standard is the Mossad's too. Remember the document numbers? They stand for project-codes-number-division-year."

"You think we're getting into something we shouldn't be getting into?" I probed cautiously.

"It's still a contract."

Sure it was a contract, and a contract is a contract. We do it all the time: assassinating presidents of foreign countries. Nothing to it!

"The assassination part bothers me," I confessed.

Joe studied my face for awhile, then, quite casually remarked, "Oh, well, don't worry, we won't have to. Here is the latest dispatch from the Iranians, or, shall I say, from the Egyptians. We are not to kill the bastard, but to remove him alive."

He handed me a typed page containing nothing but twenty one rows of numbers and hyphens, with one sentence at the bottom: 'Decoding sequence through your man in Salonika'.

"I figured it out myself." Joe smiled. "Their code is elementary: take the English alphabet, number it sequentially, then code the message multiplying each corresponding number by four. It's an equation, more precisely, an inequality–A=4A. That's all. I thought they could do better than that."

"What's the message say?"

"Here." Joe passed me the translation.

"Method of operation possible and workable. Due to certain unexpected events operation will be adjusted. The gentleman involved will vacate premises under your escort. He is not under any account to be damaged. You will be informed of destination and who will take your charge after leaving Initial area. Radio frequency will be given before you go. If you and your team are available, we offer the assignment. Two hundred and fifty thousand U.S. dollars will be immediately deposited in Handelsbank, Zurich, on your acceptance. Communications to go via man in Salonika. Drop changed. New drop at later date."

"Taking him alive presents a problem," Joe admitted. "As a matter of fact, it changes the entire game. As I see it, the Israelis have assembled a team of their own, which will be flown to Iran at the time of our assault on the 'little fortress'. We take the bastard and deliver him into the Israeli hands while still on the Iranian territory…I don't trust these guys."

"So, what's the plan?" I grew more and more apprehensive of the new developments.

"The plan is in two parts." Joe paused and extended his arms palms up. "The bullshit part, which is about seventy five percent of the scheme *Joe weighed the imaginary substance on his left palm, then turned it over as if dumping its contents,* and the real thing, which is what? Twenty five percent?" *He balanced the smaller part of the imaginary substance on his right palm and closed his fingers in a tight fist.*

The 'bullshit part' had three components–one for the Israelis, one for the Iraqis, and one for the Iranians. The Israelis would see the following. The American clay pigeon team goes to Iran via Turkey, reaches the target, extracts the 'gentleman', delivers him into the Israeli hands, then attempts to break out south to the Gulf in order to be picked up by the Greek tug boat 'Armadillo' *the arrangements had already been made.*

"The Israelis don't know that we are aware of their involvement," Joe analyzed. "To them, our Turkish entry is just another hit-or-miss attempt. If we were killed, like the British and the German teams before us, the Israelis would recruit someone else for another attempt. I wonder, who could it be? The Russians?" He laughed.

Iraqi version stunk as bad as the Israeli one. Americans, as it goes, will do anything for money. So, why not use them? Assassinating Ayatollah might grant the Iraqis a strategic advantage and shorten the war. And even if someone could trace the path of the assassin team to Iraq, no one could prove that the Iraqis were involved in the plot. Even if it failed, the Iraqis risked nothing.

"At the first interview, Abdul asked Keith if we secured the exit route after the mission has been accomplished. Keith hinted on the marshlands east of Tehran, but withheld the information on the grounds of it being highly classified. That approach gave us more clout with the Iraqis. I mean, the point of us being independent. Basically, they don't give a damn what happens to us after the mission is accomplished. As far as they are concerned, they've never heard of us."

"And the Iranian part?"

"Yeah, that's when our Iraqi card becomes a trump. The Iraqis were not involved with the British and the German teams. They are in the clear. The Egyptians, and the Israelis behind them, are not aware of our Iraqi card. They also assume that we are ignorant of the fate of the two previous teams and, therefore, most likely, would select the entry via Turkey, seemingly the easiest route. Thus, whoever the leak is—the Egyptians themselves, or someone in the Mossad, or in the CIA—that person will pass the false information to the Iranians. The Iranians, then, will be expecting us on the Turkish border."

"But what about the exit?"

"We can't go back to Iraq. The leak, wherever and whoever it is, will null our option of going south, to the Gulf. The swamp option is a joke, leaving us only one exit—north."

"To Russia?!" *Hey! I did not bargain for that, I thought.*

"No, probably not...but I'll think of something."

PASSING A STOP SIGN

"Bad news," announced Joe. "Our clients cancelled the contract."

Deep inside, I was glad, but decided to fake a disappointment. "You mean we are not gonna pass 'go', we are not gonna collect twenty thousand dollars?"

"Oh yes, we are," Joe retorted. "We just have to find another sponsor, that's all."

"And how are we going to accomplish that? Sponsors who are willing to present you with a quarter-million-dollars don't grow on trees, you know," I stated. I was relieved. A pile of gold on my kitchen table would look fine, but the odds of coming back, in my opinion, were slim.

"But we already have one." Joe grinned at me. "And you know him, Jim."

"Hah?" was my natural response. I swore never to be surprised by anything Joe said, because 'hah?', I suspected, made me appear dumb, but this one just slipped out.

"Frank Grazia, my good man. You've met him recently, remember?"

"But he's an arms dealer, not a client."

"Let me tell you a couple of things about Frank." Joe reshuffled his mental card index. "He is connected to New York Mafia."

Joe paused and studied my face in the anticipation of something similar to my 'hah?', but I had already re-composed myself, and my face became impenetrably blank.

"So?"

"Well..." Joe seemed to be slightly disappointed with the absence of any reaction on my side. "He's also buddy buddying with the Miami Mafia."

I remained silent.

"So, here is the plan..." Joe outlined another devious scheme of his.

The next week, I met Frank at the Best Western Motel on Interstate 85 near Hillsborough. *Frank preferred staying at inexpensive motels. "Not to attract any unwanted attention," he explained. But I knew better: he was a cheapskate.* The UZI greeted me exactly as it did the last time.

"Did you bring the advance?" Frank's stare lingered on my empty hands.

"No, but I brought a proposition." I decided to skip all the explanations why I came empty-handed and to come straight to the point. "The arms sale is a small fish. How would you like to invest two-hundred-thousand dollars for two-weeks time with the interest of five-hundred percent?"

Frank did not say 'hah?'. He just stared, first at me, then into space, while his brain processed the equation 'yield equals investment plus interest', where 'interest equals five times investment'.

"That's one-million-two-hundred-thousand," Frank outputted.

"Exactly."

"What kind of operation is it? Knocking over Fort Knox?"

"That's classified." I had to draw the line.

"I don't have that much cash."

"Yeah, I know, but the guys in New York have." I played my first card, the queen of hearts.

Frank seemed puzzled by my reference to the 'New York guys', "What guys?"

"The Mafia." I pulled out the ace of spades.

"I don't know what you mean." Frank paused.

"The guys to whom you gave the information about the Miami dudes with the dope–the dudes who were ambushed in Newark and killed." I played a trump.

Frank's eyes suddenly bulged, "Where did you get this information?"

"We have sources." I put the rest of my hand on the poker table, all face down. I have never blackmailed anyone in the world before.

"I'll see what I can do." Frank put his head down.

The game was over.

I called Joe, to be sure that he was home, and drove to his place.

"Please report," Joe spoke.

"I've delivered the message." I definitely did not like to 'report'.

"Could you extrapolate on that?"

"If I don't have to 'report'."

"Sorry, during an operation, I tend to evaluate everything in military terms."

"But the operation has not even begun."

"Oh yes, it has. It's in progress right now."

I related my conversation with Frank.

"He will come up with the money," Joe said confidently. "You did a great job, thank you."

Later, lying in bed, I thought of all recent events. So far, I had already established the safest passage to the country of our target, saved on arms, and, now, financed the whole operation. How in hell did I achieve all that? Joe pulled the strings, and I was only the front, the face of the operation. Joe manipulated 'factors' *his most favorite word in the English language*–events, people, me…

A knock at the door interrupted my 'Where do I stand?' thoughts.

"I couldn't sleep." Martha put her arms around my neck. "I want to stay with you tonight."

She undressed. Tall, five-foot-ten, long-legged, by no means skinny, she exuded an aura of health. Her oval, fully symmetrical, somewhat country face with a jaw, in some measure square, although definitely not manly, only added force to her genuine image of health.

She had undone her long wavy blond hair.

"I know you like me in a pony tail, but it's uncomfortable in bed," she commented softly.

"No, I don't mind. You're beautiful either with your hair fixed or undone."

She lay next to me, and God, she was beautiful! I kissed the silky-soft globes of her not too large breasts with their small nipples; caressed her wide, softly rounded hips and her exquisite mound; then my hand slid down her full, velvety thighs and up between them. Did I really need anything else in the world, besides this warm and loving, gorgeous and exciting woman–my Martha? Suddenly, the operation, Ayatollah, the gold, and Joe–all became comfortably distant, distantly unimportant, just a game. And the real thing, the truth, the beauty, lay right next to me.

Martha's lips were soft, warm, and responsive…God! I loved this woman, and she didn't even suspect how much. Or maybe she did.

"I love you too, darling," she whispered. Of course, she knew.

"Let's skip the engagement and get married right away…Well, as soon as I return from my next field trip," I said.

"Is that the proposal?" She smiled.

"Uh-huh."

"Well, give me time to think…" She paused. "Yes."

The next Saturday, Joe presented me with a few surprises. First, I answered the knock at my door, and there he was. I didn't have any other choice but to let him in.

"How do you like your coffee?" I asked him. He came unexpected and uninvited, which slightly irritated me. I had plans for this weekend, and Joe was not included in them.

"Black, four teaspoonfuls of sugar." He liked his coffee extra sweet. It kills the bitter taste, he said.

"What are your plans?" I asked. People ask this question when they intend to invite someone to join them; in such context, the tone being used is friendly. But if the tone is anything else, they mean to leave them alone. And Joe got the message.

"I didn't mean to intrude," he said somewhat sadly. "I just brought you a little present."

He placed a swollen five-by-ten manila envelope on the table. I opened the envelope. It contained ten thousand dollars in one-hundred-dollar bills.

"That's your up-front share." Joe sipped coffee. His eyes squinted and studied my face. The son-of-a-bitch knew perfectly well that I had never held so much money in my hands in my entire life.

"Yea, how about that?" I attempted to hide my surprise and a bushel of other mixed feelings. "So, Frank came up with the cash."

"In one week. That's a record."

I began feeling guilty about not inviting Joe to join me and Martha, but I fought off the feeling.

"We've already made plans for this weekend," I said. "How about joining me Monday afternoon and spending a night in my place?"

"That's fine." Joe's face brightened up. I felt sorry for him because I knew that he did not have any friends in Raleigh *or in any other place in the world.* He was going to spend a very lonely weekend. As if sensing my empathy, he muttered, "Don't worry about me. I'm gonna have a very busy weekend too. There are a lot of loose ends to tie up before going to Texas."

Of course, he lied. Knowing full well what a dedicated perfectionist Joe was, I suspected that he already had 'tied up the loose ends' as soon as they showed up.

"What's in Texas?" I inquired.

"I'm glad you asked." He seemed pleased *he set the bait and I nibbled at it.* "We all are gonna meet and train in Texas, at the survival camp near Lubbock."

A GLIMPSE OF HELL

The survival camp, located on the other side of Double Mountain River, deep in the hills, was owned by a man named Roger Guidi, a military nut and survival freak. He had to be, at least that's what I imagined. All my knowledge of survival camps came from watching movies. Thus, I expected to find the following. Roger Guidi had to be a seasoned army Colonel, retired, who, serving in the armed forces his entire life, just couldn't part with the military life-style. Take his gun away, and he would quickly develop an inferiority complex. Roger's clients were a bunch of craze-eyed kids who joined the program mainly to have fun the wild-west style. Every morning they dressed up in cammies and ambushed each other in the brush screaming 'Charge!', shooting wildly harmless, blank ammunition.

I was wrong. Roger Guidi had majored in Nuclear Physics at one of the Universities of Texas. He wore glasses and could easily pass for a young professor of mathematics. He did serve in the Marines a few years back and even attained a rank of sergeant, but quit the service.

The current survival class *we were not part of it* consisted of several middle-age males from all walks of life, two women, two couples, and a sixteen-year-old boy—all anxious to learn how to survive real and imaginary perils of life.

Our training program did not fit into the survival class curriculum, so Roger called our task a specialized application. During the preceding week, he and Joe built a crude, full scale replica of the 'little fortress'. Of course, it hardly resembled the real thing; buildings were missing. Instead, their location was marked by sets of five-foot-high stilts driven into the soil, each supporting a construction containment plastic sheet, a 'rooftop'. The guard tower and the mosque mock-ups stood higher than the rest of the 'buildings'. Roger did not know where the real thing was located, and, as I soon discovered, to my surprise, neither did the other members of our team, besides Joe, Charity, and me. Keith was not present; he would join us in Athens. The 'need to know' principle applied here as well.

The other members of our team were Dave Blount, Kurt Stahl, and Mark Zuckerman.

Dave 'Chuck' Blount, a heavyset Irishman from Colorado, with a face faintly resembling Chuck Norris', was a quiet and somewhat shy man. He kept a low profile, stayed aloof, did not participate in small talk, and, even when he spoke, his sentences rarely exceeded five words. There was absolutely nothing remarkable about Chuck, except for the fact that he had killed seventy five North Vietnamese regulars and Vietcong guerillas while serving in Vietnam.

"Is that my cot?" Chuck delayed his slow wandering gaze on Joe's face. What was he? An unthinking killing machine?

"If you like," answered Joe. It did not matter who slept on which cot, seven in total, in a tent set up specifically for our group.

"Don't take the first one," I said. "It's Charity's."

"Oh, thank you for choosing one for me, Jim." She turned to me, visibly surprised: why would I bother to select a cot for her? But I had reasons, the main one being her sex. I thought she would be safer staying in the plain view of all in the tent. Being in front of the men, I mean, instead of being surrounded by them. "Just for that, I'll take the one in the back."

Chuck pressed the cot bedding with one hand, as if not entirely sure whether the cot could support his weight. Then he carefully lowered his body on the bed.

Kurt Stahl, a former fighter pilot of the U.S. Air Force, too, had served in Vietnam during the latest stages of war. He was stationed in Thailand and had flown thirty five Phantom missions, mainly over Cambodia and Laos, and a few over North Vietnam. Although of German descent, Kurt spoke poor German. His blond hair, steel-blue eyes, long straight nose, and a firm chin placed his origin in the northern regions of Germany, somewhere close to the Dutch border. And that's where his parents came from. If his parents remained in Germany, and he was born, say, thirty years earlier, he would, probably, have served in the Luftwaffe and flown a Me-109 shooting down American and British planes over Germany during the Second World War. The way he talked about airplanes and aerial combat, it was obvious that to be a pilot was in his blood–that was his 'blueprint', his predestination. He did not fit any other mold. He could have been born before the First World War and fly next to Red Baron himself. But it was not meant to be. Whoever flew in Kurt's place during the First and the Second World Wars, were, probably, shot down in the end. Thus, Kurt was lucky to be born later and on the 'right side'. I wondered why this handsome *the handsomest man in the group*, intelligent, and successful career officer joined TRAG. What did TRAG offer this man that the Air Force could not?

"What made Kurt resign from the Air Force?" I asked Joe, when we sat at a bar later that night, and he was in a talkative mood.

He shrugged his shoulders.

"I knew I'd find you here!" It was Mark, Mark Zuckerman. "And what are you having? No, don't tell me, it's Cherry Herring, a teenage girl drink, right?"

"Why won't you join us?" Joe extended his hand and his smile.

Mark Zuckerman, an Israeli from Haifa, or an American from Lakewood, New Jersey–whichever, it didn't matter, because he held a dual citizenship–was the most colorful and interesting man in our bunch, as well as the most talkative. He claimed to be a former agent of the Israel Defense Force intelligence service and a veteran of the Six Day War in the Middle East. Of course, I didn't believe a single word of it. Mark presented a splendid example of a pretender. He was 'up and down, and over, and out…" He surprised me by revealing that he belonged to the 'most secret Masonic lodge in America'. He introduced me to the 'secret handshake' *that's how those Masonic guys recognized each other in the dark halls of their hideout lodge.* Mark's pinky folded and tickled mine.

"Are you sure you're not mixing it with the Greenwich Village gay club?" I asked Mark.

"A gay club! That's pretty good." He giggled.

Later, when Mark disappeared in the men's room for a few minutes, I observed, "This guy is the biggest bullshitter I've ever seen in all my lifetimes. An intelligence agent? With his mouth?"

"And why not?" Joe answered. "It's all in the past. Look, if he went back to the Defense Force and told them that he is a member of TRAG, would they believe him? No chance. But he is. No, I checked him out: he is on the level."

But no matter what Joe said about Mark, he was a bullshitter, likable, interesting, even intriguing, but a bullshitter nevertheless–a master of the bullshit art. Whether his claims were true or not didn't matter. What mattered was his extraordinary makeup. Intelligent, imaginative, and…imposing, Mark radiated an aura of intrusive self-confidence. The office term for this quality is 'excellent communication skills', the social definition is 'he speaks what is on his mind', and the street's is–a 'big mouth'. When Mark joined a conversation, he always had an opinion on the subject, which he stated without a shadow of hesitation. Within a minute, the conversation, somehow, shifted to a new subject, Mark's. But no one seemed to mind the shift because Mark always made it interesting.

When I meet a person, a stranger, I like to classify that person by a type. That makes it easier to remember the person. But I could not define Mark's type. I simply wasn't able to pin him down and shove him into a type box. He was Jewish. Although he was a veteran of a Middle East war, I could not imagine him in a soldier's uniform, holding an UZI or a Galil. To confuse me even more, Mark approached me once and asked, "Heard any good Jewish jokes lately?" But even this default did not apply to Mark: his degree of 'jewishness' was too great. He was clever, resourceful, and adaptable, and his features left very little doubt as to his origin. However–Mark was a renegade Jew.

As the evening progressed, the bar, the club, the country dance joint, whichever, filled with local folks–a mixture of red, blue, and yellow crossbar, cross-grain, crosshatch, and cross-stitch cowboy shirts, light Stetson hats, droopy moustache's, and fluffy skirts, plus country songs, smiles, and beer.

Kurt abandoned our stationary company and plunged into the dancing crowd. Before I knew, he was shagging with a choice sample of local fair gender. I wondered again why did Kurt join TRAG. A playboy could not be a killer, or could he? The dance stopped before the tune ran out, due to some kind of disturbance on the floor. From what we could discern, Kurt was in the middle of it.

"Uh-oh...I smell trouble," Joe commented.

Apparently, Kurt enjoyed a higher degree of success with the native girls than their escorts could tolerate. He ended up in the center of an equilateral triangle formed by three burly ranch hands. The exchange of amenities like "...and I can throw you farther than I can spit" and the appropriate response "Oh yeah?!" was quickly approaching a shove-and-pull phase.

"Let me handle this." Mark slid off his chair.

Mark's frame did not encompass more then one hundred and seventy pounds, while the 'Texas triangle' overbalanced six hundred.

"I better help them." I stood up.

"Wait." Joe held my arm.

Mark produced a pair of spectacles and promptly set them on his drooping tip nose.

"How do I look?" He slouched.

"Like a nutty professor." Joe smiled.

"Emeritus," I added.

The dancing floor dispute, meanwhile, heated up to the point of first physical contact. The tune stopped, and the dance-circle paused.

"Hold it! "Mark interrupted the friendly meeting. "You arr underr arrrest!"

Clearly, the word 'arrest' was the key word which broke up the cordial encounter. And, if I heard it right, it was uttered with a German accent. Kurt straightened up his rumpled shirt, the Texans studied Mark silently.

"Of course, I was just kidding about ze arrest," said Mark with the indeed newly acquired German accent and smiled. "I am Doktorr Schweizerr, und zis dummpkoff iz mine patient."

"I bet you a buck," I turned to Joe, "he is not going to get away with it."

But Mark did pull it off. Even more, we acquired three sympathetic Texan friends. They even invited us to their table and bought us beer. According to Mark, we were mental patients from the Lubbock General Hospital, its psychiatric ward. Mark accompanied us on a rehabilitation outing. Kurt, a long time patient of Mark, suffered from an acute schizophrenia and a delusion that he was an ace pilot, while all the time he was no more than an ordinary shoe salesman. Joe was a real fruitcake–a pyromaniac, plus suspected murderer, although that charge had never been proven. With me, it was even worse. I exposed myself on every possible occasion, wetted beds, and suffered from an intermittent amnesia.

"Where are ye from?" Texan-one asked me.

"I don't remember," I replied, feeling sheepish.

"Look at zem. Zei arr crrazies!" Mark obviously enjoyed his new role of psychiatrist. I'd say, he was carrying it too far. "Und zei don't even know zet."

"They seem normal to me," timidly objected Texan-two.

"Ya, zei seem norrmal. Zei alwais do. But zei arr crrazies."

Joe extended his hand to me.

"What?" I asked.

"Ze bet." He smiled.

I handed him a dollar bill.

We detached ourselves from our Texan friends and returned to the bar.

"I like their country songs," I commented. "There is a certain simplicity and innocence about them."

"Not me," contended Mark. "To me, they all sound the same, and you can break them into three major categories: passionate–I need a pussy, joyful–what a wonderful pussy I have access to, and sad–no more pussy."

"Those are love songs," I accentuated. "I wish you'd quit mocking them."

"Yeah, shallow. Love is only seven inches deep."

"More like four, in your case." I couldn't resist the temptation of putting Mark in his place. Joe and Kurt laughed.

"Yeah, very funny." Mark's feelings were obviously hurt, but he bounced back. "I would be more cautious, if I were you, Jim. Your secret, I mean."

"What secret?" I began to suspect that Mark was setting me up for some kind of retaliation.

"In the restroom, on the inside door."

"Yea, let's all go and see." Joe displayed a high degree of enthusiasm. Apparently, he knew Mark very well and was aware that crossing swords with Mark usually entailed dire consequences for the one who dared.

Under the circumstances and the peer pressure, I didn't have any other choice but to accompany the group to the restroom. Also, I was curious: what in the world could Mark find there that belonged to me?

Mark's face brightened up in anticipation, "On the other hand, guys, maybe we shouldn't go. Everyone is entitled to a secret."

We all squeezed into the stool compartment. And there it was, plain as day, the incriminating evidence against me. The darn inscription read, 'Missed you here yesterday, JIM.' and right below it, someone's facetious reply conclusively elucidated the rest of it, 'Sorry, I was out, pal. Had to stop by the AIDS clinic.'

"Wait, guys. That's not me. I've never been here before." I found myself explaining, and, probably, my face became red. "That's not my handwriting."

And if there ever was a time in my life when someone had a real good guffaw on my account, it was here, in the restroom of the dancing joint, where Joe, and Kurt, and Mark, and finally myself, laughed to tears.

"Even?" Mark asked.

"Yes, you fucking son-of-a-bitch, even."

We walked out close together–friends. Mark had scored a brilliant victory.

In the morning, we assembled in a classroom in the ranch house.

Our two-day training schedule included one day of the 'ground school', as Joe called it.

"What's the ground school?" I asked Kurt.

"It's what you learn on the ground before you fly." Kurt and Joe, both being pilots, liked to use the airman terminology, even when it did not apply directly.

Joe started, "First, we'll learn the weapons most likely to be encountered. Charity will cover small arms, and Chuck–rocket launchers. Then I'll acquaint you with the main task, the assault on the target. And tomorrow we'll practice the assault in the field. Any questions? None? Okay, take over, Charity."

"We have two assault rifles here," Charity began. "The M-16 and the AK-47…"

The sight of this beautiful woman instructing how to use killing tools was indescribably incongruent. I could easily imagine her giving gymnastics instructions to a bunch of schoolgirls in a gym, but here she was, expertly throwing at us such non-feminine terms like the 'bolt action', the 'muzzle velocity', and the 'killing ratio'. My God! Charity, what in hell were you doing here? What in hell was I doing here?

"How many of you know how to use the M-16?"

All, but me, raised their hands.

"Aha, good, then we are not going to waste time on it. "I'll show you, Jim, how it works, later. What about the AK-47?"

I was more than happy to raise my arm this time. Only Mark abstained, and I could see that he was slightly embarrassed by his lack of all-around expertise.

"Okay, that's good, and I'll see you, Mark, too, later."

"Even?" I turned to Mark.

"Even." He smiled.

The hand gun and hand grenade parts of our curriculum harvested enough students to warrant a lecture by our beautiful teacher.

"The Makarov pistol is probably the weapon that we are going to use. I'll show you how to take care of this lovely device…" Charity actually used the word 'lovely', as if the killing tool was something to revere and pamper and not a device to blow someone's brains out.

"Don't copy gunslingers in the movies," she instructed. "When you shoot from the hip, you are bound to miss. Aim carefully, hold your pistol firmly and support that hold with the other hand. Squeeze the trigger gently." She assumed a proper stance; her nostrils moved in excitement; her pony tail, normally playing and swaying from side to side, became motionless. "Like this…".

Finally, Charity yielded the 'podium' to Chuck Blount who was clearly uncomfortable with the role of instructor. First, he cleared his throat, trying to compose himself for the task. Then he replaced the army schematics of the M-16, borrowed from Roger's library, with drawings of a LAW and two RPG's. I wanted Chuck to inquire how many of us were familiar with a LAW, which would give me an opportunity to proudly raise my arm *I acquired the knowledge at my meeting with Frank Grazia, when I stood only one step from firing the thing*, but he never did. He simply went, step by step, through the operating instructions of all three systems. As he continued, he relaxed and restored his self-confidence.

"The Russian RPG-7, which has an extra pistol grip, is a lot like RPG-2 but better. Its shaped charge warhead can penetrate a foot of armor. But its night-sight is not as good as ours…"

I listened to Chuck, but my mind wandered. What in hell was I doing here? It was Saturday, and I should be taking my Martha out to the Crabtree Valley Mall, or another as much peaceful, place. Instead, I bibbled around in the land of Alamo. I did not want to know that RPG-2 pierced only six inches of armor and weighed ten pounds. I wanted to go back to Raleigh. That's where I left my heart.

"Are you with us, Mr. Riveaux?" Joe's voice brought me back into the classroom. I had missed the end of Chuck's lecture.

"I think so, Sir." Damn! How much I hated calling him Sir. But right now, here, in the damn hills of Texas, he was my commanding officer, shit. "I am with you."

Joe drew a layout of the 'little fortress' on the blackboard and presented the details of the assault plan. We were not going to initiate a preemptive strike, or scale up the fence.

"We don't have enough time for all that," Joe said. "Surprise and speed are the keys to the success of this assault." He paused. "Surprise and speed. Seven minutes for the strike and seven minutes for the rest of it. Seven and seven."

"Seven and seven," echoed Chuck. "That's what we used to call it in Operation Delta in Vietnam. Seven and seven–send them to hell or heaven!"

Chuck's face lit up. Usually aloof, unobtrusive, and quiet, Chuck, suddenly, came out of his shell in the open. His eyes narrowed and seemed ready to cast arrows and lightning. He stood up, and his solid figure radiated strength. Chuck blossomed: 'seven and seven' was the key to the inner Chuck, it brought memories of excitement and glory of the past. At this moment, Chuck stood in the jungle of the Mekong Delta. That's where he found a true friendship and sacrifice, discovered the agony of loss, solved the mystery of death by killing so many. That's where he left a part of himself–his soul.

All stared silently, somewhat surprised, at Chuck. In the silence, he realized that he had become the center of attention. He sat down and retired back into his shell. The pause lasted another few seconds.

"Y-y-y-eah..." Joe continued finally. "Here is how we are going to do this…"

Joe presented the plan. My part included advancing to the main building and terminating four sentries on its roof with two hand grenades.

"…there are two half-tracks in front of the main building," Joe emphasized. "Try not to damage those. We need one to break out."

The plan was extremely simple, and, to my surprise, for the first time, I began believing that we could pull it off.

Mark touched my arm and whispered, "I know where we are going."

"Go on." I was curious whether he guessed it. I knew that Mark was born in Tehran and spoke fluent Farsi, the main Iranian language, as well as some Arabic, and Hebrew. "Go on, tell me."

"The mosque next to the main building in the compound? That's Muslim stuff." Mark smiled slyly. "We're going to the Gulf, Persian Gulf. We are gonna hit Saudi Arabia or one of the Arab Emirates."

That was chance to recoup the dollar that I lost to Joe on Mark's account. Of course, I was cheating, because I knew exactly where we were going, but what the heck, I couldn't resist the temptation.

"I bet you a buck that you're wrong," I said.

Mark scrutinized my face, then analyzed the options, "Okay, it could not be Lebanon or Syria. Those are too poor. Iraq and Iran are out because those are in the state of war with each other. *Here Mark was making a terminal exclusion mistake, because he did not know Joe and Joe's reasoning: war creates confusion, which can be exploited.* Afghanistan is in a civil war. That leaves only the oil-rich Arab countries down south. And those guys have gold, believe you me, Sir, a lot of gold."

"Any questions?" Joe inquired.

"Yeah, one." Mark rose. "Shall I brush up on my Arabic?"

"Why not?" smiled Joe. "We may need it on one of our next

missions."

"What did he mean by 'on one of our next missions'?" Mark was confused.

"I wouldn't know." I extricated myself.

"If it's not an Arab country, where then?" The uncertainty obviously bugged Mark.

"Maybe Israel?" I suggested and watched how Mark's face displayed his inner worry.

"No, the Palestinians have even less than their exiled brothers in Lebanon..." Suddenly, Mark's face lit up "It's Turkey! Son-of-a-bitch, why didn't I think of it before?"

Saudi Arabia...Turkey...Iran–the locality didn't matter. The 'little fortress' could stand anywhere, and the odds for taking her would not change. And it didn't make any difference what language her defendants, or her attackers, would speak, because the odds still remained exactly the same.

"Okay," Joe concluded. "Kick their ass!"

"Kick their ass!" we responded.

The glimmer of dawn set off a chain of bustle events. I was whisked out of one of my fondest dreams by an AK series, which sounded as if someone had fired it right next to my ear.

"What the hell!" I almost fell out of my cot.

"Up, ladies, up!" Joe stood by the entrance to the tent. He lifted the AK and emptied the rest of the clip up in the air.

"Fall in! You have thirty seconds."

We lined up still pulling up pants and fastening shoes.

"Very good. Take five to pee and reassemble."

"Back to the boot camp," commented Mark.

A curious crowd of survival students awakened by Joe's AK escapade and not certain what was happening gawked at us. Elmo Elkins, the youngest of all in the camp, the sixteen-year-old, approached me and declared, "Whatever you're doing, I'd like to join you."

"Talk to the Commanding Officer." I pointed to Joe.

"Is he your Commanding Officer?" Elmo seemed disappointed. "I thought it was you."

"Maybe in my next lifetime," I professed.

Elmo left and returned a few moments later.

"He said no." Elmo complained. "You wouldn't turn me down, would you?"

"No, I wouldn't," I replied. Why not earn some easy credits here and there?

After breakfast we rode on two jeeps to our destination. Elmo was allowed to join us as Keith's substitute–we needed someone to take Keith's place during our training.

"You are not Elmo, boy," I came from left field. "You're Keith, got it?"

Joe issued weapons: pine stakes for AK's and LAW's, and rocks painted red for hand grenades. Elmo was disappointed.

"You would issue the real thing, wouldn't you?" he asked me.

"I certainly would." I smiled. More easy credits.

And for the whole fucking day, we practiced the assault. We stormed the 'fortress' at least twenty times.

"All right!" Joe hollered. "Keith is incapacitated!"

Elmo collapsed, and I added another task to mine. Then we took the plastic castle one more time.

"Good, back in the jeeps! Go! Now, Jim is hit!"

I fell on the ground and watched Kurt silently 'annihilating' the imaginary rooftop sentries.

"Another rat patrol is coming!" yelled Joe, and we modified the routine.

At the end, I was totally exhausted. The sun touched the horizon, when, finally, Joe declared, "I think we're ready for the final assault…after dinner."

That made sense: after all, our real assault was going to take place in the dark. We reassembled after dinner.

"We had a busy day," stated Joe *Amen, brother, I agreed*, "and we trained hard. But, I don't know how many of you noticed that so far we lacked one essential element." He paused, and, I guess, all of us tried to figure out what that essential element was. "This time, gentlemen and ladies, we are gonna do it…with real weapons."

"Ya-hoo!" Elmo exclaimed.

"Not you." Joe heartlessly excluded the kid.

If I have ever seen anyone totally heartbroken and close to tears, it was poor Elmo. He was being denied a chance to participate in the main event. And, first Charity, and then the rest of the team, came to Elmo's defense.

"He worked real hard, he earned it," Charity stated and we all echoed. "Let him."

But Joe did not budge.

"All right." Our pretty spokesperson declared. "Then we all refuse to go, don't we, guys?"

"Yeah, tell'm, baby…", "We stay right here.", "Elmo's in, or bust!" came from all sides.

"That's fucking blackmail," smiled Joe. "Okay, Elmo's in, and…"

Cheers and applause drowned the end of Joe's statement of capitulation. All surrounded happy Elmo. Then Roger brought AK's and the rest of the arsenal.

"These are offensive type hand grenades." Joe showed us a tin-can type object. "They blast, but they do not scatter fragments. The fuse is four seconds…"

Roger accompanied us to the training site.

"I've got to see this," he commented in excited anticipation.

Joe doused the 'buildings' with gasoline.

"For special effects," he explained.

I carried an AK, a spare clip, and two hand grenades. We all knew the routine. Now, all we had to do was to go through the motions. The jeeps already stood in position, ready for action; so were we.

"Ready?…Start the engines!…Go!…go!…go!:" Joe screamed.

Mark hurled the first grenade in the direction of the 'guard tower'. It exploded with an incredible bang and a flash. And then, as they say in intellectual circles, shit hit the fan. Another AK rattled, the second grenade was set off…flash-blast!

The Alpha team dismounted and followed the Bravo jeep into the compound. More AK's joined in…another blast…flames shot up in the sky…My heart was pounding, I was in the middle of a battle. I discharged a half-clip trying to hit the main building. Joe and Charity ran toward it, and I followed. They fell on the ground short of the target, and I tossed my first grenade. It exploded and showered us with shreds of burning plastic. I ran in front of the target to the end, hurled my second grenade, and fell on the ground…

Everything around burned. In the strange chaos of flames, smoke, and dust, I could see where bullets hit the ground and ricocheted, raising more dust. I changed the clip and added my two cents worth to the deafening cacophony of shots and explosions…

Finally, I ran out of ammunition. As if synchronized with my actions, all stopped, the 'battle' was over. The ground burned, a grayish-orange mess of dust and smoke billowed above. A deserted jeep stood on the edge of the site, motionless, as if stunned by the spectacle of flames and destruction. Human figures wandered in the shimmering melange of burning stakes, melting plastic sheets, and swirling sparks—another glimpse of hell, maybe? I suddenly realized that not all of us would be coming back from this mission. Fifty percent? Less? That percentage of casualties in Joe's operations was rather a rule than an exception. From seven of us *the eighth guy had not showed up*, which three, or four, will die? Will I be among them?

Roger approached.

"That was quite a show." He was impressed. "I bet the real thing will be even more spectacular."

Elmo jumped up and down, piercing the night air with ya-hoo!'s.

"Any casualties?" Joe asked. There were none, somehow all miraculously survived the make-believe hell session.

Elmo approached me; he was still trying to calm down from the most excitement of his entire life, "I asked Mr. Green to take me with you, but he said no. You would take me, wouldn't you?"

Elmo's eyes reflected the still burning remains of the compound and were full of hope: what if the team ganged up on Joe in favor of accepting Elmo in its ranks? After all, they did it once. I could see that Elmo would go with us, even if told of the real odds.

"No, not on this one, kid." I shook my head. I did not want to score easy credits anymore.

MERCHANT OF RALEIGH

There are many attractive cities in the world: Venice, Amsterdam, Paris, Rio, New York...But Athens is not one of them. Her unplanned streets and ramshackled dwellings are in sharp contrast with her only jewel–the Acropolis, a perfection of architectural design, a majestic monument to the Hellenic culture, standing on the hill and overlooking the city. The city built on a barren rock, grayish in the morning, yellowish at noon, and purple after sunset, lacks parks and lakes, the cosmetic particulars which add luster to a city face. Probably, such makeup, put on her homely face, could improve her looks, but, so far, no one has attempted to apply it. Athens lies spread on the plains of Athena. Perhaps, the Goddess of War allowed the ancient Greeks to found their city on her plains only because they promised to build the Acropolis. But maybe there was no deal at all; she simply conceded in her noble gesture of generosity, like when she defeated Poseidon and magnanimously allowed him to retain his honors and even offered him a place at the Acropolis.

Joe, Charity, and I flew from New York. And as usual, Joe neglected to mention one small but important detail before we boarded the plane. My ticket reserved the seat 18B, which meant that the person in 18A, by the window on my left, would be a stranger. That stranger could be almost anyone, but deep inside I hoped that the stranger would turn out to be an attractive woman; it happens once in a while. I approached my seat and became speechless: the stranger in 18A smiled at me from ear to ear.

"Elmo?!? What in hell are you doing here?" I exclaimed, completely flabbergasted.

"Going with you, Sir."

Charity and Joe sat two rows ahead of me. I approached them.

"Are you out of your cotton picking mind?" I inquired. "He's just a kid."

"He can handle it." Joe unwrapped a strip of chewing gum and shoved it in his mouth. "...smack...smack...Besides, we need an extra hand."

"Give me a break." I returned to my seat and the smiling Elmo.

"I hope you don't mind me coming with you, Sir." Elmo bent over, unfastened the small table plate in front of him, and placed tiny silvery wind-up R2D2 on its surface. "Mr. Green asked me to help you out."

"Na-a-a, of course not." R2D2 marched across the table, bravely buzzing his way straight to the edge and over, just like us.

In Athens, at King Minos, we reserved three rooms. I was going to share mine with Elmo and Mark, who was going to arrive the next day with the rest of our group; Keith, Kurt, and Chuck were to occupy the second room; and Joe and Charity *by George, she was Joe's girlfriend* shared the third.

If only everyone minded their own business, life in the world would be so much simpler. All we wanted to do in Athens was to stop, make contact with Baghdad, and proceed to our destination. But no...

I entered the lobby.

"Come with us..." an accent said. "Please cooperate, or we'll have to shoot you."

It was a straightforward request, no nonsense, no ambiguity: cooperate or die. I faced two well dressed mustached gentlemen.

"Sure," I said.

A chauffeur opened a door, and the three of us squeezed into the back seat.

"I hope you don't mind a blindfold, Mr. Green," said the taller man.

"Of course not," I replied while trying to conceal my surprise *Holy shit! They think I'm Joe.*

So, our mission was no longer a secret, and these guys kidnapped Joe *pardon my confusion...kidnapped me* in order to extract more information about the task. But who were these gentlemen? How did they know where to find us? And, the most important question, at least to me, will they let me go? The answer to the last question was 'maybe'. Using the blindfold was a good sign. If these guys intended to kill Joe, they would not bother with the blindfold. Apparently, they just wanted information. What was I going to tell them? I could simply tell them that they made a mistake—I was not Joe, period.

But, with all cards on the table, these gentlemen would not like it at all, because the whole incident made them look foolish, and, judging by the shape of their mustaches, they could become quite upset and take it out on me. Secondly, what would I gain with this candid revelation? Discovering that I was not Joe, these clowns would, almost definitely, put me 'on ice' while they collected the real Joe. Even then, they would not let me go, not until they got what they wanted from Joe. Now, knowing Joe's stubborn nature, I was certain he would not give them the information, and, judging by the thickness of these guys' mustaches, they could become very angry and put 'cement shoes' on both of us. No, my confession was not the answer. The option to play Joe seemed safer, because, first, only one head was placed inside the guillotine *or was it blindfold?*, and second, I retained at least marginal control over the events. Still, if it came down to the choice, my life or information, I would certainly give them the information. To hell with principles.

We, finally, arrived at an unknown destination.

"Watch your steps," advised the shorter man.

I could not watch anything; the blindfold was still on. I counted thirteen steps *my lucky number* while we descended. We passed a narrow corridor *I brushed against the walls a few times* and entered a room.

"You may take the blindfold off, Mr. Green," The taller man informed me. I pulled the darn thing off and faced a balding middle-aged man with puffy eyes and a theta-shape beard-and-mustache. He was silent for awhile; we stared at each other. Then, when he looked away, I briefly scanned the room. Apparently, we were in the basement, because one of the walls displayed a large water stain.

The theta-man said something in a foreign tongue, and the taller man translated, "My name is Manucher Ghorbanifar. Maybe, you have heard of me."

I shook my head. Maybe, Joe did, but I didn't have the honor.

"Well, it doesn't matter. But we have, certainly, heard of you."

Here we go, I thought. Now he is going to say that he knows all about Operation Golden Camel.

"Probably, you think that, since we are on the other side of the ocean, we don't know. But we do. We are aware of your arms-for-the-Contras link, and your Mafia ties, and, what concerns us the most, your Iraqi arms connection."

What the fuck was he talking about? The Iraqi arms connection?

"Here…" Mr. Ghorbanifar handed me several photos.

Two men, Keith and yours truly, figured prominently on all five photographs: three were taken in front of the Iraqi embassy and two in the streets of Athens.

"Poor quality," I commented while trying to think feverishly of some plausible explanation of what in hell I was doing in front of the Iraqi embassy. These guys, obviously, represented some sort of intelligence service interested in activities around the embassy. They spoke a tongue unknown to me. This tongue was not Arabic. I had a couple of Arab friends back in Raleigh and, although I did not speak Arabic, I could at least identify the language. Thus, these guys had to be either the Israelis, or Iranians. The theta-man's first name, Manucher, sounded Israelish, but his last name, Ghorbanifar, could be Iranian.

"We know that the Americans have just sold the Iraqis sixty military helicopters. What was your part in that deal?" Ghorbanifar reclaimed the photographs.

It became clear that whatever we were talking about was anything but Operation Golden Camel. And it appeared also that these gentlemen were mistaking Joe for an arms dealer.

"Helicopter transactions, Mr. Ghorbanifar, are way over our heads." I articulated confidently, as if I knew what I was talking about. "We deal in small arms only: guns, ammunition, and LAWs." *I stretched L-A-A-A-WS far into New England.*

Suddenly, I felt very important discussing international arms sales. It added even more to my confidence. I also used 'we' implying that I was not a solo player, but that there was an organization behind me: other dealers, Mafia, what have you. I began to enjoy my strange predicament.

"What kind of a deal have you signed with the Iraqis then?"

"We have not concluded any deal, it was a preliminary meeting. Mr. Abdul Kadhim Mohsin of the embassy conveyed that the Iraqis were interested in purchasing one hundred LAW's." I decided to use Abdul's name in order to add more credibility to my statements. "We said that we would check the market and inform him of the costs."

At this point, I completely fused with the character which I played *it definitely wasn't Joe, it was stronger and infinitely classier.*

"We always set a fair price." I continued bullshitting. "But we don't mind the higher bidder, Mr. Garnifar."

"Ghorbanifar." He corrected me.

The door opened, and another man, in spectacles, entered. Mr. Ghorbanifar and the man exchanged greetings in a Muslim fashion *Goddamn, they are Iranians, I realized* and Mr. Ghorbanifar presented me.

If I have ever beheld an ultimate expression of surprise, I witnessed it now. The man's eyebrows rose far above the upper rim of his spectacles.

"This man is not Mr. Green..." the spectacled whispered

in English.

"What?!" The taller man's eyes became absolutely round, like those of an owl. "But those pictures!"

Mr. Ghorbanifar, meanwhile, unaware that he was staring at an impostor, smiled.

"Are you, or are you not Mr. Green?" the taller man, with a glimmer of hope in his voice, inquired.

"Nope." I yanked the straw he tried to clutch at.

"Why?" He swallowed.

"I hated to disappoint you." I grinned sheepishly; I could not come up with a better answer on such a short notice.

Ghorbanifar still smiled, blissfully ignorant of what was transpiring in the room.

Finally, the taller man presented Ghorbanifar with the bad news: they had the wrong man. A heated debate ensued. Although I did not understand a word of what they were saying, I sensed that the debate was not centered around me, but concerned Joe. His name popped up again and again. It seemed, they were anxious to talk to Joe. I decided to interfere.

"Gentlemen," I said. "If you want to talk to Mr. Green about the arms purchases, you might as well talk to me. I am Mr. Green's business manager."

I presented myself. Instead of waiting for the uncertain outcome of their discussion, I elected to seize the initiative. I went for broke. They listened.

"As I said before, Mr. Ghorbanifar, we prefer to sell to the highest bidder. If you want one hundred LAW rockets and are willing to bid, name your price." I was in control again. Man, it felt good to be on top of the developments.

By the time they figure out what is what, I thought, we'll be long gone.

"Yes, Mr. Riveaux, we would like to bid. But first, we'd like to see Mr. Green." Ghorbanifar, clearly, did not trust this slippery American with the French name.

"All right, I can arrange the meeting," I pledged. It all was working out neatly: they wanted Joe, so, let him handle it, and I would be out of all this mess, home free.

Surprisingly, the Iranians discarded the blindfold when we were leaving the place. Perhaps, they wanted to establish a degree of mutual trust.

The Iranians released me by the spin-entrance where they had collected me an hour earlier. I went immediately to Joe's room and told him about the abduction incident. He did not seem to be upset at all by the new developments.

"That's excellent!" he exclaimed. "We can purchase the stuff from Frank and re-sell it to the Iranians with profit."

We had a dinner in the restaurant on the main floor of King Minos. The crowd at the other tables consisted, largely, of foreigners. I heard German, and French, and Arabic. I guessed, and Joe confirmed it, that King Minos Hotel was a focal point at the crossroads between Europe, Africa, and the Middle East, just like the Holiday Inn in Tegucigalpa for travelers between the Americas.

"I think we should keep distance from these guys." I cautioned. "After all, we're just about to hit their country."

"No, no, this is ideal. They suspect nothing." Joe poked at the broccoli-cluster on his plate: it was too large, and it had to be cut in two, but Joe's knife fell on the floor and was no longer usable. "They believe that we came to make a deal with the Iraqis. But if we agree to negotiate with Mr. Ghorbanifar and leave the country shortly, he will assume that we quit the Iraqis and made a deal with him, see? We can proceed then with our mission and deal with Ghorbanifar later."

"You dirty, conniving son-of-a-..." I said while fighting my own battle with the bone extension at the base of my T-bone steak. The bone refused to yield my favorite meaty part; the knife was dull.

"By the way, Jim, do you know who Mr. Ghorbanifar is?"

"An international arms dealer?" I ventured cautiously while finally winning my T-bone steak battle.

"Mr. Ghorbanifar is the chief of Iranian intelligence in Europe."

"Damn!" I was properly impressed. Ghorbanifar's importance added to what I was just about to spring upon Joe. He loved to set me up for a 'kill'. And that 'kill', always well hidden until the last moment, surfaced suddenly, producing the maximum effect on me. I usually exclaimed, "Goddamn!" expressing a mixture of exaggerated praise of Joe's wit and a good-natured annoyance at my own slow-wittedness. But now was my chance of getting even with Joe. I only had to wait for a proper moment.

"I'd like to set up a meeting with those guys before we go." Joe attempted to shove the whole broccoli-chunk, using the fork, into his mouth, but the task turned out to be much harder than he expected. Joe's mouth simply was not big enough to accommodate the chunk.

The last sentence came out completely unintelligible. That was the moment I was waiting for.

"We could do it right now, if you wish," I said casually. "Look behind you."

Joe turned around. Three tables away, facing us, sat Ghorbanifar. To me, the spectacle of a man caught with his mouth full of food is less than dignified, but, on top of that, with a stem of broccoli sticking out, is downright silly. Joe became visibly embarrassed. Finally, he managed to subdue the dogged broccoli and muttered, "Smart Alec! That's Ghorbanifar. Why didn't you tell me?"

"Well, it seemed like such a minor detail." I scored again getting even for the Honduran episode from the past, when Joe failed to inform me and Johnny of the important change in our plans on the mission to Nicaragua.

"One of these days, I'll get you real good." Joe smiled. "One of these days."

Ghorbanifar did not dine alone. With him, across the table, sat one of my kidnappers, the taller one.

"I think those guys are through with their dinner," Joe remarked. "Why won't you ask them to join us?"

The taller man introduced himself to Joe as Rafani. He translated. I couldn't help but feel uncomfortable sitting at the same table with someone whose country we were going to hit in a few days. And there was Joe, sitting like a hot shot *or was it hot shit?* and negotiating an arms deal with a couple of characters from a very hostile country. Why did he bother to negotiate at all? Who needed this piddly profit? We were going after the jackpot–Ayatollah's gold–and here sat Joe bickering over something that was of no importance. Sitting next to these Iranians, while the best thing we could do was keeping away from them as far as possible, seemed strange. Hell, more than strange–the whole thing seemed bizarre.

"...the surcharge of ten percent should be covered by you," Joe stated.

"If you can get us a hundred Phantom jet tires, Joe," Ghorbanifar babbled *somehow, somewhere in time, these sons-of-bitches had switched to the first name basis*, "we'll let you have those ten percent."

"I have no access to Phantom jet tires, Manucher, but if...", and the bargain continued. My God!

Finally, the meeting ended.

"You are not serious about those guys, are you?" I asked Joe. "What are you getting out of this?"

"It's not what you get, but how you play the game," 'bon motted' Joe. What a bullshit it was! 'How you play the game'! We didn't play games here. Just one slip by either of us, and the whole show would be over. They waited for us in Iran, those security sons-of-bitches. And, right in the middle of this grim scenario, of all things, we toyed with the Chief of the Iranian intelligence in Europe. Shit!

"Isn't it exciting?" Joe's green beady rat eyes reflected the lights of foyer candelabrum.

"You are crazy, do you know it? They get one whiff of what we are up to and they will skin our ass, shred by shred."

In the morning, we all gathered in Joe's *and Charity's* room. Joe introduced Keith. Some of the group sat on the messed up bed *I couldn't help being envious*. Charity, fresh and beautiful, with her hair fixed her favorite style, in a pony tail, occupied the only chair. God! She was ravishing!

Mark, Elmo, and I sat on the edge of the table. As if in preparation for a major speech, Joe slowly paced the floor. He stopped in front of the mirror and primped his hair in a very effeminate way. If someone, anyone from the street, entered right now and had to point out the leader, Joe would be the next to the last person *the last had to be Elmo* chosen.

"Well, it's a go," Joe said to the mirror, then turned around to us. "We're taking the early afternoon flight to Baghdad. Any questions?"

That was the major speech; Joe delivered it and waited for questions.

"Yea, one," said Kurt. "What's in Baghdad?"

"Our transition point to the staging area," Joe replied. "Okay, is everyone up-to-date with the insurance?" "What kind of insurance is he talking about?" Elmo asked me.

"Insurance is making your will and designating a beneficiary in case you are not coming back. Your fees, then, will be paid to that beneficiary." I quoted expertly because, by now, I was 'up-to-date' myself. A wheelbarrow of gold bars would be dumped by Martha's door, if...

"Well, if there are no more questions, ladies and gentlemen," Joe intertwined his fingers and cracked his knuckles. "See you in two hours."

Keith joined me in the hall.

"There is something I have to tell you, Jim." Keith took me aside. "I brought it to Joe's attention, but he doesn't think much of it. It's about Chuck Blount: the chap is mad."

"You mean he is mad about something?"

"No, I mean real mad, weird mad. Did you know that he fragged his commanding officer in Vietnam? Did you know that? And he talks weird, some nonage-rhyme nonsense like 'seven and seven, to hell or heaven'."

"It's their Special Forces stuff, I wouldn't worry about it."

"I'm telling you, watch out. He is mental."

THE PRICE OF SILENCE

It was really happening! We were on our way. As a matter of fact, we could not turn around and go back; it became impossible. We had reached the point of no return.

Until this moment, I believed that something, I didn't know what, or somebody–the outside forces–would cancel the whole thing, stop us from going any farther. The Iranians in Athens, if they got a whiff of our connection to the assassination *or kidnapping?* plot, or Saddam, if he chickened out, or any of the whole bunch of intelligence agencies, if they 'obtained the information'–any of these factors could stop our operation cold in its tracks. Also, the mission could be cancelled from within: Joe could change his mind *I'm stating this only for the sake of argument, because the son-of-a-bitch would not change his mind even if they'd threatened to put the world on its end.* And more factors could interfere. But none of these factors kicked in. As Joe said, 'We were riding a wave of risk in the ocean of timidity', which was more like 'riding a wave of doom in the ocean of hostility'.

Joe seemed relaxed and composed, even cheerful, as if our destination was not a war zone, but West Palm Beach. He and Charity sat in front of me. I was squeezed between Mark and Elmo.

"Have you ever been to Istanbul?" Mark asked *he still believed that Turkey was our target.*

I smiled. Maybe, it was a little bit sadistic of me, but I was really looking forward to seeing his face when he discovered our true objective: jumping smack in the middle of the Muslim fire and brimstone to fetch the Muslim Satan instead of sipping Turkish espresso coffee from tiny cups and relaxing under the moon over Bosporus. Elmo was quiet, perhaps he finally realized that he was getting into something which was way over his head. Keith, Kurt, and Chuck sat behind us. Keith and Kurt carried on a technical conversation on the subject of…flowers.

"…and her petals open in a double cluster, not unlike that of a peony," Keith explained.

"Yes, like a rose?" Kurt, not particularly fluent in botany, tried to 'hang in there'.

"Wake me up just before we land in Saigon," suddenly said Chuck.

There was a silence.

"Sure, Chuck. We'll take that alternate, if Baghdad is overcast," Kurt said finally.

At the airport, we were met by two Iraqi officers in identical two-shades-green-and-brown cammies and maroon berets. Their insignia of yellow-with-blue-outline wings and the same color combination parachute shoulder patch indicated their association with the paratroop branch of the Iraqi army. Later, I found out that these guys had nothing to do with the real paratroop. They were Saddam's personal bodyguards. They *all of them* had one thing in common, besides the uniform–they all brandished a Saddam-style moustache.

The officer with the more luxurious moustache approached me and extended his arm.

"Welcome to Iraq, Mr. Green." He spoke in a very pleasantly accented baritone *my stare was transfixed on his moustache instead of his eyes.*

A pause hung. *Here we go again, I thought, but I still shook the officer's hand.* An embarrassment was in the making, embarrassment not for me, but for the officer and, most of all, for Joe.

"I think you made a mistake," I said finally. "This is Colonel Green." I presented Joe.

"Major Hasan Arif." The officer did not seem to be embarrassed by his mistake, he turned to Joe and added respectfully, "At your service, Colonel."

Joe, his face slightly reddened, introduced the rest of the team. I could see the officers' surprise and even a momentary confusion when they realized that Charity was not a bystander who just happened to be around, but a member of the team. I wondered if they knew anything about our mission. We were escorted to Al-Mansour Palace hotel where individual suites were already reserved for us.

"Why in hell did you present me as a Colonel?" Joe had just began to recover from the introductions embarrassment.

"Well, he'll remember you longer." I smiled, enjoying Joe's predicament. "Besides, I thought they'd offer us better hotel accommodations, if you were a Colonel instead of a Lieutenant."

"Yeah, I guess it's all right," he conceded. "But you may continue calling me Joe."

"That's very magnanimous of you. How can I ever repay?"

Baghdad showed no signs of war. All shops were open, people walked in the streets. Darkness was coming on, and I thought the whole city was going to plunge into the ocean of tenebrous obscurity preparing for Iranian air raids, but the city ignored the war. There was no curfew imposed, no check points set up, and no lights-out decree enforced. We stopped by the bank to exchange a few dollars for dinars.

"What are ya gonna do with Iraqi money?" Joe asked me and Elmo. "Get souvenirs? We can't take them out of the country, not to where we are going."

Joe was right about the souvenirs, we could not carry anything Iraqi into Iran. But I knew exactly what I was going to do with my dinars: I intended to taste indigenous delectables. Iraqi bills could be easily transformed into a delicious variety of local shish kebab in the charming company of Charity. Elmo, too, had his reasons for the money exchange. He still carried a sizeable sum in Greek drachmas, which he preferred to turn back into dollars.

As to the puzzling phenomenon of Baghdad bathing in the sea of lights, which I thought was very careless on the part of the Iraqi military, a hotel concierge explained to me that a temporary agreement between the two warring countries, a truce of a sort, has been reached. The combatants agreed to suspend bombing and launching of surface-to-surface missiles at large cities. Thus, at least for awhile, the hurling of explosive presents by both sides stopped, and, what they called 'the war of the cities' had halted a few weeks before we arrived.

When Charity and I returned to the hotel, panicky Elmo, stuttering, informed us that while we were dining and sight-seeing Joe had been arrested and whisked away by two paratroopers.

Mark added, "Keith tried to tail them, but they stopped him and gave him rough time."

Alarmed by the unexpected development, all congregated in Joe's room.

"I don't like it," said Keith.

As the time passed and Joe still did not return, the mood of all present grew gloomier. The atmosphere charged.

"Does anyone know what in the fuck we're doing here, in Baghdad?" asked Mark.

"Yeah, I had the same question on my mind." Kurt joined in, then he turned to me, "You're Joe's close buddy. What do you know about it?"

Put on the spot, I hesitated. I couldn't tell these guys how much I knew about the operation. I couldn't disclose our final destination; only Joe could. I glanced at Keith and Charity, but they remained silent.

"I can't tell you," I said finally; I didn't want to lie.

"It isn't Turkey, is it?" Mark pressed.

The group, no longer a team, was falling apart right before my eyes. There was nothing to hold it together. I suddenly realized how indispensable Joe's presence was. Joe was the substance, the cement, which glued us into one body–a team. Without Joe, the group was just a group of incompatible individuals; without his guidance we were just an ant army marching in an endless circle. Where were we going? Joe was our link to the past and the bridge to the future. Without him the operation was only an aimless fantasy, its reward a mirage, and the victory trumpet paying a tribute to our daring–just an echo from obscurity. We needed a leader, damn! I hated this idea. The idea implied our disorganization and dependence. I always considered myself to be self- reliant and independent, and here I...we, needed a leader?! Shit!

"I knew there was something fishy about the whole thing," emerged Chuck, up to this moment aloof and quiet. "He's taking us to Hanoi, not to Saigon, right?"

Ordinarily, the flagrant absurdity of this statement would, without any doubt, have attracted everyone's attention. At this moment, somehow, the irrelevant utterance, in a strange way, had just blended in, dissolved in the air of lingering uncertainty. No one acknowledged the question, no one even glanced at Chuck. The silence hung heavily, and on everybody's mind was only one question: was Joe coming back? The time passed...

Suddenly, the door handle moved, and seven anxious faces turned toward the door. Who was it? The police? Were they going to arrest us, too? The door opened. Joe stood in the doorway. I could almost hear the collective sigh of relief.

"What's going on?" Joe inquired, apparently surprised to find us all in his room.

"Not much," I answered. "Just a flock of lost birds–off their migration path."

Charity, usually cool and composed, sprung up on her feet and almost threw herself upon Joe. Still uncertain of what had happened while he was away, Joe embraced her tenderly, "Hey, hey...Did you miss me?"

And the whole room lit up. Goddamn! I have never seen such quick reversal of the mob's mood as I have witnessed now. Keith, for absolutely no known reason, shook Joe's hand; Mark, as soon as Charity released Joe, passionately hugged him; Elmo, positioned in the corner, snickered, or cried; Kurt slapped Chuck on the back and, with a broad smile, announced, "We are not going to Hanoi, Chuck. We are going to Saigon!"; and I, myself caught in the whirlwind of emotions, which would be hard to sort out, had to admit that I, too, was happy to see the son-of-a-bitch who, still puzzled by the sentimental ado, kept on asking, "Will someone tell me, what's going on here?"

"We thought the Iraqis put you in jail," Mark acknowledged finally. "They've roughed up Keith."

"No, everything is fine."

After a while, the commotion, at last, had finally subsided. When the silence prevailed, Joe cleared his throat and informed us that, officially, we were attending the International Date Growers conference *In the middle of the war? I smiled.* and, the first thing in the morning, we'll be on our way to our staging area in Sulaimaniya, about 300 km north of Baghdad, close to the frontline.

"Here is your fucking buck," Mark whispered to me. "I know now where we are going–it's Iran."

With the long and charged suspense now over, and the happy ending granted, the mob dissolved. I was ready to leave, too, when Joe motioned me to stay. It was our 'inner circle' again–Joe, Charity, and me–like in Raleigh, ready to plan our next move.

"Check for bugs," Joe whispered, and we spread around the room searching for hidden microphones. But the room was clean.

"What I'm about to tell you is hard to believe," began Joe and paused. "I saw Saddam."

Joe related the event. He had been escorted by two 'paratroopers' to a limousine parked a block away from the hotel in a quiet, unlit side street. The awaiting chauffeur stepped forward and courteously opened the back door for Joe. The 'paratroopers' split but remained nearby guarding the limousine. The chauffeur dissolved in the dark shadow of the building.

Joe found himself facing two men. The man occupying the front seat said, "A wind changes the face of the desert."

Since Joe did not know how to react to this seemingly irrelevant statement, he remained silent.

The man continued, "It is the will of Allah to bring the wind to the desert. You, Mr. Green, are that wind."

"More like a tornado," smiled Joe upgrading the consequences of his pending operation to more realistic dimensions.

"A tornado? Very good." The man smiled back politely. "Let me introduce you to someone whom you probably know."

The second man, up to this moment sitting in the darkness of the back seat recess, bent forward and extended his hand to Joe. Joe could see his face, his handsome elongated face, dark, wavy hair, high forehead, slightly slanted hazel *or blue?* eyes, long nose, moustache, cleft chin, and no smile. The man was Saddam Hussein, the President of the Republic of Iraq.

"…salam aleikhum," said Saddam in Arabic.

"Mr. Hussein is pleased to make your acquaintance," translated the man in the front seat.

The high-level conference began and lasted over two hours. The topics discussed included military logistics for the operation and its schedule. Joe noticed that the interpreter was nervous and sweated profusely. The limo windows remained rolled up, and the heat inside was building up. Joe wondered what was going to happen to this man after the meeting. Did he sense that his participation in this sensitive discussion could be his death sentence? An eery feeling came over Joe.

The conversation turned to international politics, and Saddam talked a blue streak about the Arab unity against the common enemy, the state of Israel. Joe listened and nodded acknowledging that he understood Saddam's position on the subject. It is conceivable that this nodding was the element misinterpreted by Saddam as Joe's agreement with what he said, because at the end of this political exchange Saddam suddenly made Joe an unusual offer.

"I'll tell you about the offer later." Joe smiled slyly, realizing how tantalizing the delay could be for Charity and me.

The meeting, finally, had drawn to an end. Both Saddam and Joe, apparently, were satisfied with the results.

"I pray to the almighty Allah that he may give you health and happiness, and that my prayer may accompany you for all time to come," translated the man in the front seat and added, "That is very generous of Mr. Saddam Hussein."

"Tell him that I wish him the same," Joe reciprocated.

They parted shaking hands again, and this time Saddam smiled.

"I can find my way," Joe said to Saddam's bodyguards and walked toward the hotel. A single shot behind Joe finalized the conference. Joe did not even turn around; he just paused and then continued walking. He knew exactly what that shot meant. The services of the interpreter were no longer required. Baghdad was a rough town…

Joe finished.

"Well?" nudged Charity.

"Well what?" Joe pretended that he did not understand.

"The offer, fuck it! Saddam's offer."

"O-oh, that." Joe, the Tease, paused. "Well, Saddam offered me a position in his government as a Chief of the European intelligence. He stated that he had acquired many enemies abroad, and that I would be the right man for the job. He doesn't trust his associates."

"You mean, right now?" Charity was surprised, I was not sure how I felt.

"No, after the operation. He promised to build me a villa of any style, anywhere in Iraq, and even offered his assistance in relocating my family to Iraq as well."

"Family?" I knew that Joe's family lived in Pennsylvania.

"Yes, but I told him that I was divorced. He smiled and said that, in that case, I could bring my girlfriend." Joe glanced at Charity, and she giggled.

"Wait a minute you guys." I gasped. "You don't seriously consider a marriage, do you?"

"Well, maybe not right away," said Joe, and both smiled.

"My God!" I exclaimed. "Think of your offspring."

"What about the offspring?" Charity became curious and maybe prepared to be offended.

"Ever heard of genetics and heredity?" I probed, enjoying the suspense and the potential effect of what I was about to say. *Let's give them some of their own medicine, I thought.* "If you and Joe are both audacious war maniacs, I'd hate to see your kids. If you can destroy a country, they will annihilate the world."

"Only you can come up with the nonsense like that," laughed Charity, visibly relieved. She accepted my concerned reference to genetics as a compliment.

In the morning, we all, including Charity, were issued Iraqi paratroop uniforms, two-shade-green-and-brown cammies. With the insignia missing, we resembled a bunch of raw conscripts. Joe appeared at the door in cammies.

"Do we have to wear this?" moaned Mark.

"Yes, where we are going, we could attract too much attention in civvies." Joe produced a folded document and handed it to Mark. "Have a look and tell me what it says."

Mark read the document again and again. Finally, he was satisfied, "My Arabic is a bit rusty, but, from what I understand, it is a military pass." He paused. "But this is not a simple pass. It's a permit, authorization of the highest order. Carrying it, you can go to any place, in Iraq I mean, any time, and you may request anything you need. It is signed by General Ali Hasan al-Majid."

I watched Joe's face. It's one of those little psychological things that I picked up while studying bird behavior, observing how birds react to the unfamiliar. They may be curious, or cautious, or startled; they may approach, or study from a distance, or freeze, or take off. In that aspect, the human species is no different from any other animal. Joe's eyes squinted slightly *he digested the information: was it a comfort or a threat?*, then, while his eyes still remained in the squinted mode, the corner of his mouth moved in a faint smile *yes, the information was very comforting*, vertical wrinkles formed between his eyebrows *he concentrated: what could he do with all that newly acquired power?*, and, finally, his features relaxed, his eyes assumed their customary ratty roundness, and he smiled *damn! the opportunity knocked.*

"I wonder who this General al-Majid is," he said while still smiling to his own thoughts.

"Probably from the General Staff, close to Saddam Hussein." When Joe stepped aside, Mark turned to me and whispered, "What in hell is going on? No, don't answer that. I know, we're going to hit Ayatollah, right?"

The smart Jew figured it out. I smiled and put my arm around his shoulders, "You don't mind, do you?"

Mark sighed and, for the first time since we left Texas, smiled. "You fucking conniving bastards! Mind it? I haven't had such good news since they cancelled the 'Fiddler on the Roof'."

For some reason, Mark disliked the play and the movie. He called it 'garbage mixed with trash' and mocked the main character, "If I were a rich man…ya, ya-ya, ya-ya-ya…". He stopped then and, with the expression of utter disgust on his face, dismissed the subject, "This schmuck missed his fucking train." That was Mark's other intriguing peculiarity–the thing with trains. His 'missed the train' expression could mean 'totally worthless', or 'as dumb as a doorknob', or 'kicked the bucket', and, probably, yet more interesting interpretations.

Our group was attached to a small supply convoy headed for Sulaimaniya. Loaded in one open truck *excluding Joe and Charity who rode in the comfort of the cabin* and sitting on top of boxes and sacks, we trudged along toward the town of Kerkuk. The countryside presented very little to gawk at: sand planes, sand dunes, and more sand with a few low trees and bushes scattered here and there, and not much of anything else. Only an occasional dust devil would appear, stir up a handful of sand, and then wither away.

I sat between Kurt and Chuck.

"No place to hide," Kurt said.

"From whom?" I asked.

"From Iranian aircraft." Kurt pointed south. "That's where they'd come from, straight from the sun. Can't see them, they are on top of you before you know it."

I glanced at the desert surrounding us. Perhaps Kurt was right, there was no place to hide.

"Yeah, it's pretty bare. Not like in Vietnam." Chuck joined in. "In the delta, we didn't worry about the enemy planes, there were none."

Chuck talked in long sentences, which was unusual, to say the least. I wanted to hear more.

"Delta, you said?" I asked.

"Mekong delta. I think that's why they called our campaign the Operation Delta."

"Was it rough?" Keith expressed interest too.

"No, it was okay. I don't remember much of it. I was hit. See that scar?" Chuck parted his hair. "That's where a Vietcong bullet hit me, straight in the head. I don't remember much, but they told me that I continued on fighting. I didn't feel any pain. Probably, I didn't see anything either, because, they said, I killed a couple of our own guys too before I passed out cold."

We listened.

"They shipped me back to the States and kept me in the V.A. hospital for two years."

"Why for so long?"

"I couldn't function well. I couldn't concentrate on things. You see, they had removed a chunk of my brain. Even now, sometimes I forget where I am…But I like the circus."

The last sentence seemed to be out of place. I glanced at Keith, and he shrugged his shoulders. A long pause followed.

"Me too." Keith, finally, decided to continue the conversation.

"But they released you, Chuck. It means you're all right."

"Why are you saying that?" Chuck's face reflected a deep puzzlement.

"I mean after Vietnam." Keith attempted to re-rail the derailed trialog.

"What's that got to do with the circus?" Chuck sounded somewhat irritated.

Swell, I thought, We'll be in the middle of combat, and this guy will believe that he is at the circus.

THE FACE OF SCREAM

Major Nasif Baran saluted and presented himself to me. We had just arrived to Sulaimaniya.

"Are you the American mercenaries?" He was quite blunt about it. "Colonel Green?" he presumed *Here we go again, I thought.*

The journey had been long and tiresome. We had only stopped in Kerkuk for a bite of Iraqi army C-ration, to take a leak, and pick up another truck loaded with supplies destined for Sulaimaniya.

"No, but you may call me Lord Jim." I was irritated. I pointed toward Joe who attempted to act nonchalant.

I didn't like the guy, although I could not trace the origin of my antipathy toward the major. Maybe it was the manner of how he stared at us: curious but distant, polite but somewhat contemptuous. Or maybe I just didn't like his standard Saddam-style moustache and his dark, contact-avoiding eyes. Perhaps, however, the major was right. From his viewpoint, who were these American misfits, persons of dubious past and questionable future?

Joe produced our military pass, and the major was properly impressed. Apparently, the person who issued the pass, General al-Majid *Joe referred to him as General Majic, because his name was the key to all doors* was a mighty important individual in the Iraqi military.

In any war, military personnel, particularly those stationed close to a frontline, enjoy very few outside visitors. A company of entertainers may stop by, press and photographers may invade one's almost nonexistent privacy, or it could be us, a date growers delegation, dropping in suddenly out of nowhere.

"Is that a joke?" I asked Joe. "It's the most absurd cover I have ever heard of. Date growers? On the frontline?!"

"Yeah, it has a sweet flavor to it, doesn't it?" Joe commented with a faint shadow of a smile.

"How about the grave diggers?" I attempted to make a joke.

"No, that would be too depressing for the Iraqi personnel. I don't think any of them wanted to be buried by an infidel." Joe took my hapless joke seriously. "Besides, the date growers stuff was Saddam's idea, not mine."

"Very imaginative," I quipped.

"It's only the official line, for the enlisted personnel. The officers are aware of who we are. They have no idea of what our mission is, but they know who we are. They received orders to assist us. As a matter of fact, this morning we are going to meet the local commander."

At the Central Command Post, we were expected. A staff sergeant motioned us *Joe, Keith, and me* toward the proper door. General Yasin al-Bitar, the divisional commander, introduced his staff. Joe reciprocated by presenting Keith as a major and me only as a lieutenant. The general opened a fancy box with a row of gold-label-ringed, thick Havana cigars comfortably resting deep on the bottom of the box. Extending his hospitality one step further, the general offered coffee.

"I thought Muslims don't smoke," I whispered to Joe; he shrugged his shoulders.

The CCP walls were covered with maps: general relief maps and military maps depicting the frontline and disposition of the friendly forces and the opposition.

After all settled down with their cigars and/or coffee, Joe began, "Gentlemen, before I state the purpose of this meeting, I must point out that the location of our target is classified. I hope you understand the reason of why I am not at liberty to disclose it." He paused and scanned the row of indifferent Iraqi faces across the table. "What we need is transportation, supplies, arms, and, of course, a safe passage across the frontline. Any questions?"

Typically, Joe's speech was short, in fact, stripped to the bone, but still right to the point. All were silent for about ten long seconds. Finally, Yasin broke the silence; he turned to his officers and consulted them in Arabic. We waited. When the internal conference was over, Yasin leaned back in his comfortable armchair, puffed on his cigar and disappeared in the thick cloud of white smoke. Only his hands could be seen. Finally, out of that cloud came the question, "What do you mean by 'a safe passage across the frontline'?"

"A diversionary action by your troops, General." The smoke cloud reached Joe, and he attempted to fan it with his hand.

"You mean to attack the Iranian defenses, breach them, and clear a passage for you, Colonel Green?"

"Something like that."

The cloud slowly dissipated, and Yasin reappeared. Another pause commenced. The general's chest began moving with irregular jolts, while his face remained unperturbed. Then his mouth opened slightly, and strange gargling noises came out of it. Yasin laughed.

"You want me to...*gargle*...*gargle*...to slaughter a hundred of my soldiers, so that you can pass through?"

"You've got it!" I had to give Joe a credit for how he said it: straight, calmly, and with a cynical half-smile. Maybe, this was how he tried to get even with the general for the general's insulting laughter.

Yasin stopped laughing and for a while studied Joe's impenetrable face. Nervously, he stubbed out his cigar and, visibly irritated, stated, "To stage such operation would require at least two weeks."

"We have two days," calmly allowed Joe.

And Yasin exploded at Joe. Whatever he blurted out in Arabic, I could translate even without learning the language, with a negligible inaccuracy, to, "You Allah-damned bastard! Who do you think you are, sitting here and dictating me how to run my war?"

Both Joe and I stared at Yasin with undisguised curiosity: how many times in one's life may one have a chance to observe a ruffled up general? Then Joe poured more cold water on the glowing coals of the general's anger, "We have two days. So, let's not waste them, General."

"That's impossible. Two days time is not enough." One could almost see the steam rising above Yasin's head.

"I have a plan." Joe rose up and approached one of the maps on the wall. "I do not request a major invasion–just a limited incursion right here, south of Baneh. That's where their 2nd Motorized Infantry Division is located right now. Their 21st Tank Brigade is further south and is of no immediate threat to you, as well as their Artillery and Battle Group. You throw in just one battalion at this point and reinforce it with five tanks and rocket artillery. That's the diversion attack. Meanwhile, we go around and...give us thirty minutes to reach this point, right between the 2nd and the 5th Divisions, and hammer it with your long-range artillery and rockets for about ten minutes. That's where we'll break through."

"Wait. You intend to go right through the artillery barrage?" Yasin displayed a degree of interest.

"Is there any better time to break through? When you're being pounded by the heavy artillery, checking someone's credentials is the last thing on your mind. I don't think the Iranians will give us any trouble."

"You know, that just might work." Yasin's eyes lit up.

Thus far, it was a dialog between Yasin and Joe. The rest of us just watched and listened. But now, suddenly, all surrounded Joe by the map. He went through his plan, step by step, one more time.

Nasif stepped in, "My information is that the 2nd Division is at Sappez, fifty kilometers northeast of Baneh, and that the 5th Division would be filling in."

"No, the 2nd is at Baneh now. At least that was their objective," Joe insisted.

"We have to verify that."

"If Colonel Green is right," Yasin observed, "and the 2nd Division is at Baneh, it means that the Iranians could be massing for another offensive. If that is true, then this operation could serve as a reconnaissance-in-force. It will keep the Iranians off balance and allow our forces time to regroup."

The meeting continued smoothly.

"We have to verify whether the 2nd is indeed at Baneh," Nasif repeated.

"Do we have enough time for a recon?" Joe squinted skeptically.

"The reconnaissance is not necessary. The source of fresh information is right here, in my headquarters." Nasif gestured us to follow him.

Joe and I *and Charity, who joined us after lunch* followed Nasif into a low clay building with tiny clay-stained windows and down to the basement with clay floors. We passed through a long narrow tunnel-like hall. Steel-reinforced wooden doors on both sides of the hall, all opening inward, hid cells, some of which, I assumed, housed prisoners. The spacious, dimly lit interrogation room contained a long, sturdy, formerly fancy and shiny, and now scratched and stained, dining table. And that was all, there was nothing else in the room, which seemed strange.

"I'm ready for a desert," I joked quietly. "But the table is empty."

"Sh-sh..." hissed Joe.

Nasif left the room for awhile and returned with a dog, a white German, or Hungarian shepherd.

"What's her name?" I asked while petting this very friendly pooch.

"Zu-zu," Nasif answered dryly. I gathered he was jealous of me making friends with his dog so effortlessly.

Charity competed with me for the dog's attention. Joe did not participate in our little canine game. I paid only a fleeting notice to the fact that, for some reason, he tensed. To me, on this afternoon, the world was a bowl of cherries. The bright sun shone outside in the cloudless sky, flowers bloomed, birds sang...and I just had a delicious lunch: fish dipped in a batter generously infused with exotic Arab seasonings and spices and sizzle-fried in olive oil. My stomach purred. Hell! Sure, we were in the war, but, so far, I hadn't seen even a single trace of it. And besides, who cared! It was not our war. We were passersby here, only guests.

Two Iraqi soldiers brought in two Iranian prisoners—an army sergeant and an officer, a captain. Nasif spoke Farsi. We did not have to know the language to understand what he said. He inquired of the Iranians whether they were willing to cooperate, but received no answer. He repeated the question, and the captain responded negatively. At this point, I began having suspicions that the interrogation session could involve more that just a friendly persuasion. After a prolonged pause, during which Nasif weighed the options and the rest of us wondered which one he was going to choose, he approached the sergeant and, seizing him by the front of his shirt, shoved him toward Joe.

"You need the information, Colonel Green." Nasif spoke coolly. "You start!"

That was an unexpected twist. Joe's face reflected surprise and anguish. What Nasif implied, no, more like demanded, was beating the prisoner. He expected Joe to throw the first punch. Joe hesitated, we needed the intelligence, but at what price?

"Start!" Nasif screamed.

Joe was cornered: comply or lose face, hit the prisoner or bail out, do it Nasif's way or receive no information. That was it—the moment of truth. All waited, the suspense became so thick, that if we tried to swim through it, we'd drown.

Hit the-son-of-a-bitch now, I caught myself thinking, Hit him! Every muscle in my body tensed. Suddenly, I had difficulty breathing. I coughed, breaking the heavy silence, and all glanced in my direction. I felt obliged to say something.

"Maybe we should start with the captain," I heard myself say. "He, probably, knows more."

That statement broke the stalemate and eased the pressure on Joe. But it also dropped the ball in my lap. Nasif, now, probably, was going to grab the captain and push him toward me. Nasif turned and approached. His face was very close to mine. I knew he was going to say 'Okay, then you start it, Lord Jim.'

"Tell the woman to leave the building." Nasif spoke to me. He never even glanced at Charity.

The only inanimate object in the room–that fancy, sturdy, solid oak dining table–probably had witnessed many glamorous feast gala affairs in its long life: fifty years, perhaps a century, maybe even two. It had not always rested on this dirty uneven clay floor in the basement of a less than hospitable building. It had seen better times. Covered by a traditional Islamic red-tint-dominant tablecloth, it had served a dinner, well deserved after a long feast, to the whole family following the first sunset of Ramadan. On other occasions, like weddings, the traditional tablecloth had been replaced with an overlay made of silk. The table, then, was transformed into a sightly stand displaying a piquant fruit-and-sweets arrangement so pleasing to the eye that some attendees, particularly the very young, were unable to wait for the conclusion of the ceremony and succumbed to the temptation of snatching a delectable tidbit when no one was looking.

But the good old days for the table were no more. The Iraqis wrestled down the resisting sergeant and laid him out, spread eagle, on the table. Using telephone wire, they tied the sergeant's arms and legs to hooks fastened to the underside of the table. Only then I noticed these added-on, but inconspicuously hidden hooks, one per corner. Having finished the task, the soldiers restrained the captain who displayed the first signs of worry. The mooring exercise was accompanied by the heavy breathing of the active participants and by the excited barking of the dog. Zu-zu carried on, as if the whole fucking thing was a hilarious game. She jumped and barked rushing from the struggling trio to Nasif, then to the captain, then to Joe and me, inviting us to join the fun.

During these mysterious preparations *for what? I thought*, incidentally, accomplished quite efficiently, as if performed routinely, Nasif produced a very thick Havana and lit it. Holding the cigar in the corner of his mouth and puffing on it with obvious pleasure, he rolled the sleeves of his shirt up to his armpits. He glanced at Joe and me somewhat slyly, as if saying, "I've got a surprise for you, boys!"

The cigar, I thought watching Nasif's preparations. The bastard is going to use a burning cigar on the man's bare skin. Goose bumps ran up my spine and surfaced all over my arms. At this moment I definitely wished to be somewhere else.

Nasif bent over and introduced a new element in the game–a boot knife. He approached the captain and, holding the blade very close to the captain's face, turned it edgewise and broadside, allowing the quarry to examine all sides of the issue.

I froze. What were Nasif's intentions? Was he going to slash the captain's throat? Or face? Or poke him in the eye with the tip of the blade? Nasif diffused the suspense by simply blowing a puff of smoke in the captain's face. At the moment, the captain was not Nasif's next prey, it was the sergeant who lay helplessly, perspiring, and awaited an answer to the burning question, 'Am I going to survive that which is about to befall upon me?'. He lay on the table, a fancy oak table built to serve a man in times of quiet evening festivities and the fanfare of joyful celebrations.

The first hint of what Nasif had in mind appeared when he cut the sergeant's trousers open, from boot to belt. On the table lay not a sergeant, but a man, a handsome, well built man–a product of the human evolution through countless generations, a final result of a long, highly selective process–a proud Persian man.

The fright of all horror films I have ever watched, all put together, could not surpass the raw terror of what followed. Nasif captured the man's sexual organs in a firm grip and amputated them in their entirety–slash…and another slash…and one more slash–completing a terminal, irreversible act. Blood spurted. The man's body thrashed in intense, all consuming agony; his wrists, stripped of flesh by the shaving action of the bare telephone wire in his desperate all-out effort to free himself, bled profusely; and he screamed! His scream could not be recognizable as that of a man, but rather as one of an animal, mortally wounded, mindless from pain and fear, an alien animal. It rose in pitch, continued at the maximum level until there was no more air in the man's lungs, and then went a step further, if only it was at all possible. And again…and again…My attempt to describe this horrendous scream could be only an abstraction, a dry summary, and a faint approximation of the true phenomenon. This scream still follows me wherever I go; it haunts me in the middle of the night.

Nasif discarded the organs like a worthless scrap, throwing them in the corner of the room. The creature on the table, something other than a man, no longer screamed. It hissed and groaned, totally exhausted and hopelessly abandoned. Using a leg of the former sergeant's trousers as a rag and still chewing and puffing on the cigar, Nasif wiped his hands. Then he approached the captain.

Kneeling, the man trembled in fear, begged and promised. The faces of both Iraqi soldiers displayed no emotions. Zu-zu, who during the carving procedure cowarded by the wall and whined, had now recovered and fluttered around the room.

Joe, like me, was visibly shaken by what had happened and stood motionless. Perhaps, seeing the broken captain, today he had learned another survival equation, 'terror plus horror equals compliance'. That's what the Iranian captain was offering us now in order to survive.

We did not wish to stay for the epilogue of the drama; the main act was all we could handle. I could hardly hold my tears; I was anxious to leave. Approaching the door, I glanced at the floor in the corner, fearing to see what I wanted to see. But it was no longer there. The dog licked the blood, hungry Zu-zu had her din-din. I had to get the hell out of this hellish place, and now was not soon enough. Joe held me by my arm.

"Don't run…" Joe whispered still holding me while we walked. "Don't run, damn you!"

Outside, my half-digested lunch of fish assumed the form of a puddle of bouillabaisse right by the wall of the goddamn building.

"What happened?" Charity caught up with us in the street.

I did not want to answer, and, I guess, Joe was in a comparable mood, because he just rubbed his temples as if trying to convey that he had a terrible headache.

"That bad?" Charity did not press.

We cut across someone's backyard and a field taking a shortcut to our lodge. Heavy clouds in my mind obscured my rational view of the world. I noticed a John Deere combine parked by the edge of the field and, for a minute, imagined that I was back in North Carolina.

"That's Mr. Batten's machine," I said. "I'd like to say hello to the old fart."

"We'll do it some other time," Joe's hands held me again, "when we leave Iraq."

"Then what in hell is the John Deere doing here?" I asked. "Did they cut off his balls too?"

"Snap out of it." I heard Joe say.

But, for better, or for worse *and at what cost to my sanity?*, we had obtained the intelligence, all of it. The 2nd Motorized Infantry Division of the Iranian strike force was at Baneh, as Joe predicted. The 5th Infantry spread right below, to the southeast. And there were more developments: the 21st Tank Brigade was moving north, fast. General al-Bitar was right, the Iranians were massing for an offensive. Our preparations had to be accelerated. Instead of two days we had one, at the most.

"You and Charity take the logistics," Joe suggested. "Keith and I will work on the plan at the general's quarters."

Captain Abu "Abe" Haddad, formerly a major and combat officer, was our logistics connection. Of all the Iraqis that I had met so far I liked him the most. Not tall in stature, but with broad shoulders and bulging muscles, he exuded strength. I could read a hundred articles on Iraq, travel across the country, and still have only a vague idea of what really makes it tick, not without inside help. Abe Haddad became my Iraqi guide, a doorkeeper by the door to the inner, hidden, chambers of an Iraqi castle. He did not reveal state secrets, or reneged on his oath to Saddam–he just afforded me a peek behind the official curtains.

Abe's own story was sad. While stationed in the south, by the Gulf, he became a scapegoat for heavy losses and his superior officer's mistakes during the Battle of Beida. As a consequence of his superior officer's intrigues, Abe had been demoted and transferred to the 1st Army Corps in the Kurd's country.

"That was dirty," I commented.

"The colonel was a Tikriti." Abe made a strange remark.

"What's a Tikriti?" I had never encountered that word.

"It's the place where they all come from," Abe explained.

"So?"

"Saddam Hussein is a Tikriti."

According to Abe, Saddam placed Tikritis in influential posts in the army and the police–a common practice here, in the Middle East. One's first loyalty began with the loyalty to his immediate clan and place of origin. The Republican Guard, an elite corps within the army, consisted, largely, of conscripts from Tikrit as well.

"By the way," Abe revealed, "Major Nasif Baran is from the region of Tikrit too."

Abe drove Charity and me to the 'junkyard', as he called the temporary depot of miscellaneous war trophies taken from the Iranians during the most recent clash.

"Goddamn!" I exclaimed facing piles upon piles of small arms, boxes of ammunition, pieces of field artillery, tanks, and even two army helicopters–all intact.

Charity went literally wild at the sight of this military hodge-podge. She ran to a stack of RPG's with attached pointed green rockets, picked up one, and lovingly *my God!* caressed the fucking tube, sliding her hand up and down the length of the phallic symbol.

"Yes! Yes! That's what we need." She cried out and ran toward another pile of war tools. "Look, Jim, isn't that wonderful?!"

"We still have to sort out what we can use," Abe commented while observing Charity's excitement with mild curiosity. "Why won't you take these helicopters instead of jeeps? Wherever you are going, you'll get there faster."

That was a brilliant idea. Charity embraced it with a passion, "Of course. We can get them from the air with rockets and machine guns."

After we selected *Charity, mainly, selected—I loaded the stuff* everything that we needed for our task, we found Joe. Carried away with excitement and interrupting each other, Charity and me presented the helicopter idea.

"It's interesting," Joe commented, "but too risky."

"Any route is risky." I voiced my expert opinion.

"Our success depends entirely on stealth," Joe reasoned. "The Iranians would track the helicopters on the radar. Even if we got through, we could not approach the 'little fortress' without making a helluva racket and alerting the compound."

"But we still could sneak upon them real fast." Charity desperately attempted to salvage the helicopter idea.

"After the recent Air Force plot against Ayatollah and the attempted bombing of his Tehran residence the bastard is paranoid. I'm sure he gave explicit orders to shoot down any aircraft approaching the compound. So, no helicopters."

Charity and I were extremely disappointed, particularly Charity. She liked the idea of attacking the fortress from the air, Rambo-style. I suspected that this, on the surface very feminine, but tough as nails, woman was more of a daredevil than both Joe and I put together.

Later in bed I couldn't fall asleep. Memories of the day's events amassed and churned in my brain. The fancy dining table *or was it a sacrificial altar?* in the empty cellar, the unhuman scream of the victim, the fiendish expression on the sadistic bozo's face, the bloody knife, the limp remains of what used to be a proud manhood, and the hungry dog leaking blood on the floor flashed before my eyes, again and again. While witnessing the head-on-stake process back in Nicaragua *and contributing to it*, I had been under the strong impression that I'd seen it all. I was wrong. That session was only a 'warm-up'. Today, I had a glimpse of what they do in hell. Yes, one live scream certainly beat five dead stares...

"Salam aleikhum, Habib! " came from the outside, an Iraqi sentry greeted someone.

"Aleikhum salam," echoed in the distance.

I wanted to leave this damn place, this clay-shantee-town with its sandy, uneven streets, and never, never come back. I wished to wake up in the morning in my Raleigh apartment and listen to the enchanting endless-variety repertoire of a mocking bird outside my window, instead of hearing, again and again, as if recorded somewhere in my tired brain, this haunting, blood-curdling, brain-scrambling, unhuman scream of the sacrifice victim.

Mark snored noisily, Chuck turned over and farted. Damn! I hated all this: being here, lurking in the dark alleys of the world, where cruelty and fear ruled, and where Death roamed.

Tomorrow we were going to enter Iran on one of the most violent missions imaginable. We were going to kill. And when one killed, one must be prepared to die. Would I die?

BUGS BUNNY CROSSING

In the morning, Joe assigned us to our duties, "Charity and Chuck–check arms and ammo, Keith and Mark–transportation and gas, Jim and Kurt–provisions, water, and the first aid. Any questions?"

"What do I do?" There had to be one more task, for Elmo.

"You stick with me."

A little pyramid of boxes and cans containing dehydrated, pressed, and canned goods brought in by Abe's men and stacked on the floor of our temporary habitat awaited Kurt and me.

"Read any Iranian?" Kurt glanced at me hopefully.

"Nope," I replied staring at the scribbly lines of Farsi labels.

"Then we have a problem. How do we know what's inside?"

"We can sort them by size and color," I proposed, "then open one of each."

"Yea, that might work, but what do we do with the opened food?"

"Eat it." I had never run from an extra meal.

"Why won't we just sort the cans and then ask Mark what's in them?" Kurt turned to me and smiled. His smile was a way to say "I don't want to call you stupid, pal, but let's admit it–your idea stinks". He was not putting me down, or implying how smart he was. He was only noting "Slow today, aren't you, man?"

The inventory procedure did not take long. I called out the items and Kurt recorded, "Yellow packages, probably biscuits–ten…red cans with the fish label, got to be fish in tomato sauce–sixteen…green cans with no label…"

After adding two canisters with water and the first aid box, I concluded, "That's it."

"Let's take a break." Kurt yawned. The work was not hard or long enough to warrant a 'break', but what the heck? There was nothing else to do.

"Why not?" I echoed.

Kurt was a mystery. I knew exactly why the others had joined the mission: Joe for its challenge, Charity to prove that she could do a man's job, Keith for the excitement of it, Chuck because he simply didn't know where he was, Elmo to become a hero, and Mark for the love of gold. But Kurt did not fit any of these categories. He had met his challenge in Vietnam and, owing to his rich parents, was well off. Why, then, did he join the TRAG and volunteered for this crazy mission?

"I think I'll go for a walk," Kurt said. "Care to join me?"

"No, I've seen enough of this place."

Mark and Keith returned first.

"Your inventory is correct," Mark confirmed. "How did you figure it out?"

"Simple. By shaking each item to see how it rattles."

"We have to eat this shit." Mark made a face.

"Yes, pal, including pork." I smiled. "By the way, speaking of pork…"

If Kurt was a mystery, at least before I applied my exhaustive psychological analysis, Mark was the opposite. I could see through him. The only reason why he had joined the mission was Ayatollah's gold. Why else? I read all about the Golden Calf in the tales about biblical times. And it was not that I was unsure of Mark's love of gold, I just wanted to measure the degree of his aurous affinity. I wanted to hear it from his own lips. Why? Maybe to flatter myself on my psychological prowess and uncanny insight. But I had to go about it very carefully. Mark was smart and could easily figure out what I was up to and tell me to mind my own business. I selected a very delicate, diplomatic approach.

"How do you feel about gold?" I ambushed Mark. If one wants a straight answer, one must ask a direct question; why beat around the bush?

"What do you mean?" Slightly surprised, Mark searched my face for a clue of what prompted me to ask such an out-of-place question.

"Do you like gold?"

"I do." Yes! I should be working for the diplomatic corps.

"Now I pronounce you man and gold!" I jubilated, the results of my preliminary analysis solidified.

"However…" Mark paused just long enough for me to begin to realize that, maybe, just maybe, my conclusions were a bit hasty. "I like it not for its value, I mean converted into paper money, but for its purity. Why did you ask?"

"Trying to figure out what the hell we are doing here."

What was I doing here? It appeared that in the whole group, in the classic sense, I was the only true mercenary–I worked for profit and for profit only!

So, what did we have in the basket? A slaughterhouse sailor, a lethal gymnast, a gung ho florist, a Judaic renegade, a suicide playboy, a raving lunatic, a juvenile delinquent, and a hara-kiri birdwatcher who loved gold–definitely a winning team!

By the end of the next day we were ready to go. Our little convoy was made up of three jeeps: major Baran's, who volunteered to be our guide to the local war site, and two of our own. We reached the assembly area by one o'clock in the morning after worming through the endless succession of sandy hills, casting no shadows under the high moon. Every time we climbed a hill, the leading jeep spun its wheels and showered us with sand. Sand penetrated everything: it blinded me, crunched on my teeth, and ran between my fingers when I put my hand in my pocket.

Finally, after negotiating a wide but shallow river, we passed the gates to nowhere and entered the remains of a small Kurdish village. The wind, barely perceptible, whispered a lullaby to the desert, and the desert slept. She didn't mind the full moon, which, casting bluish light, exposed every wrinkle on her face. She didn't care that the spinning wheels of our jeeps scratched the skin of her hilly cheeks, and she didn't want to know what we were doing here, by the edge of the destroyed Kurdish village. The ruins, mixed with sand, bathed in the eery splendor of moonlight, and the gates, which had miraculously survived the fury of another obscure battle, could just as well be the gates to hell.

"We wait here." Joe scanned his map with a flashlight.

"You should start moving at one-thirty," Nasif said, stubbing out the butt of his cigar, "and reach the objective by two."

"Fall out!" Joe shouted.

I stepped behind a remnant of a wall to relieve myself–a fairly routine procedure, so routine that one hardly ever remembers it. But this time, my leak was significant, special. It could be my last leak, I thought, and if I'm to die, then I want to face the Lord with an empty bladder. I smiled; at least my sense of humor was still with me. Then I rejoined the group.

"How does it feel to be under a barrage by heavy artillery?" I asked Joe.

"I wouldn't know." He smiled. "I've never been under one."

What?!! I thought. You made a decision to go through the barrage without knowing anything about it, without ever experiencing it?

"Then how do you know that we can make it?" I inquired.

He shrugged his shoulders, as if whether we'd make it or not was irrelevant.

"Swell." The level of my apprehension increased by a notch or two while the level of my confidence slipped.

"But I've seen it being done." Sensing my anxiety, Joe tried to reassure me. "In the movies. That's how I came up with the idea."

"Are you kidding me, man?"

"I've seen it too." Mark joined in. "Also, I've seen it being done in one of the old cartoons."

For me, that was simply too much. These guys believed they could survive the barrage because Bugs Bunny did?!!

"I'm gonna drive the jeep," I stated firmly, "since it seems that I am as qualified, or unqualified, as anybody else around here."

"I have no objections." Charity lent me her support.

"That's the spirit!" exclaimed Mark.

"All right," Joe agreed, "you drive. You think you can handle it?"

"Piece of cake." My confidence level began to catch up with the level of my apprehension. *At least I'll be in control, I thought.*

We bibbled around for another long ten minutes, and then it was time to go.

"Good luck, gentlemen...and lady." Nasif shook our hands. His grip was firm and reassuring. At any other time, I would, probably, have had to fight off the impulse of wiping my hand clean after this handshake, a handshake with the man who, using this very hand, had emasculated another man. But now, in the face of what we were about to confront, Nasif's deed did not matter. The ordinarily unspeakable act of mutilation, monstrous in its form and revolting in its process, suddenly lost its significance. Values do change in the face of death, I had to admit.

"Thank you." I answered the handshake.

"Mount up! Let's go!" Joe hollered. Ready or not, we were going to plunge into the dark abyss called Iran.

We followed the river upstream, east, for awhile, then turned northeast, directly toward the point of our crossing into Iran. Suddenly, on the other side of the hill a series of bright flashes sketched the outlines of scattered clouds above. A few seconds later came thunder. Strings of tracers crossed the sky.

"Keep going," said Joe calmly. It was no big deal, just a few Iraqis were putting their asses on the line in order to save ours. The diversionary attack commenced.

We climbed up the hill. The air shook up violently–something exploded in the dandelion blossom, probably an Iraqi tank hit by a LAW rocket. Scratch one tank crew! Our jeep dipped in a hole, jumped, and nearly overturned.

"Keep-your-eyes-on-the-road!" Joe yelled at me.

There was no fucking road. We burned the hills in the night with the headlights off. The terra firma shimmered, shadows moved, pointing away from the flashes of the night battle. I had to make an effort to take my eyes off the captivating display and keep them on the ground and the zebra shadows ahead.

A spray of pink tracers hit the ground in the battle zone and ricocheted low over us. From the second jeep came 'Yahoo!'–Elmo in ecstasy; that was all we needed now.

"Watch the kid; he's gonna fall out of the jeep," exclaimed Mark.

"But it is so beautiful." Charity commented in awe.

I couldn't believe my ears. These guys were looking at the battle as if it was no more than a show, a harmless pyrotechnical display, while in reality, although we couldn't see it, people were dying only a half-mile away. A tank crew was incinerated; those beautiful pink tracers maimed and killed before leaping majestically up in the sky.

"We're too close. Turn right ten degrees." Joe advised.

We passed the hill and dived into the moonlight. The battle behind us intensified. A tremendous explosion advertised the demise of another Iraqi tank.

"Ready?" asked Joe.

"Ready for what?" I completely forgot that the battle was only a diversion and not the main event.

"…three…two…one…zero!" Joe counted off the seconds on his watch.

A rustling moan of incoming artillery shells and rockets *I couldn't compare this wailing symphony of death with anything I knew*, introduced the main event.

"Let's go!" Joe screamed.

A series of blinding flashes straight ahead opened the second act of the unfolding drama. Only spectators up to this moment, we were about to become its participants. The air jolted and, as if we had suddenly entered a gigantic sound chamber testing base, continued trembling and vibrating with tremendous power. The next second, a wall emerged—a wall of mangled soil and dust, flame, smoke, and thunder. As we sped toward the wall, it grew wider and taller and the thunder became a roar.

"Go around it!" shouted Joe. "Skim the edge."

"Oh yeah?" I heard myself say. "That's not how they do it."

The wall drew near.

"To the edge!" screamed Joe.

"Ri-i-ight!" I screamed back and plunged smack in the middle of the fiery wall…and the shit really hit the fan. The Lion of Babylon no longer protected us. Instead, he was ready to pounce upon us and tear us apart. They've cancelled tomorrow. If there was hell, we were right in its center. Orange flashes, suddenly and randomly, came from all sides. Each flash carried a punch, a kind of a punch which jolted one's innards and almost exploded one's brain—another sensation incomparable to anything I knew.

"Ha-ha!" The world had shrunk to the size of a football field. Of course! I could see the gates, just like the gates to the Kurdish village. What kind of gates were they? To heaven? Or to hell? And there stood Saint Peter, in an Iranian uniform, guarding the gates. I hit Saint Peter with the jeep's bumper. He somersaulted and fell. The poor bastard had never had a chance to spread his wings and dart off to safety. We passed the smoldering remains of a truck, which, apparently, had sustained a direct hit. The jeep plowed into a barrier of freshly excavated soil and sailed over a trench.

"Ha-ha!" The time and space intermixed. Perhaps, we had returned to the starting point of the Universe, the Big Bang. I could see flashes, but could not discern the explosions. Instead of 'bang! bang!' I heard only a loud 'SH-H-H'. The air was no longer air. It became a hellish orange blend of gases and dust, probably a primordial dust, permeated with an acrid smell—the mixture of freshly plowed soil, burnt rubber, and picric acid.

Another flash-smash of a close hit showered us with chunks of dirt and sand…and then suddenly…I was in the clear. The jeep raced down the hill. I saw the moon and the stars—the stars of the new Universe!

"Slow down." That was Joe's voice. My God! I wasn't alone!

"Stop the jeep. You, goddamn maniac, you almost got us killed."

The air still consisted of vibrations and thumps, though less loud.

"What happened?" I asked.

"You tell me." Joe studied my face, as if he had never seen

me before.

I had nothing to tell, because I did not understand what took place; why did I go straight through the barrage–a test of bravery? Temporary insanity? A suicide attempt? I was confused; nothing made sense.

"Where is the second jeep?" Mark asked.

The barrage stopped all at once, but its effect in the form of a heavy grayish cloud on top of the hill still lingered. The cloud hugged the hill and slowly expanded. Silently, we watched the cloud. It held our friends captive. Maybe, they still circled inside in search of an exit, or had crashed into a deep trench, or their jeep had been smashed by a rocket, like that truck, that we had passed during our maddening race through hell. Maybe they had died, all of them: Keith, Kurt, Chuck, and little Elmo. They had died because of me, because they followed me. I started shaking.

"Should we go back and check?" I tried to hold my shivers. Hell! If they had died, the mission was over. It would be pointless to continue. Four against the fortress?!

"Their jeep could be damaged." Charity agreed with me.

"All right, let's go." Joe nodded.

I pushed the pedal, the wheels whined and spun, and the jeep whirled around like a worked up horse in a Texas rodeo.

"E-e-easy now!" I don't think Joe liked my driving style. But what the hell!

Suddenly, trailed by a tail of dust, Keith's jeep emerged from the cloud and proceeded speeding straight at us. I closed my eyes anticipating a head-on collision, but the jeep roared by, barely missing us.

"Whew! It's crazy." Mark sighed with relief. "Their brakes must be gone."

We turned around and finally caught up with the jeep. And here, at the foot of the hill, I witnessed the bullshittiest dialog of all times.

"What kept you?" Joe asked casually as if the whole thing compared to crossing the street and the delay could not be attributed to any extraordinary circumstances.

"The bloody tire blew out, slashed by a shrapnel." Keith replied just as casually and spat to the side. He might as well have said 'Yeah, the picnic back there was pleasant. Cheerie-o pip-pip, we had a very good time.'

"You passed us in as much of a hurry as if your asses were on fire."

I noted from the sideline, trying to make a dent in the machismo wall and inject at least one cubic centimeter of ordinary human emotions into this solid bulkhead of exaggerated masculinity.

"The bloody brakes gave out." Keith easily brushed off my stealthy foray.

"Told you," whispered Mark.

"You can't drive without the brakes in these fucking mountains." Joe peered under the jeep. "Need a flashlight." He wasted a minute or so and declared, "Maybe the hydrolic line is busted."

"This make doesn't use any hydrolics; it's all mechanical." Elmo surprised all. "Let me see."

He pushed Joe aside gently and disappeared under the jeep's belly. We suddenly had an expert kid automechanic on our hands. Joe looked at me, I glanced at Keith, and Keith shrugged his shoulders.

The kid peeked out, "The brakes don't pull cause the link is broken. But I can fix it."

"Good show!" exclaimed Keith, suddenly displaying a flood of ordinary human emotions: relief, joy, enthusiasm–just to count a few 'forbidden' feelings. For a moment, just for a moment, he lowered his macho shield. Then, realizing that he committed an unpardonable sin, he quickly regained his cool. *My God! These guys were making me sick. I knew very well that they were hyped up and scared as much as I was—my hands still trembled—but no, they refused to admit it, as if there were shame in being scared.*

"Okay...it's fixed." Elmo, smiling, emerged from under the belly of the wounded jeep. "Give it a push. Go ahead, try the brakes."

"What was it? That mad dash through the artillery barrage?" Keith turned to Joe; I could detect a note of detached concern in his voice. "We could have skirted it, you know."

"Talk to the crazy bastard." Joe motioned toward me.

Frankly, I did not remember much of what had triggered my decision to go through the wall of fire, or of the hell inside, through which we had passed. I remembered only bits and pieces, only brief glimpses into another reality. The process resembled the act of diving and surfacing, or, maybe, running through a burning house and smashing through the back door.

"It was bloody great!" Keith suddenly awarded me a full credit for the deed resulting from my temporary insanity.

"The lunatic's almost got us killed." Joe attempted to dim the shine of my glorious-whatever-I'd-done. But the credit was due, whether he liked it or not. After all, we had made it in one piece.

"I didn't mean to upstage you," I said to Joe, deep inside enjoying his creditless predicament.

"Uh-huh," he responded.

"So, what do we name them?" Charity interjected.

"Name what??" Joe seemed to be irritated. I could only guess what bothered him: the fucking exhibitionist could not count as his the most daring, courageous, and expertly accomplished deed *at least in Keith's opinion.* He had to yield it to someone else–me.

"The jeeps." Charity explained. "They did a great job, they deserve names."

She couldn't have found a better place and time for this kind of mental exercise–assigning pet names to jalopies. The urgency of putting more distance between the hell-hill and us did not exist. Maybe we should vote on the issue and then have a snack before proceeding any further. Maybe these guys were right. What was to worry about? One way or another, we stood on the road of no return, about to plunge, head first, in a spiral spin, into a black hole.

The moon hung motionless above the still expanding dust cloud. When we pierced through that fiery wall of primordial dust, we had crossed our Rubicon.

"Greased Lightning," Elmo came up with, patting the hood of jeep Bravo.

"Yea, that fits." Keith agreed. "What about the second jeep?"

A short debate ensued. Joe pointed out that the jeep's name should be commensurate with its military function. Mark went for the Eagle. Kurt offered the Flying Nun. Mark told Kurt, "Stay out of it; it ain't your jeep."

Charity giggled, apparently anticipating the effect of what she was about to say on us. All waited for the surprise.

"Even if it sounds somewhat milquetoasty, I propose to name our chariot the Kitten," Charity declared. She crossed her arms and hunched her shoulders as if chilled and herself became a cuddly little kitten. "She purrs like one."

The naming hassle would, probably, have continued, if I didn't step in.

"Guys, guys! Listen, it ain't a good idea to stick around here any longer."

The dust cloud from the top of the hill, slowly rolling down the slope, had finally reached us.

"Let's get the hell out of here." Joe agreed.

"Amen, brother," echoed Mark.

Leaving behind the settling down dust cloud and the distant pitter-patter of machine guns, we embarked on a star-crossed journey of the damned. A sequence of two vehicles, now christened Greased Lightning and Kitten, nose-to-tail, both pockmarked by shrapnel of the hellfire artillery barrage, entered the hilly passage between the Alborz and Zagros mountains. The vehicles carried weapons, a few supplies, a lot of fuel, and a team, a Waldorf salad–a strange mixture of nuts *Joe, Keith, Mark, Kurt, Elmo, and me*, fruits *Charity*, and vegetables *Chuck*, a tutti-frutti bag of individuals having only one thing in common–reaching the goal, whatever that goal might be.

RAG DOLL STOP

After traversing a plain, we found ourselves on a narrow, tortuous, sinuous mountain road of the terra incognita. I drove. Joe, fumbling with a flashlight, was trying to locate the road on the map.

"Here it is; we are right where we are supposed to be." I did not share Joe's jubilation. Who designed that we were supposed to be here? Joe? Not really; he followed the path set by someone else, by someone who wished to alter the balance of power in the region. Even though our mission had been cancelled, and Joe had changed the objective, the path remained and we had to follow it to its natural end. We could choose a different road, or stop for a brief repause, but the path led to the same destination–the fortress!

I listened to the cicada symphony–a preamble to our death march with no postlude.

"Snap out of it," Joe said.

Wasn't that what Karl said to Hans? Wasn't our ride a replay of another sequence of events leading to the end of those two German guys? We had crossed into Iran very early in the morning just like they did. Our road was like theirs. And I could see the turn ahead where the Iranians, probably, set up a road block to stop us. In a few seconds, I'd discern a yellowish round fuzz spot–the deadly signature of a straight-incoming rocket, and then it all will be over…

"Ph-r-r…Upch-hoo-o-o!" came from the back seat. Mark applied the Valsalva maneuver unsuccessfully. His feeble attempt to hold the sneeze resulted in a sticky mess all over his hands, the uniform, and his face.

"Damn!" he muttered, quite embarrassed.

"That's gross," commented Charity and lengthened the distance between herself and Mark.

If Joe's advice could not snap me out of my doomsday mood, Mark's sneeze did, at least partially. I was not alone in this fix! I was in the company of people I liked. Hell! If we went, we would go together. If there was anything to face in another world, we would face it together, all of us: Joe, and Charity, and Mark, and me. We would share the good and the bad together.

"Here." I handed Mark my handkerchief. Under different circumstances, I would not, probably, offer my handkerchief to anyone. No, sirree, I would not like to see someone's snot in my hankie! But now it didn't matter. If we all went to hell, who cared about the handkerchief? "Use and dispose of it properly."

The rest of the contents of my inner pocket included a bundle of hundred-dollar bills *I never carried a wallet*, a comb, and my passport. The comb, having survived the rough climate of my inner pocket *its pressure, heat, and humidity*, all bent and twisted, but still usable, offered a hint as to the current lifestyle of its owner. The passport, exit-stamped in Greece, did not reflect our Iraqi visit. That brought an interesting question: let's say, owing to incredible luck, we survived the mission and emerged in Saudi Arabia *with gold?!*. What kind of a reasonable explanation could we offer the Saudi authorities as to where, in the fuck, we came from? But…there was nothing to worry about, we were not going to make it.

It was four o'clock in the morning when we finally stopped by an abandoned mosque off the road by a nearby Kurdish village *destroyed, of course, in the course of war.*

"Welcome to Lut Tall *Desert Hill*, population zero!" said Mark.

The village was destroyed, but the mosque had survived somehow. My probing flashlight revealed a structure of a raised brick design and mosaic dating, probably, back to the 14th century: beautiful work of abstract shapes, geometrical forms, and Arabic lettering.

Fagged out after the raucous night, I lay on the stone floor of the mosque, but I couldn't fall asleep. Joe and Charity stretched out next to me; the other guys occupied the niche.

"Tu-whit to-whoo," came from the outside: the local owl warned its feathered neighbors not to intrude on his turf.

"So far so good," said the incurably optimistic Joe.

So far we were lucky, I thought. Particularly on that damn hill. Why did I, so recklessly, plunge into the fiery wall? What made me do that? The frenzy of war? Everything starts with war and ends with war. We loathe and worship it. We created gods of war: Mars, Athena, Tyr…We are both conquerors and victims, and gamblers. We play war, then we rest, and then we play it again. Is that what our mission was about? We played with fire like butterflies in the night–a very dangerous game. Our wings could be singed, we could fall into flames and burn just like those silly butterflies.

Joe sighed.

"I've got to take a leak," I said and was startled by the mosque's response '…leak!…leak!…leak!' The mosque was 'blest with' one intriguing quality: in spite of its relatively small size, the main chamber of the mosque created a sonorous echo, perhaps owing to its mihrab, a niche extending south and indicating the direction of Mecca.

Outside, the darkness diffused slowly. The sublime zodiac light in the east, over the serrated skyline of distant mountains, began painting orange on the dark blue.

Later in the morning, Joe and Keith disappeared in the opposite directions–to reconnoiter in the neighborhood. Since there was very little to do for the whole day *we intended to travel only by night*, I, too, decided to have a look around. The village ruins, which lay downhill, below the mosque, seemed harmless enough.

"Care to join me?" I asked Mark.

Elmo tagged along. We explored the village. Many months had passed since its destruction day. Rain, wind and sand had smoothed out the rough edges of its ruins. Elmo picked up a doll, a Raggedy Ann look-alike, and carefully cleaned her stained painted face.

"Now you have a girlfriend," smiled Mark.

The main street, and the only street, cut the village in two. The street's surface, compacted sand, showed no recent tracks. Instead, it displayed a checkerboard pattern of peculiar indentations. Elmo playfully initiated a game of hopscotch trying to avoid stepping into the indentations.

"Stop!" Mark suddenly screamed, startling me. "It's a mine field."

Elmo froze with his arms spread, as if lowering them could set off a mine. He still clutched the doll, Raggedy Ann's legs dangled helplessly.

"Don't move. Just stay where you are." Mark rolled up his sleeves in a magician-like fashion, and I wondered why he did that. Was he going to disarm the mines? "Don't panic, Elmo. Turn around…slowly…Now, walk this way, slowly…"

Finally extracted from his deadly hopscotch predicament, Elmo, visibly shaken by the incident, smiled sheepishly, "Oh boy, that was close…"

Joe, who had already returned from the reconnaissance detail, did not seem to be surprised by our report about the mined village.

"Search the mosque for booby traps," he told Mark.

I was not ready to give up on my exploration quest. I guess I simply wanted to be alone, even if only for a short while. I descended to the bottom of a ravine and was pleased to find a creek and a pond, rare in this arid country. And here, my first encounter with a local resident took place. I circumvented a thick bush and surprised a stork; no, he was not a stork, but, voila, a heron. We both quickly sized up the situation. He did not seem to be afraid of me.

"Ardea Purpurea, a purple heron," I whispered, classifying the bird.

I don't know if he heard me and what he thought of me, but his striped rufous neck stretched, his black crown swelled, and his tuft went up like in courtship.

"Oh no, not again," I said, recalling a similar episode in the Nicaraguan jungle. "I can see that you are just another dumbfuck, pal."

He listened but didn't say anything.

"Scat!" I decided to end the date.

Maybe his feelings were hurt by my remark about him being not the brightest bird in the world. Keeping one eye on me, he walked toward the water and disappeared in the tall grass. Back at the mosque, I cornered Mark. I simply had to know.

"Tell me honestly, do I resemble a heron?"

"What in the fuck is a heron?" he asked back.

"It's a bird which looks and walks like a stork."

"I don't know." Mark scanned me up and down. "I don't think so." I detected a note of uncertainty in his voice. "Why?"

"Never mind." I did not want to go into the details of my encounter with the heron. And I was slightly irritated by the uncertainty where I stood in relation to the heron family. I promised myself, the next chance I get, to read more about herons, particularly their mating habits.

The day dragged on. I was bored. I stepped outside and joined Joe who stood silently and chewed on a grass stem.

"What time do we move?" I asked.

"If you say-so," he answered. Apparently, he was not listening to me. I followed his gaze and discovered the reason for his inattention. Charity and Kurt stood aloof at the distance, obviously too close to each other. She laughed at something he said.

"The rain in Spain falls mainly on its plains," I recited.

"That's interesting." Joe commented as if my statement made any sense, then, as if waking up, he turned to me, "What did you say?"

"Never mind." I understood Joe's concern: he was jealous of Kurt, who, obviously, was making a pass at Charity. The incident added another random factor to Joe's already complex Iranian equation. "Don't jump to conclusions, man. Often things are not what they seem to be. Panda is not a bear, but a raccoon, did you know that?"

Joe smiled, "No, I didn't. Thanks though."

"Hi, guys." Charity approached. "Are you talking about me?"

Joe and I responded at the same time, Joe with an evasive 'no' and I with a timid 'yes'.

She laughed. Seconds hung, one, two, three…silence set in…suspense grew…A little drama was unfolding right before my eyes, I could sense it. What will it be? The moment of truth?

And suddenly, totally unexpected, absolutely out of character, in the wrong place, and at the wrong time, Joe said tenderly, "Love you."

This 'love you' was not a simple confession, or a due attempt to please Charity, or a feeble solicitation for a 'love you too', but a final vow, a total surrender, a signature under the ultimate statement forfeiting one's life.

And she answered quietly, "Yes, I know."

They embraced.

"You guys make me sick," I said trying to hide the fact that I was touched by what I'd witnessed.

"Yes, Kurt wanted to take me to bed," Charity blushed. The dynamite drama was diffused, the suspense shortcircuited. She had said no to Kurt. Joe attempted not to show his tremendous relief, but his delayed, half-suppressed, quivering sigh revealed his true feelings toward Charity.

"I was looking for Chuck." Keith approached. "He is nowhere to be found."

"I think I saw him walking down the road toward the village." I remembered. "I'll find him."

Life would be hell, if no one could ever have a moment of solitude. I surprised Chuck behind the remnants of a wall. He stood up and stared at me like a ram at new gates. Matted hair covered his sweaty forehead, and stems of dry grass clung to his unbuttoned pants. Apparently, Chuck was unwilling to wait for his next wet dream.

We walked up the hill.

"No privacy," grumbled Chuck. "In the jungle, I could beat the meat behind any bush, VC or no VC, man."

LAST SONG OF THE SASSY DWARF

We were almost ready to continue our journey–jeeps loaded and bladders empty–when the whole world turned into one continuous, massive, loud shout.

They came out of nowhere, running and tumbling down the hill, falling into and jumping over crevices and holes, and seemingly seeping out of nooks and crannies of Mother Earth herself–a hundred of them, all screaming at the top of their lungs.

"Don't shoot…don't shoot!" Joe shouted, and I wasn't sure whether he addressed us or the Iranians who came down on us in overwhelming numbers. Neither side had fired a single shot. We were quickly surrounded and disarmed. The jeeps were confiscated.

"What do we do now?" I whispered.

"These guys are not Iranians," said Mark. "They are Kurds."

"What's the difference?"

I was surprised by the fact that Joe did not put up any resistance and allowed us to be captured like rats in the bag.

"What's going on?" I asked him.

"These people are friendlies…" he paused, "I hope, and could be useful to us."

"How do you figure?"

"Well, look at the village below, most likely their village. It was levelled by the government troops."

We were taken farther down the road, in the general direction where we intended to travel anyway. We walked. The road snaking in the narrow gap between steep mountains practically squeezed its way through until it finally broke out into a valley. The suddenly open view under the cloudless sky was breathtaking. The chocolate-gray, dusky ribbed hills, studded with virescent tamarisk, sloped gently into the valley. Across the valley, where mountain shadows could not reach, the hills bathed in the fading rays of the falling sun. After the pressing confinement of mountains, where shadows ruled, the valley presented a genuinely welcome sight.

The soldier walking next to me exclaimed excitedly and pointed to the bottom of the valley. I discerned a cluster of whitish structures– a village. Our mountain pass journey was almost over.

The village, originally small, just three stone-and-clay dwellings, now expanded adding to its register two rows of rickety huts built of corrugated tin and dilapidated plywood. It enlarged its roster by about two hundred vagabond Kurds, mostly war refugees. The village also became one of the camps of the Mojahedin Peshmargas, the Kurdish resistance organization. The middle of the three original dwellings served as the resistance headquarters.

Names, usually escape my memory. But I do remember faces, the images of persons I meet. Usually. Their most striking traits become a platypus-nose, a bandy-legged Kurd, a twerp with scabies, and a sassy dwarf–maybe not very flattering names, but I remember persons better that way.

Two of our numerous armed escort entered the centerpiece building. We waited. Platypus-nose returned alone.

"Are ze you ze in charge?" he asked me in pig English.

"No, but he is." I motioned in Joe's direction.

Platypus-nose paused staring at Joe evaluatingly, then he said, "Ze captain wants to meet viz you."

Joe acknowledged with a nod.

Both started walking toward the dwelling when Platypus-nose suddenly stopped, turned to me, hesitated for a moment, and finally appended, "And ze you too."

Joe seemed worried by the pending encounter with the local power broker, the Kurdish commander. Obviously, he could use my help, and I was available. Could he find a better source of support than me? Not in a million years. I knew how to handle these clowns; I had accumulated a vast amount of experience in these matters back in Athens *my kidnapping*. So I said, "Let me handle this."

Joe's face reflected a touch of surprise. Perhaps, in Joe's opinion, my willingness to place my head into the lion's mouth was out of character.

"Are you sure you know what you are doing?" Joe expended three you's, emphasizing the importance of what I was about to take upon myself.

"Piece of cake," I replied confidently.

I had a plan. I was going to tell the commander that we, eight American volunteers, came to join his valiant effort to overthrow the oppressive regime of Ayatollah Ruhollah Khomeini. Yes, that was it. We were righteous idealists who came to fight for the just cause.

Taken inside, Joe and I faced not one but five Kurdish gentlemen sitting on the other side of a long table, not nearly as fancy as the one in the Iraqi intelligence headquarters. Illuminated from below by a menorah minus three candles, the men's faces acquired a spooky appearance. Their larger-than-life silhouette shadows cast on the wall behind them only emphasized our total lack of options and the precariousness of our position.

The man in the middle said, "Explain!" *meaning 'who in the fuck are you, and what in the hell are you doing here?'*

I don't know why, maybe the combination of candle light and eery shadows confused me, and five ghostlike spooky faces intimidated me, but instead of putting our claim on the noble principles, I mumbled something to the effect of us making the wrong turn at Albuquerque and winding up here by mistake.

Joe barged in, "My friend, Major Riveaux *Joe instantly promoted me to a higher rank, maybe having learned the value of titles in this part of the world*, is making a joke. We are American mercenary team. Our task is to free the remaining American corporate hostages in Tehran."

I had to admit that Joe's version beat my Albuquerque stuff. According to Joe, we were going to strike the target on Khiaban-i Jamshid, close to the former American Embassy still occupied by the Revolutionary Guards, get the hostages, and head south, to the Gulf, where the tug boat Armadillo was ready to pick us up *Clever, I thought, all the facts fit*. Joe added, for good measure, that this was another mercenary operation financed by Ross Perot, the American billionaire.

"I don't know how you managed to cross the front line from Iraq," the man in the middle said, "but I can guess."

"That was the Major's part." Joe motioned toward me, finally granting me full credit for my glorious *totally insane* deed.

"I have seen the fresh shrapnel marks on your vehicles; they tell the tail." The man in the middle smiled and introduced himself. "Captain Aryafar."

Captain Aryafar was one of the top commanders of the Kurd liberation movement. The panel of judges broke up and joined the accused. No charges were brought against us. In fact, all five appeared friendly, and one of them, with a crew cut and shifty eyes, even offered me a long, skinny cigar. I declined. The owner of the shifty eyes was none other than the local commander, Major Khartul, I forgot his first name.

We were free again, and I stepped outside. My sensitive nose led me to the second building holding supplies and housing a kitchen. I could imagine that activity in the kitchen never stopped: feeding two hundred hungry Kurds, plus guests, was not an easy task. I promptly proceeded to establish a friendly contact with the kitchen personnel, but the language barrier somewhat hindered my success. A book of recipes attracted my attention. Although I could not read Farsi, I didn't have any problems in identifying the dishes disliked by the head chef. Those were marked by a tiny drawing of a peeing penis, as if commenting 'pee on that one!' and I hoped that was all it meant.

"What's for dinner?" I asked, putting down the X-rated cookbook. *My motto has always been 'Take good care of your stomach—without it you're dead'.*

Later, at the dinner, I felt slightly apprehensive eating the stuff our hosts served us.

Joe sat silently, holding his AK on his lap *our weapons had been returned.*

"What's the problem?" I sensed there was one.

"Let's go outside," he said.

We stepped outside.

"This son-of-a-bitch, the commander, asked me to leave Charity behind." Joe squinted in a disdainful smirk, clenched his teeth, and hissed.

"Maybe the guy was joking." I tried to justify the unbecoming behavior of the Kurdish commander.

"No, he meant it." Joe wearily rubbed his chin, giving an indication that the problem had not been solved.

"Does Charity know?"

"She is trying to brush it off as a nuisance thing."

After dinner, our hosts, Joe, Keith and me gathered around one table. The conversation centered around the Iran-Iraqi war. Maybe the subject fascinated Joe and Keith, but I had no interest in it whatsoever. Still, just to fit the image and fulfill whatever was expected of a person with the rank of major, I decided to stay for a few minutes and then leave.

"The last October, there was a fierce fighting west of here," Khartul said. "The Iranian tank brigade, let Allah cut their hands off, tried to dislodge the Iraqis. An all-tank formation, without infantry support. They were mauled pretty badly."

Khartul suddenly turned to Charity and smiled. She reciprocated politely.

"The Iranian commander apparently hadn't read Rommel's book

on panzer warfare," 'George-Patton'ed Joe.

Khartul continued, "And the Iraqis, let Allah break the tracks of their tanks, just dug in instead of using the opportunity to reverse the offensive."

Khartul moved closer to Charity.

"That sounds familiar." Keith joined in the analysis of the local tank warfare. "They used to refer to the British army as the 'lions led by donkeys'. Here, tigers and panthers are led by jackasses."

I had enough of all this military rubbish, and I certainly disagreed with Keith's unfair evaluation of the Iraqis.

"What about our crossing?" I turned to him. "The Iraqis gave us a top-notch support. Don't you agree?"

My unexpected offensive seemed to inflame Keith.

"What do you know about…?" he flared up, but Joe interrupted him.

"Hey! hey! Guys, hold your horses. This is not the place to argue. Cool it!"

Khartul, meanwhile, paid more attention to Charity than to our brief clash. He placed his hand on Charity's knee. She moved her leg and freed her knee gently.

"Well…" Khartul let her go. "A few days ago, the Iraqis massacred three hundred Iraqi Kurds, and Ayatollah's soldiers are attacking us right now north of here, near Urmiyeh."

"Something should be done about it." Joe reached for his AK. His statement could be interpreted two ways: a suggestion to respond to Ayatollah's attack on the Kurds, and a warning to the commander to keep his hands off Charity.

Up to now, the sphere of my curiosity did not cover Khartul. Unlike Aryafar, Khartul did not possess an attention attracting personality, or looks. Crew cut like Aryafar, but shorter, and plain as grain, Khartul did not project an imposing MacArthur image befitting a commander. He rather smacked of Joe—a nobody. But an ordinary man could not become a commander of a large fighting unit. Probably, like all other plain persons in the world, Khartul simply had to work harder to get where he was.

"Would you like to take a sitz bath?" Khartul turned to Charity. "We have one in the next tent."

Charity blushed, "No, thank you."

"Then may I offer you a sample of our native entertainment?"

As if on cue, a dwarf carrying a banjo-like musical instrument appeared at the entrance. He bowed to Charity *and I began to suspect that the show had been staged for her benefit*, strummed the banjo, and surprised us with a pleasant high tenor. One had to accept the unaccustomed oriental style of seemingly discordant banjo tones, unexpected vocal combinations, and the offset rhythm of the song. The song, accompanied by a fluidity of facial expressions, communicated the tortured inner emotions of the dwarf.

"Is this a love song?" I turned to Mark.

"I don't speak Kurdish," he shrugged his shoulders, "except for a few words...He sings about dark mountains, a blue moon, and a maiden. I guess it is a love song–one of the 'I want your pussy' variety."

"That's cynical."

"Cynical!? Picture that midget on top of Charity." Mark chuckled.

"Shut up, you dirty-minded schmuck!"

"Oh yeah? What about yourself?"

"Well..."

Frankly, I suspected, no, hell, I knew, that we all were Charity's secret admirers. We all yenned her, though were afraid to reveal our true feelings toward her. Except for Kurt. The clumsy Iranian uniform could not hide her luscious figure, perhaps a little too heavy for competing in the Olympics, but perfect from any other view. And her face, the face of an angel, was so incongruent with the rough events she was part of and places she ventured into *like this God-forsaken, barren valley in the dump-mountains of war-torn Iran*. At the same time, her sensuous lips and sensual smile conveyed another, non-angelic, facet of her nature, and more. At times, when she ired, her large blue eyes squinted and iced *just like Joe's, but that's where their similarity ended*, giving a strong hint of still another side of her personality, barbarous and cruel.

Khartul's condition *struck with lovesickness*, meanwhile, deteriorated to the state of uncontrolled drooling over Charity. The unmistakable symptoms of this malady manifested themselves in the enlarged outline of Khartul's quick-action self-hardening device. He ignored the sleeve-pulling act attempted by his second-in-command, the twerp with scabies, who observed his commander's decomposing conduct first with detached interest and then with growing alarm. Only a poke in the ribs by Aryafar had finally brought Khartul back to his senses.

The dwarf-tenor from Saqqhez–the Kurdish Tin Pan Alley–

finished his 'blue-moon-over-Zagros-mountains' serenade to Charity, approached her, and ceremoniously kissed her hand. All applauded, she smiled.

Soon after this sample of the Kurdish show biz, Khartul approached me, "I have to talk to you."

Joe and I exchanged puzzled glances. I shrugged my shoulders and followed Khartul out of the door.

"They said that you are the colonel's business manager," Khartul began, and I wondered what he was up to. "I am ready to negotiate, do business."

I was at a loss as to what business Khartul had in mind.

"It is not going to be easy to reach the hostages," he continued. "There are several hundred Revolutionary Guards, they are all over the place, may Allah do bad things to them."

Khartul paused, probably preparing to come to the main point.

"We can handle that," I stated confidently and sincerely, knowing that we did not have to handle that.

"It is not going to be easy." Khartul put his hand on my shoulder. "But I can help."

A strange thought crossed my mind. Was it Charity that our 'negotiations' were about?

Khartul went on, "I can stage a massive attack on their headquarters—a diversion. You, then, can take the hostages and slip out. And none of you will have to die."

"Forget it," I said. "She is Joe's scag."

"Scag? What is scag?" Khartul snuffled.

"A girlfriend."

We walked between tents in silence. Finally, Khartul cleared his throat and said, "I can arrange an accident. Then you will take command."

It was surprising how he came out in the open and proposed Joe's assassination. Perhaps, it was something I said, or how I said it, which Khartul misinterpreted as my dislike of Joe. But whatever the reason, here it was—the offer on the table and I in the corner. If I said no, Khartul, presuming that I would tip-off Joe, could initiate some sort of preemptive action, and my personal safety could no longer be taken for granted. The 'yes' was out of the question.

"Let me think about it. I'll give you my answer in the morning."

"Of course." Khartul was satisfied.

I found our group in the central tent vacated for our benefit. Joe met me at the door.

"We've got to get out of here...now!" I said. Then I related the state of my 'negotiations' with Khartul.

"I suspected something like that could develop." Joe smiled dryly.

"It can happen tonight."

"Aryafar is leaving in the morning. Khartul is not going to do anything until after he is gone. Let's get some sleep."

"Look, Khartul expects my answer in the morning."

"So?"

"Fuck it! What shall I tell him?"

"Tell him that you're delighted with his plan."

I couldn't sleep well; every little noise outside the tent woke me up. Someone approached the tent on my side. Clunk! Was it the rifle bolt? Pushing a cartridge in the chamber? A twig snapped. Was it the assassin? A bubbly spray hit the dust–it had to be a guard, taking a leak. Then swish-swish...the outbound footsteps faded...and all was well. Finally, I dozed off.

Clear peach-and-blue sky and crisp mountain air hinted on a beautiful day. In the distance, I could see snow-covered mountain peaks. The last night I'd met only a few inhabitants of the village. Now, on the way to the outhouse, I encountered more. A humpy zebu flopped his ears chasing flies away, a puppy whimpered, a pinto kicked the dust, and a Persian cat displayed interest in me. As I walked by, the cat's large, greenish-yellow, unblinking eyes followed mine cautiously. Finally convinced that the stranger presented no threat to him, the cat arched his back and yawned. In a coop behind a tent, the loud cackling of several hysterical chickens advertised to the world that one of them had laid an egg. The rest of them made a lot of fuss about it.

On the way back through the village, I met a few specimens of its human component: black-shawled women, men with sunken cheeks and unshaven chins, and ragamuffin kids–the owners of the zebu, the pinto, the puppy, the cat, and the chickens.

Breakfast passed in a subdued, almost solemn, atmosphere, maybe because there was simply nothing to talk about. Khartul sat across the table. This morning he wore a dressy native tensil-woven turban. I tried to act nonchalant and did what Joe suggested. When my eyes met Khartul's, I nodded communicating my 'yes'.

Joe appeared calm.

"Let me stick by you," I said.

"No, that would be too obvious. Do the opposite–keep away.

And don't worry about me, will you."

After the quiet breakfast, the village life picked up the pace. Aryafar and his aide packed their gear, loaded their jeep, wished us luck, and disappeared, leaving behind only a slowly settling dust trail. We had to get ready ourselves. Keith and Elmo attended to Greased Lightning and Kitten, preparing them for a long journey.

Mark and Kurt cleaned their AKs. Chuck disappeared behind the outhouse seeking monastic isolation to finish the job I had interrupted back in the village below the mosque with its phallic tower. He soon reappeared, in a weltschmertz mood of sentimental sadness owing to the loss of certain precious bodily fluids.

I surveyed the village. Unlike in the throwaway American culture, nothing went to waste here. Every wooden board, every tin sheet, and every nail was put to use.

"YR224," I read on the wall of a hut. A section of an airplane fuselage was used for the wall construction. That airplane, Iraqi or Iranian, was shot down in the neighborhood of the village.

On the edge of the village, I spotted a seemingly out-of-place contraption—a tall pole with a carriage wheel on the top. The wheel and the long rope fastened to its frame could spin on a spike. I remembered seeing something similar to this device on my uncle Sammy's farm in Canada. His kids had a good time riding it like a hang-on-to merry-go-round.

Kids over here are no different from Canadian kids, I thought.

Back in the tent, I found Joe, Charity, Mark, and…the dwarf!

"He is like flypaper, can't get rid of him," Joe complained.

"Oom taruh ambarooh koronel," said the dwarf.

"What did he say?" I asked Mark.

"I don't know, something about protecting Joe."

"He must be a good guy." I smiled patting the dwarf on the back.

The dwarf made a comment, something to the effect of me being as big as a mountain, and I joked, "Tell him that he can climb me any time." My offhand joke seemed to insult the dwarf. His little arms began flying up and down, he made a tiny fist and waved it at me. I tried to apologize for my crude sense of humor; I didn't mean to insult our newly acquired Kurdish friend. I definitely liked this sassy dwarf.

Keith entered and reported to Joe that our vehicles were gassed up and ready for the journey. Suddenly, a crowd roar reached us. It came from the side of the village where I had spotted the hang-on-to merry-go-round. It subsided, then it grew louder again. We listened.

Out of breath, wide-eyed, and shook-up, Elmo appeared at the entrance.

"They are...hanging someone," he announced.

"They couldn't find a better day," Mark commented cynically.

Elmo was wrong: it was not a hanging event. Hanging is too simple, too civilized. I've seen how it's done in the movies: the body falls to the end of the rope, the neck snaps, and the whole fucking thing is over. There is little entertainment in hanging. Asians are more inventive; their taste in entertainment is more refined. In the western theater one has no control over the events on the stage. Actors have it all. A few shows allow limited audience participation, like questions and cheers, but nothing of substantial nature, nothing to brag about after the show. Here, by the hang-on-to merry-go-round, the roles were reversed: the audience controlled the stage, and the star of the show had no say whatsoever in what was going to happen next.

In this village, the event was a show. The hang-on-to merry-go-round was a theater stage and the crowd around it an unruly audience.

The show was already in progress when we arrived. The stage held no curtains, no lighting, and no sound equipment. The star of the show, a half-naked Iranian soldier taken prisoner by the Mojahedin forces, was suspended upside down from the hang-on-to merry-go-round. Although he seemed relaxed *a few punches in the face contributed to that condition* and was surrounded by a friendly crowd *everyone smiled*, I suspected that deep inside he was, at least slightly, apprehensive.

A force applied to a mass suspended from a stationary point in the gravitational field sends the mass into circular motion. The stronger the force, the wider the circle and the faster the motion. The show, based on that principle, continued with no commercial interruptions. The star played his part well: he swayed enthusiastically and rotated around the pole, playfully spinning in the process just for the fun of it. That spinning momentum made his part a bit easier to play—some punches aimed at his face missed the target, probably owing to a relatively low skill level of some members of the audience. In the middle of the play, the star attempted to deviate from the script and covered his face with both hands, but the audience screamed foul. One of its members used a club to straighten things out. After this timely corrective action the star pretended that his arm was broken. It acquired its own lifeless swaying momentum. In one of the memorable scenes, the star improvised again, emptying his bladder over himself and mixing his urine with blood. Surprisingly, the audience approved his impromptu and rewarded him with loud cheers.

We were part of the audience. Keith maintained a stony face. Mark licked his lips and swallowed as if his mouth became dry. Elmo's face reflected the expression of ultimate surprise, the expression he would probably wear if told that his daddy was not really his daddy, ask the milkman. Charity sobbed. The twerp with scabies offered her popcorn *it was a show, wasn't it?*, but she graciously declined. Kurt and Chuck were not present. Kurt, I knew, courted one of the local Kurdish girls, and Chuck, probably, masturbated again behind the outhouse. Joe and the sassy dwarf left before the end of the show. And I, and me, and myself were confused. I loathed the cruel thrills of the mob and pitied the victim, but I also knew that the victim had participated in the raid on another Kurdish village.

"Where is Joe?" Charity pulled my sleeve.

"I'd like to know myself." The 'show' had absorbed me so completely that I forgot that Joe's life was almost as much in jeopardy as the life of this unlucky Iranian bastard still hanging on the end of a thick, bristly, spliced, twice-laid rope *yes, sometimes I see that rope in my nightmares* and receiving the 'Lazy-Susan treatment'.

"I'll go with you."

"No, find Kurt and Chuck. I have a feeling that we'll be leaving in a hurry."

Joe could not be found in the tent or in the mess hall. I began to worry; what if Khartul had succeeded? The next logical place to check was Khartul's headquarters. Joe could be in trouble right now and desperately needing my help. The hut was built with a single entrance, and I approached it cautiously. The door gaped open. I cocked my AK, the action bolt clicked. Now! I stepped in. Coming in straight from the sunlight, I could hardly see the interior.

"You should do it in advance, before you approach the place." Joe's calm voice startled me.

"What the hell!!?"

"Watch you steps."

I tripped over a body on the floor. As my eyes slowly adjusted to the poor lighting conditions of the interior, I discerned another body slumped on the table, the same table from which five spooky faces stared at us the last night.

"Do what in advance?" I asked.

"The AK bolt, I heard it."

The body on the table was Khartul's. His throat was slashed from ear to ear–Joe's favorite method of silent killing; the victim doesn't scream. Khartul's fancy, tensil-woven turban soaking in the pool of blood on the table drooped over its edge. Joe picked up the end of the turban to clean the knife *and his hands*, then just dropped it.

The other body, on the floor...

"Not the dwarf! " I exclaimed. "For God's sake! He tried to protect you."

"I couldn't take that chance," the cold-blooded son-of-a-bitch replied. "He surprised me."

At this moment I sincerely hoped that from now on the ghost of the innocent dwarf haunted Joe, just like the ghosts of those two boys whom he executed in the swamps of Nicaragua–his continuing nightmare, his private hell.

"Look what I've found on the shelves." Joe handed me a stack of documents. "Something about the Yankee-Romeo-two-two-four. See what that is."

"Who gives a damn about the fucking plane! Let's get the hell out of here."

"You're right. Lock the door, that will give us more time before they discover the bodies."

"There is no fucking lock here."

The rest of the group waited for us in the tent. Charity bit her fingernails.

"I'm worried," she said.

"Don't." Joe embraced her shoulders tenderly *right after killing someone?!*. "It's all fixed." *Yeah, dead fixed, including the dwarf.*

Kurt was able to scrounge two round watermelons, probably a present from his new Kurdish girlfriend. He handed one to Mark, "Here, one for Kitten's crew."

I don't think Kurt had scored, but Chuck, judging by the blissful absentminded expression on his face, apparently did. Elmo, after seeing the mob in action, had slowly recovered from the state of shock. When several shots, signalling the ending of the final act en passant, reached us, he twitched nervously.

"Let's go."

We drove by the 'theatre'. The mob was scattering. The body of the Iranian soldier lying on its side in the dust no longer had a face. We gawked at it, but no one commented. Several kids tried to keep the pace with our vehicles. The R-rated show, which they had been allowed to watch, was over. To them, the passing of our caravan was a mere intermission before another show. They shouted and laughed, and waved to us, as if what had happened by the hang-on-to merry-go-round was an ordinary event, which they had seen many times before and were going to see again. No, there was a difference between the local and Canadian kids.

We passed the sentry who saluted us. No one else paid us even passing attention–come-and-go was the local lifestyle. Two miles down the road, we crossed a dilapidated wooden bridge with no creek flowing under it.

"Stop!" the son-of-a-bitch shouted.

Sure...'Keith, blow up the bridge' comes next, I thought.

"Keith, blow up that sucker," the son-of-a-bitch ordered.

How did I know that? Shoot this, blow up that, kill the dwarf.

"Mark, take the wheel," said the son-of-a-bitch.

Of course, Mark was a better choice at the wheel, he could follow the Farsi road signs. Charity sat in the front, and I rode in the back seat, next to the son-of-a-bitch.

A thump of the blast behind us and its raspy multi-echo in the nearby hills let the world know that the bridge was no more, like the dwarf.

"I had to do it," the son-of-a-bitch said, he knew what I was thinking about.

I did not answer. I did not want to talk about it; more than that, I did not feel like talking at all. Instead, I rummaged through the documents that Joe found at Khartul's headquarters: an invoice in Hebrew, a signed price list in Farsi, the airplane registry and maintenance papers in Spanish, and a Pilot Log and the pilot's personal notebook in English. The cargo plane Yankee-Romeo-two-two-four was neither an Iraqi nor Iranian aircraft. As I sifted through the papers, a drama unfolded, a story emerged–a skullduggery classic about a clandestine operation, one of those which seldom surfaces and which the john-in-the-street never hears about.

Ali Akbar Hashemi-Rafsanjani, the Speaker of the Iranian Parliament and the leading figure of the dissenting faction had tried to establish contacts with the Americans–a potential supplier of arms and spare parts for the American weaponry already in Iran, which was bought originally by the former Shah. Curbed by the law forbidding arms sales to Iran, recently passed by the U. S. Congress, the White House dealt through the Israelis. The Iran-Contra affair was in the making. The Israelis closed a contract with Iran through a French firm–a secret deal worth $200 million. Israel would sell to Iran 106mm cannons, mortars, ammunition, communication equipment, and Phantom jet tires.

A British arms agent had chartered an Argentinian cargo plane YR224. Flown by two British mercenaries, the plane landed in Tel-Aviv. On July 11, 1981, the loaded plane took off for Tehran. It made three runs via Turkey. On its return after the third run, something happened.

According to the Pilot Log, the plane was hit by a cannon fire from a strafing unmarked military jet. The resulting damage was extensive, one engine caught on fire. The pilot changed the course to 180 degrees *straight south* in the effort to reach the closest airfield.

The log ended with a chilling entry: "YR224 is losing altitude…We are going to die…now…"

Yankee-Romeo-two-two-four crashed in the hills near Zafar-abad.

I experienced an eery feeling that, somehow, the YR224's destiny intertwined with ours. Perhaps, that feeling sprung from the coincidence itself–the slim chance of our paths crossing in the most unlikely place. Their flight and our mission had the same roots, and both were created in the chain of the same events. But I could be wrong, maybe the answer was much simpler: our paths crossed because we were of the same breed–adventurers and mercenaries–all attracted to the same trouble spots, like butterflies to fire. YR224 had crashed and burned like a butterfly. If we should die soon, we would, probably, meet the crew of YR224 at the wait station wherever that place might be.

WHEN THE SKY SPLITS

I was so engrossed in the YR224 papers that I missed the moment when we reached a larger road and merged with the local traffic.

"Just like in California," Charity commented. "And…almost as hot."

The traffic had slowed down to a crawl.

"What is it?" Joe inquired impatiently.

"It's a military convoy of some sort," Mark replied.

With no wind in the valley squashed between hills and no significant motion to create a windwash, we began to realize how hot it was. The global warming effect was getting to me; my icecaps began to melt.

"How about a slice of cool watermelon?" Mark suggested.

"Not a bad idea–watermelon," echoed Joe and proceeded removing his knife, the same blade he had used to cut two throats only an hour ago.

"Are you kidding me, man?" I held his hand firmly.

"Oh." The son-of-a-bitch remembered. If I didn't stop him, he would use the knife. "May I borrow yours, Charity?"

"Don't cut any for me." I was disgusted with Joe's casual attitude toward the killings and indiscriminant use of his knife–to cut bread, a watermelon, a throat!

The vehicles ahead, one by one, dropped out, turned off the road. The distance between the convoy and us shortened until we became the convoy's tail.

"Shall I pass them?" Mark asked.

"No, that's our lucky break. Stay ri-i-ight behind them." Joe rubbed his palms together, happy with the piece of luck fallen in our lap. It was our lucky break; the convoy, among other things, carried wounded. Greased Lightning, with the cross painted on her side, blended perfectly with the medical convoy. Check point sentries at Najafabad and Baba-Sorkh just waved us through.

In Bijar though, the convoy turned south, to Hamadan, and from then on, we were on our own again. At Bijar we had reached the midpoint between the front and the main highway at Zanjan. By Joe's extrapolated guess, we had to pass two more check posts before hitting the main highway–a problem-free road all the way to Tehran.

"So, what have you discovered in the papers?" Joe asked me.

"That you were right to be cautious of the CIA and Mossad."

"Of the Mossad?" Mark turned and glanced at me and Joe.

"Precisely," I said.

"Not exactly." Joe stepped in. "The CIA and the Mossad are fine by themselves. It's the combination of the two you have to be cautious of."

"What do you mean?" Mark and I voiced at the same time.

"Both are equally powerful in the Middle East, with the Mossad holding a slight edge over the CIA. It's like two housewives in the same kitchen–each having her own recipe for every dish."

"Which one sent us?" suddenly asked Mark.

"Neither." Joe laughed. "This is my operation."

But was it Joe's operation? I questioned it for the first time. Granted, it has been set up by Joe, but was it really his operation? TRAG could not send a team to assassinate a president of another country. It seemed inconceivable to me that Joe could hold so much power in his hands.

We approached the next check post at Qajaz. Here we had the first opportunity to find out whether the identification papers obtained for us by Nasif were valid. Both sentries stared more at Charity than at the darn papers. She granted them a smile. The shorter one made a joke, Mark laughed, and both Joe and I smiled, pretending that we understood what the shorty had said. We were free to proceed.

"What did the short dumbfuck joke about?" I asked Mark.

"About Charity. He said that his dick ached, and he suggested that we leave the nurse with them, to take care of the problem."

"I declare!" sneered Charity. "Don't you men ever think of anything but sex?"

Finally, we had successfully negotiated the last major obstacle, the town of Zarrinabad, where we could have been stopped. The sentry, however, didn't want to bother checking the 'medical team' obviously coming straight from the front and which by then, had passed at least three check points already.

"Borou! borou! *Go! go!*" he shouted.

Murphy's Law is like a cheetah. It blends with the background quietly stalking, setting up an ambush, patiently waiting…One never knows when and where this tricky, treacherous beast will strike. A muffled puff from under the jeep followed by a swerve off the road signalled an emergency.

"A blowout!" Mark announced.

"Swell," I said.

We had a spare tire.

"No big deal." Joe sucked on the tip of a chocolate bar in a somewhat whorish manner.

Greased Lightning parked right behind the lame Kitten.

"We'll fix it." Our wiz-kid-mechanic volunteered.

Brakes squeaked, I turned and froze: a large military truck carrying a dozen or so soldiers stopped behind Greased Lightning.

"We have company," I said quietly.

"No shit!" Joe, finally, stopped slobbering over the chocolate bar and put it down.

The Iranian army captain approached me. I was getting used to the phenomenon that my 'commanding' appearance projected the image of the one in charge. The captain addressed me in German. That seemed odd, why should he? The sad story of the German mercenary team ambushed not far from this place came to my mind. Could there be a connection between the event and the captain? Did he know something about us we wished he didn't? One way or another, our Iranian medical team masquerade was over; it simply wouldn't sell anymore.

"Was ist das?"

Shall I dump the whole thing on Joe? I thought; I was tempted to do exactly that. I glanced at him. A chocolate streak ran down the side of Joe's mouth–a sight not entirely congruent with a commander's image. Back in college, my psychology professor once said, "One of the ways to gain an upper hand in the shaky circumstances is to throw your adversary off balance. It can be achieved with an element of surprise. Surprise always disorients an individual, even if only briefly. For example, you may pretend to recognize the adversary. Now, he is damn sure that you and he have never met, but there you are, claiming that you have. He is confused."

"I don't speak German." I turned to the captain. "Are you Captain Mahallati sent to assist us?"

I was not going to repeat, ever again, my pitiful performance at the Mojahedin headquarters, where I panicked and tried to joke my way out by stating that we made a wrong turn at Albuquerque. I had learned my lesson. Besides, I discovered that scary things are not as frightful as they may seem, once you get to know them. Like those five spooky faces on the other side of the table back there, at the

Kurdish village.

"No, I am Captain Taheri." The captain spoke perfect English.

"Doesn't matter, have you brought the radiation detection equipment which we have requested?"

I glanced at Joe and Mark standing next to me. They seemed puzzled by this strange conversation with the captain. I read in Joe's eyes 'What in hell is going on?'. But I had a plan. We could pass for a medical team while on wheels, but face-to-face, the story wouldn't wash down even with the flat Iranian beer, which Abe, thoughtfully, had stowed with the rations. Our non-Iranian origin could not be concealed.

"I think you are taking us for someone else." The captain smiled. "We do not have the equipment. And who are you?"

"I'm afraid I cannot disclose that, but if you call the Defense Ministry…"

At this point, Mark stepped in. He spoke Farsi. I observed the captain's face. First, the captain became interested, then his facial expression reflected a shock. Both men, taking turns, excitedly pointed in the direction where we came from. I was intrigued, could Mark figure out what I had in mind? Finally, the captain walked back to his truck. The truck passed us and we followed it.

"What did you scare him with?"

"I said that I was from the Ministry of Public Health."

Mark paused and lit a cigarette. "Then I told him, confidentially, that Saddam Hussein had exploded an atomic device at Baneh, wiping out an entire Iranian infantry division. That was what you had in mind, wasn't it?"

"Something like that." I smiled *yes, Mark had figured it out.*

"Goddamn! " Slow Joe finally caught on to what was transpiring. "That ploy just might work!"

"I don't know." Mark hesitated.

"What? What is it?" Joe nudged him impatiently.

"Well, I told the captain that we, the international fact finding team, were, probably, contaminated with radioactive dust while in the field…Just to keep them away, you know."

"So?"

"The captain is going to make arrangements to decontaminate us."

"Swell," I said. "What do we do now?"

What could we do? Clearly, we should not accept the captain's provision. That would be equivalent to stepping into a lion's cage with a hungry lion inside. Yet if we'd turned down the decontamination procedure, our refusal could alert the captain. Gunning down the captain and his detachment in the truck in the plain view of continuing traffic would end our mission. Besides, where could we run?

"We 'decontaminate'" Joe smiled, and I knew why. To him our dangerous predicament became a game, a challenging game of wits, another twist in the deadly maze, this time called the Golden Camel. He did not invent the game, but he surely liked to play it. "We need a shower, don't we?"

The truck turned right; we did the same. A recently built dirt road brought us to a barbwired compound the size of a football field–from all things, an ammunition dump.

"You think we can get away with the fib?" I asked Joe; the sight of the barbed wire had added to my apprehension. "The captain can dial any number in Baneh and receive an answer."

"I've already checked into that. I told the captain that we have to call Tehran, and he said that they don't have a phone."

"Oh yeah? Look over there." In the descending darkness, we could discern a radio antenna on the roof of a small trailer.

"That could be a problem." Joe agreed.

As we passed the gates and entered the compound between the communications trailer on the right and a long barn-like structure *soldiers' billet* on the left, we faced two underground ammo depots. Three smaller structures past the billet on the left housed a kitchen, a shower compartment, and a well. A motor-powered electrical generator hummed behind these structures. We all parked between the trailer and the depots. Oh yes, there was one more structure at the far end of the facility, past the depots–an ever-present, my all-time favorite third world essential–an outhouse. I think I had developed an outhouse complex in Honduras, on my previous TRAG mission. I noticed that I paid more attention to outhouses than to national monuments. Half of the roof on this one was missing adding a weather factor to its utilization.

We disembarked and joined captain Taheri. Astonishingly enough, although the main reason why we were brought to the compound was the decontamination process, Captain Taheri did not insist upon our compliance with the procedure. He simply offered the shower facility and left it up to us whether to use it or not. More than that, he invited us all for dinner.

"I want to show you the real Iranian hospitality," he said, and I wondered what he meant by 'real'.

The second-in-command, a man with a bearded face and hairy arms *and hands, and neck, and, probably, the rest of his body*, invited us to join him inside the communications trailer doubled up as the officers' quarters. According to Mark, the man was a counterpart of the Iraqi Baath' political commissar, the unit's Islamic 'spiritual leader', a link to heaven, so to speak, although I preferred to call him the Missing Link.

Oddly, the outside lights, including the search beam, were turned on *in war time!?*

"You realize that this is a setup?" I whispered to Joe.

"Yes, I know. Mark is outside, to keep an eye on things."

Captain Taheri joined us. At the table, he requested a moment of silence in the memory of the fallen at Baneh.

"...*something*...of Mecca and the tomb of the Prophet, may God's peace and blessing be upon them." Taheri ended the brief eulogy, referring to the fallen in the manner as if they were alive.

All commenced chewing *tasty stone-oven baked flat bread and fried fresh water fish.*

"What is it? Always Friday in the Middle East?" I whispered to Kurt.

Taheri initiated a conversation.

"I have a friend who majored in Nuclear Engineering at the North Carolina State University in Raleigh," he said, mainly addressing me and looked at his watch.

"Oh?" I knew very little about NCSU besides its outstanding basketball team, the Wolfpack, shooting for the national championship.

"Yes, he was always afraid that someone would use the bomb sooner or later." Taheri continued addressing me, exclusively. Joe attempted to join the conversation, but Taheri simply ignored him, which, as they say in the intellectual circles, pissed Joe off.

Maybe, in a certain perverted way, I enjoyed Joe's predicament: he was the true commander, but could not declare it and had to remain on the sidelines. We played a card game, but Joe could not use his trumps. I, meanwhile, cheated.

"A nuclear bomb is not a plaything," I declared. "Look at Dr. Green *all looked at Joe*, he used to work at Los Alamos laboratories, which makes him one of the fathers of the bomb. But here he is— strongly against its use."

Of course, Joe was too young to be one of the fathers of the nuclear bomb, but what the heck! We played games, at least I did. I invented the game, so I could change its rules.

"You invented the nuclear bomb?" Taheri turned to Joe, and I smiled inside. *You wanted the ball, Joe? Here it is.*

"Yes, I did," firmly stated Joe.

Joe's confident declaration, totally incongruent with his baby face, seemed funny. I couldn't hold my smile. Charity giggled, Elmo chuckled, and in the avalanche fashion, all including Taheri and even the Missing Link who did not understand English, laughed.

Joe had not anticipated the effect of his serious statement on the audience. He was uncertain how to respond. Finally, he succumbed to the newly born, absurdly comic mood at the table and laughed himself. We played with fire, and, realizing that his claim on fame was a bit farfetched, Joe backed out of it.

"No, of course I did not invent the bomb. I wasn't even born then." *He gave me a dirty look.*

Now, when all attention had shifted from me to Joe, I could slip out and keep my scheduled appointment *greatly overdue* with the outhouse...and to make my generous contribution to its already sizeable collection of both ancient and modern artifacts. Then I returned to the table.

"Ps-s-st..." Kurt poked me in the rib gently and thrust a note in my hand.

I read the note stealthily. In Joe's handwriting, it said, "These guys came from Baneh! Keep smiling."

"Swell," I said aloud.

So, Captain Taheri and his entourage came from Baneh! The smart weasel had played along with our nuclear holocaust scheme from the beginning. He probably had already radioed for reinforcements. That's why he kept looking at his watch. We'd been had.

"We missed the train," said Mark. He was the one who, during my brief absence, brought Joe the disturbing news after talking to one of the guards outside.

What was it with us? Why did we have to rediscover Murphy's Law again and again? Why couldn't we just take a back road to Tehran instead of getting into a mess on every fucking hill? Perhaps, they didn't build peaceful roads anymore, and the search for one would be roughly equivalent to a dog's hopeless search for a blue hydrant. We were on the roads where another law applied, Joe Green's Law, a derivative of Murphy's Law: When you look for trouble, you'll find it.

A guard entered, looked us over, approached Taheri, and whispered a message into his ear. I caught a word 'farangi' *like a cunning race of aliens in Star Trek*–the Europeans, *us* in Farsi. Taheri nodded and smiled.

"Now." I think it was Joe who said it.

From that point on, events picked up speed. Keith who sat next to Taheri *both facing me* shrugged his shoulders, at least, that was what I thought he did. Taheri's facial expression changed from a smile to surprise. Keith, calmly, stood up, locked Taheri's head between his forearms, and, with a quick twisting motion, snapped the captain's neck.

"Crack!"–that was all–the sound my knee joint makes when I bend my leg.

Taheri's body slumped on the table, and now I could see a knife in his back. Both the guard and I, equally astonished by what had occurred, stared at the captain's lifeless body. Joe, meanwhile, tackled the Missing Link. The rest of the group, one by one, exited the trailer.

"Let's go." Mark pulled wide-eyed Elmo by the back of his pants.

"Take care of the guard," Keith dropped casually while exiting the trailer.

Scores of 'experts' on the subject of fighting, or, as they call it, hand-to-hand combat, attempt to analyze the process in terms of natural responses: when your adversary makes a certain move, you must apply a certain defensive countermove and, if successful, follow up with your own maneuver *strike or run*. It sounds easy, and, if you are a professional fighter with the blood temperature close to that of a snake, you may apply this technique with a reasonable chance of success. It doesn't usually work for the rest of us. Rational responses in hand-to-hand combat are a myth. Logic and continuity become hard to pin down, one's perception of reality is fragmentized, chunks of time are missing, temporary madness takes over…The memory of the combat becomes only a series of snapshots and short episodes.

I had not intended to hurt the guy unless I absolutely had to when we entered the introductory phase of the combat. This phase was no more than getting acquainted–a relatively lazy tug-of-war for the possession of his carbine *I forgot where I put mine*. Predictably so, he resisted my initially feeble, then reasonably coercive, and, finally, determinedly forceful, dispossession effort.

That phase was brief; we both realized that there was more at stake than his carbine. The guard took the initiative by kicking me in the shin, and I winced with pain. Since the contact scored below the belt, I called it a personal foul.

"S-s-so that's-s-s how you wanna play it?" I hissed and kicked him in the knee.

He issued a 'rebel yell' but did not let go of the carbine. Having scored in that manner, both the guard and I attempted to repeat our initial success using the same approach, but all kicks missed: we had learned from the experience. Clearly, new tactics had to be devised.

A brief lull in action, during which we just stared at each other and breathed heavily, offered us the opportunity to reexamine the options. I could not come up with any meaningful game plan, but the guard himself put all the trumps in my hands. I don't know whether he had a new plan, or simply decided to give the old tactics another chance, but he suddenly, with all his might, pulled the carbine *and me with it*. The inertia did the rest *well, I pushed a little bit, too*. His body slammed against the wall, and his eyes glassed. His cap fell on the floor, and his matted hair clung to his sweaty forehead.

I stared into his dark expressionless eyes. My God! Did I have to kill this man? Could I? I had killed before, back in Nicaragua, but that was altogether different game, a Shooting Gallery game, like in arcades. I could not see their faces, they were targets. But here, I stared into a man's face—no games, no targets—a human face. If I let him go, he was going to kill me...I pushed the carbine in his face, his temple caved in...

"Will you stop...*puff*...this tomfoolery and give me a hand!" I heard Joe's plea.

I don't know which 'bits and pieces' Joe retained in his memory, but, I'm sure, they were not pleasant ones. The Missing Link, being heavier and stronger than Joe, had pinned him to the table and was in the process of repossessing his knife. Suffice it to say that the knife, while both parties struggled for its control, was considerably closer to Joe's throat than to the Missing Link's.

I gathered the leftovers of my anger for the next task; Missing Link's body sagged.

"Thanks." Joe freed himself. "I owe you one. Let's get out of here."

"Shouldn't we destroy the radio station?" I found my AK and discarded the guard's carbine.

"It doesn't matter. I told Keith to light the fuse. When the dump blows, the whole shebang goes up with it."

We stepped outside. All was quiet. Two soldiers walked by, apparently oblivious of the trailer incident. Incredible as it may seem, Taheri had not informed his garrison of the threat that we might present. Perhaps, he did not consider us dangerous, or simply didn't wish to tip us off. I wasn't even sure whether he had radioed for reinforcements. It could be that we made a mistake, we mistook the captain's hospitality for a trap. Maybe we didn't have to kill the captain...and Missing Link...and the guard. My Lord, what had I done!

Warm breeze breathed from the south, the moon played peekaboo from behind a few thin clouds, the air itself whispered, "Pe-e-ace." What had happened inside the trailer was unreal, hideous, absurd.

"Look over there." Joe pointed in the direction of the gates. Headlights of two approaching vehicles flashed in the distance only to be masked by the last hill.

"The reinforcements," I said.

"Squeak...squeak...squeak..."

"What is this fucking creaking noise?" I asked.

"An old windmill behind the billet. Here..." Joe handed me several hand grenades. "When the lights go out, take the windows."

And the lights went out, only to be replaced with the lights from hell: neat pulsating muzzle flashes of AKs, messy white-fading-to-orange bursts of hand grenades, and sprouting fires. The sentry booth went up in flames, with the sentry in it, a truck blew up, the kitchen shack lit up inside like a Halloween pumpkin, then exploded...

I did not run, I sidestepped in front of the billet while delivering my deadly presents through the window glass.

"Down! Get down! " I heard Joe's screams. Hell, what did he know? I was just doing my job.

Windows exploded, one by one. I fell on the ground. The window next to me burst and breathed fire like an angry dragon...flying glass cut my hands, I smelled singed hair, my own hair. Screams from the inside of the burning building pierced my brain.

"Yeah! You feel the heat, you motherfuckers...Ha-ha!" I realized that it was crazy to laugh: those poor bastards were burning inside. But I couldn't help it.

A soldier ran out of the billet. His uniform smoldered. I stood up, pointed my AK at him, and pulled the trigger. The AK recoiled with a series of soft thumps. The soldier's head exploded.

Flashes and fires pushed the night deep into the hills. A sequence of secondary explosions inside the billet, mixed with human shrieks, the discord of shots out of sync with their own echoes from the nearby hills, a brief swish of a launched rocket, then a blast–all merged into a mad symphony of war, a symphony composed in hell. I ran toward the trailer.

"R-r-rip-p-p!" A spray of bullets hit the side of the trailer a split second after I fell on the ground next to Kurt and Chuck.

Two soldiers ran out of the burning billet; Kurt and Chuck squeezed off short bursts.

"Seven and seven, to hell or heaven," mumbo-jumboed Chuck.

Elmo serpentined toward us.

"I killed one! I killed one! Did you see that?" He announced jubilantly, as if exclaiming, "Look! Look! Daddy bought me a Tonka truck."

"Kids." Kurt smiled.

"Let's go!" someone shouted.

Kurt got up and ran toward the parking area, Chuck and Elmo followed. A jeep backed out in the open and sped in my direction, Joe feverishly twisting the wheel.

"Get in, let's go!" Mark stood up in the front seat and waved to me. Charity sat in the back.

I climbed over the side and dived into the back seat. A powerful blast in whatever was left of the billet added to my momentum, and I landed with my face in Charity's lap. Somewhat reluctantly *Charity's lap was comfortable*, I sat up.

"Are you all right?" Charity turned her head, and her large, deepseated eyes reflected a miniature orange ball of another explosion. Suddenly, I could not take my eyes off her beautiful face. Straight blond hair, now in casual disarray, high vertical forehead, delicately curved and slightly pug nose, full lips, and long neck–features ordinary in their individuality and exquisite in the composite– belonged to the girl sitting next to me on the back seat of a speeding jeep, in the midst of continuing fiery destruction and death. A flash of another explosion alchemized Charity's hair into a gold mane. I turned only to witness a dying fireball rising into the black sky and a luxurious silver sparkfall cascading down and fizzling out into nothingness before reaching the ground.

"It is so beautiful," she whispered.

We crashed through the leftovers of the gates and turned right on the road around the compound and away from the approaching convoy carrying the reinforcements. Greased Lightning finally caught up with us. We passed the creaking pinwheel of the burning windmill. Charity raised her eyes toward the spinning circle of flame and smiled serenely, and I suddenly knew why Joe loved this girl. Not only was she the girl of his dreams, she was the girl in his dreams; he had told me about her.

We sped through the night. Suddenly behind us, an unbelievably bright, quasar-blue flash transformed the night into a day. A shock wave had almost pushed my insides through my spine and nearly split my head open. The ammunition dump blew up!

"Damn!" Joe commented.

Another blast, almost as powerful as the first one, shook the hills. I stared at the blazing inferno behind us, a violent hodge-podge of exploding bombs, rockets, and ordnance *a few even up in the air*, and bursting napalm containers—a mish-mash of fiery dandelions and flashes accompanied by an eery roar.

"How beautiful it is!" Charity exclaimed, sitting next to me.

Greased Lightning had its own inferno enthusiast, Elmo, who excitedly jumped up and down in the back seat and, at times, was dangerously close to falling out of the jeep.

We left the road and crossed a valley in an attempt to reach the highway. The sky on our left, behind the hill, flared up from time to time, and each flare initiated a cacophonous discord of whispers, and moans, and screams, and hisses, and whistles, and booms of burning, rocketing, and exploding ordnance. This hellish ruckus attested to the fact that the activity in Dante's estate was far from over.

Joe turned to me and began, "Concerning the dwarf..."

"Screw the dwarf!" I interrupted. I did not want to hear any explanation or excuse why Joe killed the dwarf—it was no longer relevant. The whole Kurdish episode seemed trivial in comparison with the ammo depot events. Here, we killed. I killed... How many did I kill in the billet? Ten? Fifteen? Twenty? After that, who cared about the dwarf?!! So what, therefore, was the point of discussing him?

"Screw the dwarf," I repeated.

Joe seemed puzzled by the sudden reversal in my attitude toward the dwarf's death and, for a minute, was silent. Finally, as if answering his own thoughts, he said, "Shocking events alter one's moral values." He paused. "Don't they, Jim?"

"Not exactly." I wasn't ready to grant him credit for his

penetrating analysis. "Shocking events only overshadow one's moral values, and even then only temporarily."

That was a lie. I did not want to admit the truth even to myself. Intuitively, I knew that the change in my attitude towards the dwarf, more accurately, towards his death, was permanent. Joe was right, events, significant in magnitude, altered the related moral values. I was no longer outraged by the dwarf's killing, I was only saddened. But did it mean that other events, big enough in magnitude, could make my own death to me less significant? Did it mean that the value of life itself was relative? Relative to events? Relative to causes?

WHOM GODS PROTECT

The crack of dawn barely outlined the jagged profile of the mountains far in the east, when we finally crossed the bridge to Zanjan. The traffic on the road to Zanjan was light at this early hour. We had encountered no road blocks, or check points, or anything out of the ordinary. Flashes of explosions on the horizon behind us *the ammo depot still burned* did not alarm anyone here–things of this nature are expected during the war.

I was tired, but I couldn't sleep. My fogged consciousness floated suspended somewhere between the inside of this little kettle called a jeep and the thirty miles back where I had burned my ticket to heaven. In my mind, I was doing a hand grenade electric boogaloo dance in front of the barrack. The barrack windows breathed fire, I could feel the heat, the soldier's head exploded in a million pieces, the guard's face caved in as if it had no bone structure. Reality merged with fantasy and current events mixed with recent memories.

"Mark, you take the wheel," Joe spoke. The brakes squeaked, and the jeep stopped.

"Wake up, Jim." Joe turned to me. "Fill her up, we are almost out of gas.

"Okay." I crabbed out of the jeep and unsnapped a canister attached to her side. Then I did exactly what I was supposed to do– fill up the tank.

"What in hell are you doing, Jim!?" Joe's exclamation whisked me out of my refueling process confusion. "Don't you see? There is no gas in that canister, it has a bullet hole in it."

So, I was pouring imaginary gas. Damn! What was the matter with me? What in hell was I doing? Couldn't I see that there was no gas in the canister? The fucking thing indeed had a bullet hole in it.

"I thought there was a little gas left on the bottom." I tried to sell Joe a face-saving explanation for my 'funny' actions and salvage a few chunks of my shattered, supposedly stable image.

"Okay, use the other canister." Joe bought my fib. "Then get some rest, will you."

I had to pull myself out of the murky cloudland of my tired imagination and take new bearings on real things before I was convinced that I was firmly standing back in the real world. We started moving again.

Greased Lightning has changed her driver, too; Elmo took the helm. Maybe it was a mistake to allow Elmo to take the wheel this time, because he, like all kids, wanted to be the center of attention, and, out of the blue, initiated a horseplay. Greased Lightning suddenly overtook Kitten, and Elmo snooked at us thumbing his nose and fluttering his fingers, "Beatcha!" Passing through the hell-barrage, being taken prisoner by the Kurds, witnessing a gruesome execution of the Iranian soldier, and killing for the first time—all these world image shattering events—had not changed him a bit. He still remained a kid; he wanted to play.

"Quit it, Elmo! Get back there, now!" hollered Joe, and, turning to me, added, "Goddam kid will get us in trouble."

Fork-tailed swallows with swept back, pointed wings darted effortlessly from side to side above us in the newly-born, pale baby-pink sky, when we made a turn to find a place for camp and rest until dark.

I still couldn't fall asleep, even on the soft, comfortable sand. I blamed my insomnia on the brightness of the surrounding dunes and refused to admit to myself that the real reason why I couldn't sleep was my anxiety. This 'picnic' by the river could be our last stop on the road to the vanishing point. Eight could not fight the fortified fifty and win. And now, when my curtains were about to fall, I had lost my pass to heaven. It was gone, finito, kaput. When I incinerated those soldiers in the barrack, I had burned my ticket with them...If I had to face the Lord, I could claim that I didn't have any other choice but to do what I did, that I was a victim of circumstances. Defending my position, I could also point out that those soldiers were going to die anyway three minutes later in the dump explosion, which, incidentally, was not set off by me. But would it wash? I didn't think so.

"Hell, it's too late to change anything anyway." I said to myself aloud.

For whatever reasons, no one else slept either; they didn't even give it a try. I joined Joe and Charity, and we formed our usual trivalent modicum, our troika.

"Care for some tea?" Charity offered. Actually, she did not offer but asked, because the only place where I could get the tea was by the campfire where a tin kettle swung suspended over the flames. Charity always was the center of our group; one way or another, everything revolved around her. Of course, she was aware of her special status, and

I don't think it pleased her, because she wanted to be just one of the guys, but not being able to change what was natural, she finally accepted it. If she needed a refill of tea, I readily volunteered to take her cup and fetch her more tea. When she talked, Joe and I watched her full lips move, her slender hand float in a gesture, and soaked in her every word.

What held Joe and Charity together? I don't know. Maybe, the trade itself. Their union was built on the base of mutual understanding and support, and, at the same time, curiously so, on the component of friendly competition and showing off.

Charity sat across from Joe and me, and here, on the sand, in the shadow of the jeep, clad in the drab-green garb, she did not project the image of an angel, even with her angelic face. She was a woman, a beautiful woman, beautiful and sexy and desirable. When she turned, I could intercept Joe's sliding glance on her attractive posterior, and I couldn't help but wonder how he could allow a woman like that to join the suicide squad, to go on this crazy mission, and probably die tonight. How could he sacrifice her? But she knew the score and she still volunteered. Why? Maybe it was she *could she be?* who was taking us to the valley of her shadow, if she was Miss Death.

She pouted and conveyed, "I wish I could have a cone of icecream."

"Cherry vanilla?" I asked, glancing at Joe.

"No, strawberry."

"In Raleigh," Joe and I said at the same time. I guess we both remembered a similar conversation, which took place at the Contra camp, back in Honduras. We smiled.

"Up-p...ch-o-o!" spelled out Mark, this time not attempting to suppress his sneeze and not making a mess. "I think I'm getting a cold and a sore throat."

The sun baked the bright blinding sand around us. Mark and Elmo sat under a short, twisty, almost leafless tree, which hardly supplied any shade.

"A perfect cure for a sore throat: cut it," 'Alfred-Hitchcocked' Elmo. *That's Joe's specialty, I wanted to say.*

"You're a pretty mixed-up kid, Elmo. By the way, do you know what day it is today?"

"I have no idea. Monday?"

"Wednesday. It's Wednesday, my dear boy. During the Inquisition times, they used to burn witches at the stake on Wednesdays. Did you know that? That's why they call it Ash Wednesday." Mark bullshitted.

"Really?!!" Elmo's eyes opened widely.

"Yeah, and the first guy that they burned, his name was Elmo, Elmo-the-Kid."

Thus, mutually annihilating each other in mock scenarios, the two, both satisfied with the outcome of the friendly feud, settled down and stretched under the shadow-imitating tree.

"I have to call my mom," Charity said *it seemed so strange to hear the word 'mom' in the place like this, so far away from where all our moms lived*, "and tell her about…you know what."

That 'you know what' was the unmistakable sign that Charity and Joe wanted to exclude me from their conversation. I got the message and made myself scarce. I joined Kurt who sat by the little campfire *and boiled water for Charity's tea*. Chuck lay on the other side.

"Po-o-oh!" Chuck farted.

Both Kurt and I glanced in his direction, but made no comments.

"I see they eased you out," Kurt noted.

"No, that's not it." I covered up. "I wanted to walk down to the river and see the local bird population. That's where those swallows get the mud to build their nests. Care to accompany me?"

"I would not advise it." Keith who was out to 'recce the terrain' joined us by the campfire. "Women from the village on the other side are washing linen in the river. They might spot you."

"Po-o-o…o-o-oh! " came from Chuck's side.

"Will you stop that!" Kurt apparently had enough. He had sat next to Chuck in the back seat of Greased Lightning all night and, I suspected, could relate horror stories about his chokedump ordeal.

"Sorry, must be something I ate at the Viet village." Chuck apologized.

"I found flowers," Keith produced a scrawny bouquet, "desert daisies."

"For me!??" I faked a pleasant surprise.

"No." Keith blushed. "For Charity."

"Forget it, man," Kurt interjected. "It ain't gonna work. I've tried."

"Wait, chaps. I am not making a pass. I just thought she might like them."

"Yea, why not?" I sided with Keith. "She is a woman, ain't she? Go'n'get her, tiger!"

"You'd better do it." Keith turned to me. "I am not very good at it. You do it."

"Hey, wait a minute!" Kurt was ready to contest my commission in the flowers delivery, but, suddenly, for no apparent reason, changed his mind, "No, that's fine."

Perhaps he realized that his attempt to bring Charity flowers could be misinterpreted as another pass. As far as I was concerned, however, I didn't mind upstaging Joe in the gallant matters. After all, I had upstaged him in the military, twice already.

"By George, I'll do it," I said leaving the less fortunate.

"Po-o-o-o-oh!" came from the campfire site.

I wished we could stay here longer. The sun, the sand, the swallows, and the light breeze from the river—all were the components of a peaceful outing that had nothing to do with war. But we didn't come here to have a picnic. we had to go.

The main highway to Tehran had little traffic. In the descending darkness, we left the main highway before reaching Tehran. I drove.

"Kill the headlights," suggested Joe.

The cold hand of fear touched my heart. Yes, we were on the final leg of our journey. The moment of reckoning was near.

"The damn moon is too bright," Joe complained. "I wish there were more clouds."

"At least I can see where I'm going," I disagreed. I worried about the oil pipeline lying ahead. What if it simply rested on the ground, neither buried nor elevated? Could I negotiate it? Make the jeep jump over it? My worries were justified: the pipeline lay flat on the ground like an endless snake slithering its way between the hills and over them.

"I planned to dynamite the thing, as a diversion," Joe disclosed, "but decided against it: what if we delay, and it blows before we reach the target?"

"Yes," I echoed absentmindedly, not reacting to the irrelevancy of Joe's statement: in order to collect on such diversion, one had to be on the other side of the pipeline. I searched for a ravine where we could pass under the darn snake.

"Good show!" came from Greased Lightning, when I finally succeeded.

"Bear right," Joe said. "I'd prefer to stay clear of the mid-road roadblock."

We reached the road to the little fortress sooner than I expected.

"Kill the engines." It became awfully quiet, too quiet: no wind, no traffic, and no lights—just the silent moon hung dispassionately, observing the sand dunes and the two vehicles resting in an awkward position, facing across the road as if trying to make up their mind whether to go to the fortress and probably never come back, or get the hell out of the sandy trap.

My thoughts scrambled. How could one express the gloomy awareness that some of us, maybe all of us, were going to die? One simply can't, words become an insufficient means to convey one's feelings. Time stops. The 'before' comes to a screeching halt together with time, the 'now' hangs in the air of uncertainty, and the 'after' becomes irrelevant: one must first pass the 'now' to reach the 'after', hoping that the 'now' is not going to be the end.

"Too late; they've spotted us." Joe turned to Charity. "Implement plan A."

I was not aware of plan A. Charity and Joe leaped out of the jeep, and Keith joined them on the ground. I observed with utter amazement while Charity unbuttoned her shirt and pulled it off. The bra followed. With her breasts bared, Charity stood in the moonlight like Selena, the moon goddess herself.

"Wow!" Mark gasped.

The rat patrol was coming from the left, from the mid-road roadblock.

"Sit tight." I think it was Joe who said that. I sat in the trance-like state watching Charity. I didn't care where and for what purpose Joe and Keith obtained empty beer cans first, *I thought those were concussion hand grenades*. Perhaps they attempted to sell the idea of a drunken party to the Iranians.

Then things happened fast. The rat patrol whirled around and stopped by Charity, both occupants of the jeep gawked at her ample bare breasts; Joe and Keith produced pistols, pressed beer cans against the muzzle, and shot the Iranians. Tong! Tong! And the show was over.

"A souvenir for you." Joe tossed me the double-spent beer can, a makeshift sound suppressor.

The little drama was over, just like that. Tong! Tong! The end. No attempt to take cover, or conceal the weapons, no warning, and no screams—just simple everyday straightforward, almost casual, killings.

Charity dressed…and the moon hung motionless. I stared at the bodies in the jeep. Its large caliber machine gun pointed at the sky as if preparing to shoot down the moon.

"Well, let's go, we don't want to be late." Joe leaped in the back seat.

"Yea, let's not be late for the circus show." I heard Chuck say.

Yes, we didn't want to be late for the show, the big show, which was yet to come. And more than ever I wished to be somewhere else, preferably in North Carolina, instead of facing the little fortress. Maybe to Chuck it was only a circus show, but to me, the reality of the battle just about to unfold, seemed utterly terrifying.

We turned right, away from the mid-road roadblock, and headed toward the 'little fortress'. It grew menacingly larger as we approached it, its walls seemed formidable, and its gates as solid as steel. We neared the gate roadblock, a crossbar, and stopped.

"Well, here we go..." said Joe.

And we let the rat out from under the hat. I watched the trace of the outgoing rocket, a pernicious projectile aimed at the guard tower. In a moment, the tower dissolved into a bright fireball. Meanwhile, Charity, armed with her charms and an AK, took care of both sentries at the gate roadblock. Another rocket burned the gates. Then Greased Lightning splintered the horizontal beam of the no longer manned roadblock and, picking up speed, crashed through the still burning leftovers of the gates.

"Let's go!"

Things happened with incredible swiftness. The radio shack on the left, hit by Mark's rocket, split open and burned. Its antenna hesitated for a moment, as if trying to make up its mind whether to remain standing or fall, then it bent, broke in half, and crashed to the ground. The windows of the barracks on the right burst and breathed flames and smoke, just like those of the ammo depot barracks.

Joe, Charity, and I ran straight toward the main building. Joe sprayed the door with bullets, then flung it open, and both he and Charity pranced inside. With a swing–more like a mindless robot motion than a planned intelligent move–I tossed two grenades, one after the other, up on the flat rooftop of the building hoping to take out the sentries. The body of one, with a heavy thump, hit the ground next to me and splashed the dust. A bullet grazed the wall in front of me and ricocheted. I don't know why I ran my fingers over the fresh dent: maybe to find out whether it was warm. It was not.

"Get the hell...*swish-bang!*..." Mark joined me, his primary task of silencing the radio station had been completed successfully.

"What?!" In the hubbub around us, I couldn't make out what he said.

He pulled me behind the half-track, "Are you crazy? Those bastards...*Bang! Kaboom!*...Take cover!"

Soldiers, some in underwear, spilled out of the barracks' windows and the gaping, doorless doorway. One emitted a piercing shrill, and ran toward the garage. His boots smoked. He reached the corner of the barrack and attempted to seek shelter behind the overturned wire-mesh trash basket, a marginal safety, to say the least. I pulled the trigger, and he slumped over.

I felt uncomfortable lying at the corner of the main building: the broken up ground crunched under my elbows; they kept sliding into little potholes with sharp edges and hurt, making it hard to aim. I heard a stifled groan and turned. Mark's face rested on the ground and he breathed the dust. The side of his neck was open, the blood gushed.

"Looks bad." Kurt joined us.

"Yeah, it seems...I've missed the fucking train..." Mark coughed. Blood mixed with foamy saliva spilled over the corner of his mouth.

A bullet hit the wall above us and whined ricocheting toward the Holy Shrine.

"It's those bastards by the garage." Kurt armed a pineapple hand grenade borrowed from a dead Iranian soldier and tossed it.

"Take cover!" The grenade exploded, sparks blossomed, but, in the mixture of dust and smoke, I couldn't see how much damage it caused.

On the right, by the armory, Keith and Chuck, two cold killing machines, processed the raw material, human flesh—a small pile of bodies obstructed the barrack's doorway, a slaughterhouse entrance. Apparently Chuck forgot that he attended a circus show.

Stages of death...anger, denial, bargaining, depression, and acceptance? They did not exist. There was only agony.

Then the carousel of death picked up speed. I aimed at the barracks windows; the windows shot back at me. Like two-inch hail, bullets hit the wall and the windows above, shattered glass fell and cut my hands.

"You motherfuckers!" I heard suddenly. Elmo, wearing a bandanna, which probably signified that he was ready for action, charged toward the barracks in the open.

"Down! Down, Elmo!" Keith screamed.

Elmo stopped and, with a wide swing, tossed a hand grenade into one of the windows of the barracks. He didn't live long enough to see the results of his truly heroic *and damn foolish!* deed. The results were devastating: a secondary explosion inside the barracks sent burning debris and the body of one Iranian through the windows.

"Awesome!" Charity's voice distracted me. She and Joe stood by the wall.

"Get down!" I shouted. They looked at me surprised, as if I had said something silly, then crouched next to me. Joe glanced around: where was the picnic spread?

"What are you trying to prove!?" I screamed. "That you can die?"

"No, nothing..." Joe paused and squeezed off a shot. "Nothing like that."

I was dumfounded, not by what Joe said, but by what he did while pausing in the middle of the sentence: he shot a running Iranian sideways. He did not aim and hardly even glanced at the running target. That shot was the most coldblooded, casual killing I have ever witnessed.

"The bastard is not here," Joe announced. "But the gold is. Would you like to have a look?"

Yes, sure, right in the middle of the battle: important things first.

And then something happened, something that I am hesitant to relate even now–it was too unreal. But it happened, I know it did.

Charity stayed behind. Joe and me walked toward the main building and the burning half-track. Joe walked in front of me about ten yards ahead. That's when it happened. A hand grenade landed right behind Joe.

"Look out!" I screamed, falling on the ground.

The fiery flash and Joe's silhouette blended with a vision, a vision of an incredibly beautiful woman standing in the middle of the explosion. What the hell!? I thought, totally astounded by the vision. She stood in the heart of the blast as if protecting Joe from its lethal effects, to which she seemed impervious. She protected Joe with her body. I noticed that, for a moment, I couldn't see Joe. I could see the burning half-track on the other side of the blast, but not Joe, as if, for a second, he wasn't there at all, as if the woman had created a time lag within the explosion, and, for a second, Joe lived in another time, another dimension. Joe fell on the ground, but somehow I knew that he wasn't harmed.

I spotted the soldier who tossed the grenade and discharged a sequence of shots in his direction. The soldier leaned heavily against the wall of the main building and slowly slid down leaving on the wall an uneven blood smudge. Then I approached Joe.

"Did you see her?!" I asked.

"See whom?" He should not be able to hear anything after being so close to the explosion, but he heard me.

"The woman who saved your life."

He was silent. He either did not want to talk about her, or simply didn't know. Finally, as if probing in the dark, he asked cautiously, without looking at me, "A beautiful blonde?"

"Yes! Yes, the blonde!" So, he did see her!

"I see her in my dreams." He paused evaluating what he had said impromptu, then added, "No one saved my life, I was just lucky."

And I never dared to ask any more questions although I had a myriad of those. Why did she save Joe's life? And how? Where did she come from and where did she go? But, mainly, who was she? Joe's guardian angel? Or Miss Death who, following some unknown design, postponed his demise until later? From all I knew about Joe, death continually followed him, staying just one step behind and making him the main cause of terminal events. Could Joe be the instrument of death?

Joe simply continued walking. We entered the building.

Flat pine boxes with a pressed-in, snakelike Farsi treasury stamp on the side were stacked neatly by the wall, not in the middle of the room, where I had expected to find them.

"Care to lift one?" Joe grinned.

I picked up a box, it was heavy, about eighty pounds, "We can't remove the whole thing."

"Yes, I know, we'll take sixteen. I am sure Ayatollah won't mind sharing."

Leaving the main building, I suddenly realized how quiet it became outside: no more explosions, or shots, or screams—only the fire rustle. I glanced in the direction of the barracks, but no one stared from the windows, I scanned the roof edge of the main building, but no one peeked over: my hand grenade silenced the sentries. Kurt examined the results of his own foray by the garage. Keith and Chuck stood motionless by the armory, cautiously observing the barracks, which now really started catching on fire. I glanced at my companions. Their sweaty, dust-covered faces were ghost faces, as if we ourselves had died and rose from the grave.

We stood in the middle of a spellbinding panorama of burning buildings and vehicles all painted sienna, almost orange, in the eerie glow of hell fires.

Suddenly, Chuck screamed, and his AK came to life. Keith collapsed on the ground.

"Seven and seven! To hell or heaven!"

I stood stunned. Was it for real?! Chuck started walking toward us.

"Hit the dirt!" Joe hollered, and I fell in the dust. I couldn't see, I didn't want to see what happened. I was terrified. I heard shots, but I didn't move, I couldn't. A century passed. I was dead in the sand, but they couldn't find my body. There was no hell or heaven, there was no wait station–just sand, endless sand.

"It's okay, Jim." Charity kneeled next to me. "It's okay."

"Did it happen?" I asked.

"Yes, it did." She lowered her head and cried.

"And Joe too?"

"No, he is all right."

"It could have been my best operation." I heard Joe screaming. "But this piece of shit had to mess it up."

I stood up. Kurt approached. The absurdity of what had occurred was very hard to comprehend. Remus, the son of Mars, was slain by his twin brother Romulus. Joe finally calmed down. He seemed to be upset more by his stained record than by the loss of our comrades.

"We'll load the gold after the mop-up." He passed and dropped coldly, without looking at me, "We have two minutes...no survivors."

What did he say? The mop-up? What was that? Oh, yeah, killing the wounded. I think Joe practiced it in the past, in the mountains of Guatemala. Johnny told me about it. The guys from the mountains of Guatemala! Now I was...we were the guys from the dunes of Intiab.

Like a robot, I changed the clip, "I'll start from the barrack."

"Yea." He nodded and walked toward the radio shack.

A wounded Iranian, with his right arm mangled and lifeless, stared at the muzzle of my AK. I pulled the trigger.

"This is for Mark." I said.

His buddy, with a shattered knee, attempted to reach for his rifle.

"And this is for Keith." The man's head exploded from the other side, and the globs of his brain fell in the dust.

The next body moved.

"And this is for Elmo."

Another wounded squiggled by the wall. I approached.

"And this is for Karl Steiner." The body contracted in a spasm and then relaxed. The Iranian was barefoot, he died with his boots off.

I walked from one body to another maneuvering between these man-made obstacles like a hunter in the maze—the maze of death—trying to detect a sign of life still ebbing, pulsing, and when I found one, I extinguished it. The Holy Shrine observed my actions silently.

I passed Chuck's body. In anger, Joe emptied the whole clip into it. Chuck's belly resembled a bowl of noodles in tomato sauce spiked with mustard. The nauseating smell of gut spew and spilled blood followed me as I walked slowly on the playground of death.

Joe and I met in the middle of the court. We didn't say anything to each other, just exchanged glances. Charity and Kurt observed us silently and dispassionately, as if waiting patiently, wondering when in hell our boring task would be completed so that we could proceed with the more important matters. And the moon waited patiently, too.

We loaded the gold on the surviving half-track very conveniently parked by the entrance to the main building. I touched the allah form—four-crescents-and-a-sword—painted on its side.

"Well, that's it." Joe scanned the scene of unbelievable carnage. The second half-track was in flames; Greased Lightning steamed abandoned by the entrance. Two structures burned, and the Holy Shrine leaned against the main building, as if stunned by what had transpired in the compound. "Let's get the hell out of here."

I took the wheel. The engine roared, and we, trampling bodies and leaving behind a thick billowing smoke and dust trail, sped out of the compound. The little fortress was assailed, conquered, and, at least partially, destroyed. Its garrison was totally annihilated.

"Leave the road, turn right," Joe ordered. "No lights."

We left the little fortress not a minute too early: a convoy of vehicles from Tehran was speeding toward it.

"Are you going to tell us now where we are going?" I turned to Joe.

"Of course." He smiled. "When we reach the road to Qom, turn left."

"Left!?" I gasped. "Left is to Tehran."

"Oh, yea, did I forget to mention? That's where we are going. But hurry, we don't have the whole night."

"Are we freeing the corporate hostages too?"

"No, not this time. We'll let Perot worry about them."

The image of the inner yard of the little fortress etched on my mind. My God! We did all that? I did it? I searched for the signs of remorse inside me, but could find none, could find nothing but a hollow void, emptiness, as if my soul were no longer in my body. I felt no pity, no sorrow, no guilt, and no fear. What had happened to me?

VICTORY ROLL?

We rode in silence. Joe merely dropped, "To Mehrabad Airfield", and silence prevailed again. Apparently no one wished to talk. Joe stared at the road ahead as if hypnotized by it; even when he muttered 'To Mehrabad Airfield', he didn't glance at me or anyone else; he simply made a statement: that was our next destination. Here and now, everything had to be taken one step at a time, like in the mine field, and the next move could be made only after the previous move had been accomplished successfully.

Charity bent over so that her face touched her knees, and her hair cascaded to the floor like a golden waterfall. I couldn't see whether she rested, or cried, or simply wanted to be alone with her thoughts. Kurt reclined in his seat and gazed at the skies as if he prayed. And I, with my hands on the wheel, my eyes on the road, but my mind back at the little fortress, rode stunned and numb inside. It wasn't the loss of Mark, and Keith, and Elmo, and Chuck, that shook me up. Something else bewildered me. After participating in the hideous act of killing the wounded, I expected to find myself to be overwhelmed by emotions of guilt and sorrow. But instead, just like in Nicaragua, I experienced a sort of satisfaction, a comfortable feeling, like going home after an exhausting work day. Tired and empty.

We crossed railroad tracks and passed the soundly sleeping town of Rayy uneventfully. Contrary to all expectations, no one chased us, or attempted to set up a road block, or even gave a damn. We did not encounter a single person in the street or traffic on the road. Unobstructed, we entered the suburbs of Tehran–a maze of broken up streets, shabby structures, dun buildings, acrid smell, vacant lots, and dogs scavenging in refuse and startled by our headlights *I had turned them on.* I whistled, and one dog responded with a flaunting howl!

After passing the Bazaar and the city park, we entered a diagonal street.

"At the star-intersection, go straight," Joe said, finally breaking the silence.

The street merged into a wide, tree-lined, well-lit boulevard. All were silent. I wondered if we could ever talk about what happened at the little fortress.

We followed the boulevard until it, suddenly, broke out into the open square unbelievably vast and empty, except for a gigantic all-dominating monument, a Sassanian arch, a gateway tower.

"A pantheon to the Islamic revolution," Joe said. "Go around it."

"What?"

"Circle it."

"A victory roll." Kurt emerged from his trance-like state of grace and smiled.

"You got it." Joe nodded.

And, suddenly, something happened, something strange, almost absurd. I have seen such a quick mood reversal in our group only once, at the hotel in Baghdad, when Joe returned after his mysterious rendezvous with Saddam Hussein. Then, it swept me too.

"A victory roll?!" Charity lifted her head and laughed.

"Yes, why not?! Go, Baby!" Kurt stood up and manned the Browning machine gun mounted on the half-track.

It was crazy! and exciting! and elating! and daring! and reckless! Why in hell we were doing this, instead of speeding to the airport without delay, every minute counted? But here we were, circling the tower as if it were the center of the universe.

Charity laughed and jumped in her seat; Kurt aimed the machine gun at the arch, 'Go! Go!'; Joe pushed my shoulders, 'Faster! Faster!'; and I, laughing myself, twisted the wheel left and right, and around. That was our victory roll! We had defeated the fortified fifty, we had won! We beat the 'before', we smashed the 'now', and we conquered the 'after'.

Our excitement subsided only after we reached the airfield. We approached the airport from the back, cutting across a small grassy field. The wire fence section by the general aviation ramp seemed breachable.

"Well." Joe took one deep breath. "One more task."

"Duck." The wire mesh tore easily.

The airfield lay quiet, the usual hiss-and-whistle of commercial airline jet engines was absent, probably due to the war conditions. We parked the half-track behind a hangar and, forming a line, rounded the next corner. Two rows of parked airplanes presented us with an ample choice of transportation.

"That turboprop Cessna in the second tie-up looks good," Kurt remarked.

"Yea, you fly her. I've never piloted a turboprop," Joe admitted.

"Only if we can get the keys and charts."

"Shall we?" Joe turned to Charity.

Charity handed me her AK, then unbuttoned her shirt and loosened up her hair. I understood that she was going to repeat her mid-roadblock performance.

"Good luck," I said.

Charity entered the office building casually as if she owned it, and Joe followed her ten seconds later. I listened fearing to hear shots from the inside of the building. But after a few minutes, which seemed like eternity, Joe re-appeared at the door and motioned Kurt and me to enter.

We passed a dead sentry by the wall. His arms were spread haphazardly, rag-doll-like. He crouched sideways peering at us upside down and smiling mischievously as if saying 'See how much fun I'm having? You wanna play more?' His throat was cut from ear to ear, Joe's unmistakable mark, and the dark puddle on the floor still accumulated blood. Joe bent over the sentry's body and calmly, with no hurry at all, wiped the blade of his knife onto the sentry's shirt, one side at a time. He then tilted the blade in the light, examining whether it was clean of the blood stains, and finally all done, satisfied, shoved it into his ankle sheath. That gesture closed the final chapter of the sentry's life, permanently.

We proceeded down the hall, and through the sliding glass partition I discerned the interior of the flight office. Charity was already inside *her shirt was buttoned up again*. The muzzle of her M-16 borrowed from the dead sentry in the hall touched the flight attendants chest. The attendants' arms, raised high in the air, were trembling.

The scene, in a strange way, was magnificent. I wished that I could film it. Charity's long straight blond hair fell casually over her shoulder, her nostrils moved in excitement, her large blue eyes, with a touch of squint and cold steel, studied the attendant's face. A thin straight line of her tightly closed mouth convincingly suggested that the line between life and death for the attendant was very thin indeed. How would I name this scene? Beauty and the Beast? No, that didn't fit. The Goddess of War! That's what she looked like, that's what she was, the Goddess of War!

We entered the office, and Joe stopped by the string of keys on the wall.

"What was the Cessna's id?" he asked Kurt.

"I think Lima-Delta-two-five-zero-niner."

"Yea, that's it. Get the keys and charts." He turned to the attendant. "Is she fuelled up?"

The attendant answered in Farsi, apparently he did not understand English.

"Since he does not speak English, he is of no use to us. Shoot him," Joe ordered.

The bluff worked.

"Yes, yes…it is full of fuel, Mister."

The attendant had miraculously acquired knowledge of the English language. But this revelation did not save his life. What followed was predictable, although it still took me by surprise, so fast it happened. The whole process came to pass within three seconds, from the goddamn beginning to the fucking end. Joe stepped forward *one second*, spun the attendant sitting in the swivel chair *another second*, and slashed his throat *one more second, maybe even faster*. The attendant went to the floor, gargling while falling. One, two, three.. his hands clutched his throat…four, five, six…he attempted to get up…seven, eight, nine…his stare became fixed…ten…he collapsed. He was dead in ten seconds, no final agony, no twitching, nothing at all.

We exited the office, and Joe replayed the cleaning blade routine using the dead sentry's sleeve this time.

"I'll bring the half-track," I said.

Loading the plane's cargo bay with our precious aurous booty proceeded uneventfully. We shoved in the crates, one by one, when…

"…aza kavir ezbollah! Es ist?" came from the dark, which probably translated to the international 'Who in the fuck are you, and what in hell are you doing here?'

"Hit the deck!" hollered Joe and sprayed the darkness with a series from his AK. The darkness responded with screams of pain and a muzzle flash of its own. Someone's hand grenade burst nearby, and the Piper parked next to our Cessna went up in flames.

I returned the fire, and the muzzle flash died, "…and this is…for Chuck." I couldn't blame Chuck; in his condition, he didn't know what he was doing. He was a victim himself, a casualty of war, of the faraway war in Vietnam, which had never ended for him.

Kurt lifted the next crate. A tracer hit its side and disintegrated in a bright pink flare. The split board revealed the contents of the crate: a row of gold bars shone red and orange, reflecting the fire of the burning Piper.

"Start the engines! Let's get the hell out of here." Joe appeared from behind the tail of our Cessna. He pulled the chocks from under the airplane's wheels.

Charity was already inside the plane. Kurt followed her. For a moment, he slumped as if trying to catch his breath.

"Can you fly her?" Joe questioned.

"Yeah...I think so." Kurt straightened up and climbed inside the cabin. Joe and I followed.

Engines whistled gently, sneezed, and finally started.

"Add pitch..." Kurt said to himself and coughed.

The plane began taxiing smoothly. Joe feverishly latched the door, then he positioned himself in the co-pilot seat. Sirens filled the air, I could hear them even over the roar of the airplane's engines. Utility trucks and security jeeps hurriedly crossed the field from all directions. One jeep almost clipped the Cessna's wing speeding by us on the way to the burning Piper. A flair, then another one, shot up high in the sky, blinding the moon. Mehrabad Airfield sunk into total confusion.

"Take the unlit runway," suggested Joe.

The airplane accelerated smoothly. Tracers crossed in front of us, then a rocket streaked by, awfully close to the wing, and fireballed one hundred yards ahead. The fuselage rattled and debris fell in my lap.

"Anyone hit?" Joe inquired.

"I don't think so," Charity responded.

The air stream whistled through several bullet holes in the side of the plane.

"Hang in there!" Kurt slowly pulled on the controls, the Cessna's nose lifted, and the airplane gently separated from the runway. We were in the air!

"Hug the terrain," advised Joe. "We must slip under their radar."

Two tracer strings passed us on the sides and died in the sky.

"It's beautiful!" exclaimed Charity.

I turned to her, and we embraced and kissed, again and again. We made it! We accomplished the impossible, we beat the odds. And the gold we carried was our prize.

The plane wallowed.

"Are you all right?" Joe turned to Kurt.

"Yea, I think I sprained my left shoulder, but I'm okay."

Charity and I could not resist the comfort of back seats, and soon

Joe joined us too. Outside the window, Demavend, Tehran's Fujiyama, shined blue in the moonlight. The mountain appeared much closer than it actually was. Could it be that the Sassanian arch design was inspired by Demavend, or whatever they called the mountain in the ancient times, and the Pantheon to the Islamic revolution dominating the endless square was the mountain in its own right?

The plane banked, changing course and climbing.

"Where are we going?" I asked.

"To a little country you, probably, never heard of–Kuwait."

I don't know what came over me at that moment, maybe the excitement of our successful getaway, and the 'victory roll' around the Pantheon had something to do with it, but I turned to Joe and couldn't stop myself from saying, "About a century ago, you asked me whether I'd like to join TRAG...count me in."

He smiled, "I knew you would get around to it."

The plane wallowed again.

"Check if Kurt is all right." Joe glanced at me.

Kurt sat upright holding the controls and gazing straight ahead.

"How is it going, buddy?" I asked.

He did not answer. I followed his gaze: what did he see ahead of us? The wing sliced a cotton puff, then the plane cut through a cloud patch. What did he see that I didn't? There was nothing out there except for the pale moon racing the plane in the no-win contest.

"Are you okay?"

But Kurt did not respond. And suddenly, I don't know where they came from, the creeps ran down my spine. I'd seen that kind of gaze before, in the Nicaraguan jungle. The dead Sandinista then stared through me.

"Swell," I said and sunk in the co-pilot seat. We were flying with a dead pilot at the controls.

"What's the problem?" Joe appeared.

"El Cid." I pointed to Kurt.

"What?"

"The pilot is dead."

Charity joined us and stood holding to my seat with both hands. She observed Kurt silently, a tear rolled down her cheek.

As if Kurt's death were totally irrelevant and the guy might as well not even be here at all, Joe studied the gauges, "The autopilot is on...210 degrees, right on course...I'll fly the plane."

"Let me put him in the back." I reached for Kurt's seat belt buckle.

I was slightly irritated by Joe's non-concern about Kurt's death.

"Leave him." Joe stopped me.

Charity and I returned to the back seats. The plane flew smoothly in the still air, which only whistled gently through the bullet holes in the fuselage.

"I don't understand." Charity curled up in the back seat and covered her face. "I don't understand any of this."

She sobbed, and I sat down next to her.

"I think Joe is just paying respect..." I tried to rationalize Joe's request to leave Kurt at the controls. The idea of leaving a dead pilot at the live airplane controls, even only as a symbolic gesture, still bothered me, no, hell! it didn't bother me—it gave me the creeps!

"No, not that." Charity put her hands down and side-glanced at me, then she covered my hand with hers, "I mean us being here...and them being dead."

I still didn't know what she meant. Perhaps she wondered how we had survived the mission, or felt guilty that we did and 'they' didn't, or simply tried to make sense of all recent events...

The plane, suddenly, shuddered and dived. I saw bright flashes, smoke, and flying debris.

"We are hit!" Joe screamed.

Balancing between the of seats, Charity and I attempted to reach the cabin. The plane leaned in a steep right bank, its right engine burned leaving a billowing white smoke trail, the left engine sputtered. I glanced below: we glided over the Gulf, we were so close to our goal, and so far from it!

Joe cut the power and feathered out the damaged engine's prop. The plane slowly leveled off. Kurt now leaned forward as if studying the flight control panel. Again, creeps ran down my spine.

"Who strafed us?" I asked.

"A military jet, I don't know where he came from...We'll be ditching now." Joe turned to Charity and, as if saying farewell, whispered, "Love you."

She embraced him from behind, "Love you, too."

"Hey, hey, what about me?" I felt left out.

"We love you, too." Charity embraced me and kissed me on the lips.

"Okay, get in your seats." Joe killed the second engine. "It's gonna be rough..."

We watched the twinkling moon path on the water below. It was getting closer and closer. We were coming straight onto it, as if it was some kind of a magic, silvery runway. Intermittently, it seemed solid, then it sparkled and played again as we were approaching it, fast...

END